The Unburied Dead

Zombies and the Bronze Age Collapse

Book 2 – The Sea Peoples

CHRISTOPHER CLARKSON

ISBN: 9781791581534

DEDICATION

For Kasih.

1.

'You swore an oath!' the huge captain bellowed in accented Nesili as he paced up and down the deck, whip in hand, swishing it threateningly in front of people's faces. The captain's horned helmet and huge woolly black beard made him look more like a fierce beast than a human being.

The refugees from the beach stood in two lines on the sweltering deck, facing each other nervously and trying to keep their balance as the ship pitched and rolled on the chop.

Sweat poured off Ani as he struggled not to faint in the blistering heat.

Armed sailors holding long bronze swords encircled the new recruits. Crossed straps of thick leather lay across their otherwise bare brown chests and shoulders, black leather pants clad their muscly legs, their bare feet were browner than the wood of the deck, and their heads were covered with strange flat-topped leather helmets rimmed with brightly colored feathers. They looked like hardened warriors and experienced sailors whose sweaty skin seemed to glisten with a salt crust. The situation felt tense and extremely dangerous.

'Do you think we took you in out of generosity? Don't be fools! Your world has collapsed as has ours. We survive now by strength and arms alone! You fight with us to earn your keep, or you die!'

He paced down the line, staring each man and woman in the face.

Ani tried to stand tall like the others, but in truth, he felt small in comparison to the strong-limbed adults that had been taken aboard, and Purdu he feared looked even smaller. He was exhausted and his stomach ached with hunger, which prevented him from reaching his full height.

The captain stopped in front of them and looked them up and down distastefully. 'Who let these runts aboard?' he growled as he eyed their small, lean bodies.

There was a howl of laughter from the crew. Mezarus took a step towards the captain, but the man next to him pulled him warningly back into line.

'Are we going to fight the demons?' Purdu asked quietly as the Captain continued to scowl at her.

The captain suddenly burst into scathing laughter. 'Demons? You mean the gurglers? Are you simple child? No demons. They have nothing for us. We fight for what we need, for food and equipment. To put it simply, we kill, and we rob to survive!'

'But that's horrible!' Purdu said in disgust.

'Silence!' the captain snapped, holding the end of his whip under Purdu's chin and lifting it until her mouth was firmly closed.

Ani noticed Mezarus squirming, his fists clenching and his face turning red.

Suddenly the captain strode away to Ani's great relief. Mezarus also relaxed a little.

'Every man, woman,' and he quickly shot a look back at Ani and Purdu, 'and *child*, will fight for their living. You fight for the group! We fight for each other! We fight to survive! This is your life now. If you wish to leave, or do not wish to fight, then by all means go. Land is ten leagues that way.' He pointed towards a small cloud clinging to what must be a distant island.

'We will arm you,' he continued, still pacing the deck. 'We will clothe you, and we will feed you. In return we expect loyalty!'

Ani thought he could hear every stomach aboard rumble at the mention of food, for no one had eaten in hours, or more likely, days.

'But first you must fight!' the captain continued. 'Each person must prove themselves one of us, one of the Sea Peoples! To be one of us you follow our rules. There will be no escape and no cowardice. Does anyone wish to leave?' he growled in a low and deadly voice, eyeing each of the thirty or so strong, fit-looking men and women of many shades standing to attention on the deck. No one flinched, but still, he waited. Minutes passed and someone finally staggered from the heat. His neighbor caught him as he sagged to the deck, and tried to lift him back to his feet, but failed.

The captain spun around with a look of pure malice on his face. 'That man!' he yelled, pointing his whip and striding down the deck to the man who was struggling to back get back on his feet. 'Throw him overboard!'

A murmur of distress ran through the new recruits.

'You can't!' Mezarus said, stepping forward in anger.

'Silence!' the captain screamed and brandished his whip again.

Mezarus glared challengingly at the captain for a moment, then stepped reluctantly back into line as the captain paced up to him and stared him in the face, their noses practically touching.

Several armed men descended on the kneeling man and hauled him to the edge of the ship. He was too weak to protest. Ani could see Mezarus tearing into his own thighs with his fingernails as he watched.

'Weakness of any kind will not be tolerated!' the captain yelled into Mezarus' face. 'Do your duty. Do not complain. Be strong. Fight or die. Those are our rules.

Or we will discard you.' He spun around to face the blubbering man now being held tightly by the rail. 'Over the side with him!'

There was no murmur this time, only looks of dread and horror on the faces of all the new recruits.

The man was lifted bodily and thrown over the side without ceremony, the armed sailors returning immediately to their former positions as if nothing had happened.

Purdu uttered a small cry of despair under her breath as the spluttering cries of the drowning man died away and were swallowed by the sea. Ani reached down and squeezed her hand in sympathy and in warning. She fell silent.

Anger and loathing were etched into Mezarus' face, but he continued to look straight ahead and avoid eye contact with the captain who stood a few paces away watching him.

'Does anyone else wish to sit down… or speak?' he asked loudly, again pausing for a long time as his eyes swept the deck and settled on Mezarus.

Mezarus bit his tongue, and finally the captain seemed satisfied and marched to the stern of the ship where he climbed into the raised fighting castle. 'Then we eat!' he shouted.

Everyone looked around in amazement at this unexpected proclamation.

To Ani's surprise, crewmen slipped through the crowd of recruits to an opening into the hold. They began pulling the lids from barrels stored below deck and handed up loaves of flat round bread to their starving passengers.

Ani and Purdu raced forwards. Ani was so famished he savagely snatched a loaf of bread from a crewman and ran to an unoccupied space to devour it. The bread was not fresh but was wholesome and filling. He finished the loaf in seconds then hurried forward again as water skins were handed around.

Once everyone had eaten several of the flatbreads, they were dismissed for the time being, and soon most of them were lying on the deck digesting and trying to hide in their own shadow to escape the burning sun. As Ani lay and rested, a tall, dark-skinned man with strong limbs and a charismatic face walked amidst the recruits.

'The captain has fulfilled his part of the bargain,' he began saying calmly as he walked among them. 'Soon you will fulfill yours. You will either become one of us or die trying. We are a day's sailing from our next landing, an island called Alasiya. It has not yet seen the horrors we all know so well and there we will find much food and new recruits, if they do not prefer to die. The town will be walled and well-defended. You must be ready to fight your first battle there and win! Many of you may die, for this is the price of your freedom from the beasts. So, rest now - you will soon need your strength. Later we shall begin training. I am Karisto, your sergeant at arms. Soon you will either love life, or you will no longer care.' He strode off back to the stern and entered a low cabin beneath the rear castle, separated from the deck by a heavy curtain.

*

Ani lay and rested for some time, but he could not sleep. He was deeply anxious about the thought of imminent fighting and the killing of innocent people. This idea was repugnant to him and he could make no sense of it at all. Why should others die to feed them? How could he and Purdu possibly survive a battle with people ready to fight to the death to defend their homes? He felt only horror and sorrow. He lay wishing the sun would lower on the horizon and give them some relief from its unwavering intensity.

He lifted his head suddenly at the sound of dragging metal and heavy thuds. Men were handing out swords, spears, small round leather shields and armor.

'You too!' a young man said as he dropped a pile of armor in front of Ani and Purdu. It consisted of small leather breastplates with disks of bronze riveted to them. Another sailor handed each of them a blunt sword.

The armor was heavy, and Purdu tried to help strap Ani into it. Even with all the cords pulled tight, it was far too big and made Ani look like a partially retracted tortoise. Purdu laughed at the sight of him.

Ani marveled at the sound of her laughter. It had been weeks since he had heard her, or anyone for that matter, laugh.

Mezarus meanwhile had been given a large coat of soft leather with what looked like strips of ivory sewn onto it, and a helmet made from the same materials. He looked completely unrecognizable in armor, and his normally friendly and open face looked hard and fierce.

'I do not like this,' Mezarus said, feeling the long bronze sword in his hands. 'Who are we to fight? I won't kill innocent people.'

'Nor I!' said Purdu. 'How would we be any better than demons then?'

Ani nodded, but in his heart, he knew not doing so could get them all killed. He was also aware that others were listening. 'You shouldn't say that so loudly,' he whispered to Mezarus and Purdu. 'They made it clear we will be killed if we don't fight.'

'We can run,' Mezarus whispered back.

Ani nodded but was deeply troubled. From what had happened earlier he knew these were no idle threats. 'If they see us, they will kill us,' he replied worriedly.

'We will wait until the time is right. We stick together so we can go when it is safe.'

Ani looked around nervously to check no one was listening. Everyone seemed preoccupied adjusting their ill-fitting armour.

They were soon organized into pairs and the sergeant at arms instructed them on the basics of hand-to-hand combat, including footwork, thrust and parry, shield defense, and the use of a spear to stab or deflect an attacker's weapon. They also practiced the formation of a shield wall.

Ani could see the training was too simplistic and could not possibly prepare them to fight experienced warriors. Still, he knew it would serve him much better than knowing nothing at all, for it was all new to him.

He was sparring with a dark-skinned woman much taller than himself. Like him, she was terrified at the thought of real combat. She cowered every time Ani brought his sword tip near to her.

'It's OK!' he reassured her. 'I'm not going to hurt you. It's just training. It's only a practice sword.'

'It's still dangerous,' she replied in fear, 'and it won't be training tomorrow. I was a house slave. I can't fight. I'm going to be killed, aren't I? I can't even defend myself against a boy. I'm useless!'

She was right. Ani easily overpowered her every time as they sparred. 'Don't worry,' he reassured her again, 'we'll all protect you. Everyone will look out for you. Remember what he said? We fight for each other.'

Ani understood her fear, and it made him sad. The look of dread on her face made her already look like a victim, and he imagined there would be no place for that tomorrow.

Thinking of death made him think with deep sorrow of Amuurana, Sidani, and Lelwan. He wished so hard they were here that his heart ached, his throat tightened, and tears ran down his cheeks. He was distracted by his grief, and at that moment the woman caught him hard on the head with her sword. He winced in pain and fell to his knees. It was suddenly very obvious that he had to force these terrible thoughts from his mind if he was going to survive. The dangers were just as real as they had always been, and he needed to focus on that. He knew he was no match for a large and experienced warrior, and he had to find something else within him - something that would keep him alive. He looked over at Purdu and saw her pinned beneath her partner – a gangly man with a hairy chin who seemed to be taking some pleasure in his victory. She flailed and gasped for air before the man finally stepped back and she caught her breath. Surely, they wouldn't really make a small girl like Purdu fight against grown men? It was unthinkable brutality. She would be slaughtered, as no doubt would he. He preferred their chances against the demons. He would have to protect her, and maybe Mezarus was right, that running away was their best option.

He also feared for Mezarus. He knew Mezarus could kill demons, but he had no idea how he would fare in a real battle. He had also sworn he would never kill innocents, and that could put him in real danger. As Ani watched he easily overpowered his own sparring partner each time. Perhaps there was less to worry about in his case.

'Tomorrow, each of you will fight in a group of ten,' the sergeant-at-arms cried over the noise. 'Your group will contain some of our crew. You will follow their commands or expect a spear in the back. There will be five groups.'

'What about the other ships?' someone dared to ask as everyone stopped fighting and reflected on this new information.

There was a tense silence.

'Ignore them! These are your family you see around you now. You fight for each other,' the sergeant replied irritably.

'What if there are too many defenders?' another man asked anxiously, fear loosening his tongue.

'Silence!' the captain yelled angrily from the castle.

'If we are overwhelmed, we will retreat to the boats,' the sergeant replied angrily. 'You will use your shield defense and retreat in a line, as we have practiced.'

'When will we be given real weapons?' the gangly man with the unshaven face asked the sergeant as he strode by.

'You will not be given weapons. We have no weapons for you. You will pick them up as we acquire them.'

A fearful muttering suddenly broke out on deck.

'I am dead!' the slave girl muttered despairingly next to Ani.

'Silence!' the captain yelled again, this time climbing down from the castle and striding down the deck. 'If you fail to obtain weapons you will die with only a shield to defend yourselves. You must kill to obtain a weapon. You must pass this test to become one of us!'

To Ani, the people assembled on deck now looked like caged animals awaiting slaughter. People searched the horizon desperately as if weighing up their chances of survival should they jump overboard and swim for land instead.

'Rest now, and save your strength for the morning,' the sergeant said and dismissed them.

*

Morning brought a light fog and a calm sea. A runny fish stew was served to everyone on board, but it's odour and unidentifiable floating bits did little to soothe their churning stomachs. Some were already being sick overboard. The crew was quietly filling quivers with arrows, sharpening their long bronze swords and preparing their own equipment for the raid.

The new recruits adjusted their armor as best they could and nervously went through the moves they had been taught again and again.

'We have the perfect cover for our surprise attack,' the captain explained in hushed tones as he took a position by the mast. 'You will go ashore in the small boats. Follow your group leader's orders at all times. If all goes to plan, many of you will soon join our number as equals, and we will eat well tonight! From now on there is to be total silence!'

Ani and Purdu embraced nervously before they climbed down the ropes to the little boats that rose and fell ever so slightly beside the ship. A helmsman already sat in each boat clutching the steering oar, and the five boats quickly filled with their cargo of ten people each. The helmsman was apparently also to be their group commander, but three of the crew joined each boat. They were heavily armed with bows, many arrows, and swords, and each brought a covered clay pot filled with smoldering coals into the boat with them. They took up the oars and began rowing towards the shore, barely visible through the dim mist.

Ani could hear the rhythmic surge of small waves against the beach as they steered into a narrow cove. To his horror, peaking through the trees back from the beach was a high wall that looked hopelessly unassailable by unarmed and inexperienced troops without ladders or proper weapons. What chances did they stand against such a bastion, he wondered?

As they approached the beach Ani noticed other small boats rounding the headland and joining them in the cove.

'Who are they?' someone asked from the front of the boat.

'From the other ships. We fight together but do not let them steal our victory if you wish to eat tonight. We will race them for the spoils,' the helmsman, their commander of ten, said with a wicked smile.

Their boat rammed against the shelly beach and sent everyone reeling. Those in the front of the boat climbed reluctantly out, unsure what to do next.

'Advance!' the captain-of-ten ordered savagely.

The experienced crew jumped out of the boat and set off at a jog towards the walled town.

'Follow them, you numbskulls!' their captain commanded. 'Unless you want a spear in the arse, that is!' he said as he picked up a long spear out of the bottom of the boat.

Ani and Purdu were the last to climb over the side. They jumped into the warm water and waded reluctantly to shore.

Unexpectedly, one of the boats from the other ship ground onto the beach right beside them. A man jumped from the bow and onto the sand well before the others, as if eager for battle. He wore an ugly, bloodthirsty expression. Or was it conceit, Ani wondered. Then suddenly he realized he knew that cruel expression, though most of his face was covered in a heavy helmet. He knew who this unpleasant looking man was. It was the Gal Meshedi.

2.

Silence. There had been nothing but silence for a week. Or was it just a few days? He couldn't tell. Either way, it felt like an eternity. There was no light, and it was impossible to tell how many days had passed exactly. For the first while he had heard noises outside the cell - then nothing.

His hunger was paralyzing. Before it had been an all-consuming, angry, desperate, stomach clenching drive to do anything required to satisfy it. Now it was a state of being, a catatonic lack of anything. There was no escape. No use in fighting it. No energy left to even think about it. At least there was a tap in the cell, or he would already be dead.

He lay staring up into the darkness. How long this would go on he could not tell. He no longer cared. He just wanted it to end.

He had been promised an interview, an interrogation, or whatever it was going to be. He didn't mind which. He had just longed to get out and see light and people and food. Now it looked like that was never going to happen. Perhaps they were psychologically softening him up for interrogation, or maybe he was being punished in a way befitting his crime. Or maybe he was just being left to die. He had considered these unhappy options again and again, a growing sense of dread as he did so, but finally, he had succumbed to the mental oblivion of starvation.

He realized his eyes had become set on a fixed point in the darkness. Sometimes he imagined he was looking through a window at the night sky. Other times he fooled himself into thinking someone was staring back at him. In his darkest moments, he imagined he had succumbed to INS, and that he was trapped in a body that no longer communicated with his brain. What horrors that body, remote and alien, was committing he dreaded to think. But then his stomach would cramp, or the spiny bedframe would grate against his backbone and ribs, and he would again be aware of his corporeal self.

*

There was a strange shuffling noise, alien to his ears. He wondered for a moment if it was just his own breathing becoming more labored, but it was not that. It was outside the cell. It was slow and irregular and seemed to pass right by his door. Then it was gone. He strained his ears, listening for it with all his remaining strength. There it was again. Now there was something that also resembled a low moaning. No, it was not moaning, it was more like a guttural gurgling sound.

In his state of deterioration, he figured it must be a trick of his mind. He had begun to hear voices too, he was sure. Or maybe they were what passed for dreams in his state of delirium. This was just another of those delusions. But the sound was back! It was passing his door again, and there again was the unpleasant gurgling that sounded like the death rattle of the terminally ill.

He rolled over. It would not stop and now the sound was becoming distressing, even frightening. To drive it out he shoved his head deep into the fold of what passed for a pillow, but he could not banish it. Was this part of the torture? Were they trying to frighten him or send him mad?

'Who's there?' he rasped at last, his voice hoarse and faint.

The shuffling stopped. He listened.

'Go away!' he did his best to shout, but his voice was feeble and thin to his own ears.

Then he heard the distinct sound of sniffing. Something was sniffing at the door. There was the sound of fingernails grating on the cell door. The sniffing continued, and now the gurgling was back, louder. The scratching grew faster and harder, and the gurgling became a rasping wail.

He wrapped the pillow tightly around his ears, but the scratching turned to a loud banging, echoing deafeningly through his cell. The door began to shudder, and the wailing became a high-pitched whine.

'Go away! Leave me alone for Christ's sake!' he cried in anguish, wishing it would stop. But it did not stop.

*

His mind was snapping. There was no escape from the incessant banging, scraping and wailing.

'Make it stop! Go away!' he cried repeatedly, his hands over his ears, rocking back and forth and banging his head against the wall until it throbbed. To have come so close to death from starvation, and now this! He felt ready to dash his own brains out on the floor rather than listen to it a moment longer. Then there was a sudden muffled bang, followed by silence.

For a moment he did not register that his torment had ended. He could still hear the wailing and banging in his ears. But the silence eventually permeated his senses.

Now there was a metallic grating sound, and he heard the door handle begin to turn. A sound he had waited eagerly for over many days. Now it was with utter dread that he realized the door was opening. He drew himself up on the bed hard against the wall, trying to hide in the darkness. But there was nowhere to hide. He knew that thing at his door must not find him!

Then another sensation hit him. Light. There was light. A torch beam appeared in the door opening and swept across the wall. It fell on him, caught him in his terrified huddle, banishing the darkness that was his only hiding place.

'No, please!' he begged, his mind in pieces. 'Leave me alone!'

'Michael?' a thickly accented voice called quietly.

3.

Arla stood at the huge glass windowpane that was as long and tall as the room itself. Her arms were folded, and she was frowning, as she had been for the last half hour. The bleached white buildings of Jerusalem sprawled over the hills in front of her. The Dome of the Rock and the pink stone of the church steeples and minarets of the Old City shimmered faintly in the distance.

'You had no right to force me to leave,' she said angrily.

'Arla, there was no choice, you know that. The streets were clogged. The airports were about to close. If we'd stayed any longer, we'd never have gotten out. Our last chance to get back here safely was slipping away. The Israeli Air force was threatening to shoot down anything that came within 50km of the border.'

'James needed me. He had no one there. I wanted to be there for him at the end.'

There was an uncomfortable silence for a moment before Ariel spoke up again. 'If you'd stayed any longer, we both know what was going to happen. Did you really want to see that?'

'Of course, I didn't *want* to see it, but he needed me. I love him, Ariel, do you get that? Or has Mossad made you heartless as well as secretive?'

'That's not fair.'

'I need to find Michael,' she said brusquely, changing the subject.

'That shouldn't be too hard,' Ariel replied, sounding heartened at the change of subject. 'Didn't MIT haul him away after the explosion?'

'Yes.'

'Well, I assume they've got him locked up in Ankara somewhere. I can find out. What do you want with him?'

She spun around and returned to the long boardroom table behind which Ariel was sitting. 'He can get us access to the Centre for Bioterrorism. If they've developed a cure, we need to have it.'

'That's my sister! Are you sure you don't want a job here?'

'And end up like you? No thanks. Anyway, I wasn't thinking about the greater good. I was thinking about James.'

Ariel sat back in his chair and placed his hands behind his head, looking despairing at the return to the former subject. 'And what good do you think that would do, Arla? We both know what the disease will have done to him by now. I'm sorry to have to say it, but you need to forget about helping him. He is well past that now. They may even have terminated him. Turkey is in a real mess. I'm sure they're well beyond trying to help a sick archaeologist and are more at the incinerating whole neighborhoods stage.'

'You really are a callous bastard aren't you!'

'Don't be like that. If I could help him, I would.'

'Then find me Michael!'

*

Arla flicked through the notes she had scrawled in her dig diary by James' bedside before she had been forcibly dragged out of the hospital kicking and screaming by her brother and his 'helpers'. She couldn't remember all the details, but the gist was there. It was a thoroughly mind-blowing account of the final days of the Hittite empire, right down to the last moments in the tower when the scribe had somehow found a scrap of moist clay on which to write the last words, 'They come!' A final, almost illegible word on the tablet, had read, 'Sidani.' She knew it was a name, but it was not one she had heard before.

Now she examined her notes in detail, Thompson's irritating but strangely haunting words coming back to her: 'You're the archaeologists, aren't you supposed to be finding out how it all ended?' At the time she had wanted to throttle him, but now she nodded to herself and searched frantically for answers in the lines James had translated. His words had been faint at the end, but she could tell he had realized something. Something of great importance. She had not been able to get from him what it was, and now she felt it was up to her to find it for herself.

She read and reread the notes, but whatever it was James had seen was not revealing itself to her. There was mention of two children, a smith, and a Meshedi captain. They had fled the burning Hattusha to a mountain fort but could go no further. Trapped, the account had ended abruptly, except for the ominous final words, 'They come!'.

Arla could not help but imagine those final minutes, trapped in the tower, the door shuddering and about to give way as the dreadful host forced its way in. She had seen what had happened next with her own eyes: the brutally cannibalized bones; the decapitated heads of INS victims heaped by the forced open door, no doubt cut from their bodies by the Meshedi captain in his final stand; and of course, the final resting place of the scribe, the warrior, the children and so many others. It made a chill run down her spine, even in the hot evening air of her apartment.

She checked her phone again, hoping for news from Ariel, but there was nothing. Where was Michael, she wondered with bitterness. She was almost angry at him for his disappearance now that she needed him urgently. Thompson had also dropped off the radar; either flown home or secreted away somewhere safe in the face of the catastrophe that was unfolding throughout the world. But Thompson had said the cure was nearly there and would reverse the spread of INS. Was it just arrogance or platitudes he was spouting? Or did the CBT really have the drug she would now sacrifice anything for?

*

Her phone buzzed violently. She opened an eye. The silver plaque was vibrating noisily on her stomach where she had dropped it after a final vain check for a message from Ariel before dozing off on the couch. Ariel's name was glowing brightly on the screen.

'Took your time, didn't you,' she croaked sleepily into the phone, then sat up, threw her hair back from her face and forced herself awake.

'I'm sorry, it was harder than I thought.' He sounded tired. There was something else in his voice as well.

'What's up?'

'The thing is, I couldn't find anyone to talk to.'

'What do you mean, were they stonewalling?'

'No. I mean there was nobody there. I called dozens of numbers, then had my colleagues look into it as well. There's simply no one there!'

'It's late, I'm sorry I don't think I'm following you. What are you saying?'

'I'm saying, Arla, they're gone!'

'Hang on, who?'

'Everyone! I tried the US embassy, the General and District Directorate of Security. Even MIT. Nothing. Zilch. No one there.'

'Are you saying what I think you're saying?'

'Things are unbelievably bad in Turkey right now. It's total chaos. No one is at their station. People have fled. I know this because I'm here.'

'What? You're back in Turkey? Are you insane? You're putting yourself in massive danger. Why?'

'Because I do what my sister asks me to, and no one was helping me. I can't talk more now; I have to move on. There's something strange happening in the street outside. I think I've found someone who can help me. He's meeting me soon. I'll ring when I know more.'

'The phone networks will stop working soon if it's as bad as you say.'

'Don't worry, I've brought one of ours. Stay safe my sister.'

'Be careful!' she tried to say, but the line went dead.

4.

Ani followed along behind the others, keeping close to Purdu. He was aware of the captain with the long spear bringing up the rear, checking for stragglers that needed prodding, or worse.

Ani searched the ragged lines of advancing recruits for Mezarus. He found him trudging forlornly along behind their group leader, his shield hanging limply at his side. The others in his group cowered behind their shields as they drew nearer to the walls. Ani and Purdu had not been given shields and were totally unarmed.

Ani also kept an eye on the Gal Meshedi. Fortunately, he had not noticed them but ran eagerly up the shelly slope towards the high stone wall set back from the beach. Behind him was a line of men that Ani also recognized as the Meshedi from Hattusha. If what the captain had said was true, these battle-hardened elite warriors were sure to claim the spoils and the rest of them would go hungry! Ani was keen to keep well away from them, but an idea suddenly came to him. He knew he and Purdu stood little chance of survival in open combat alone and unarmed, or even with the pathetic group of untried recruits in their group of ten. If, on the other hand, they edged closer and at some point, fell in behind the Gal Meshedi and his men, they were sure to meet with little resistance, as the Meshedi would cut down all in their path.

Ani tugged on Purdu's loose breastplate, trying to lead her a little off to the side to tell her his plan.

Purdu shot him an enquiring look.

'You there!' came the bark of the captain behind them. 'Stay in the group!'

Ani sighed and altered his course back in behind the others. He found himself behind a huge dark-skinned man covered in armor that looked like serpent scales. He glanced quickly down at the children, then snorted to himself and ran on, faster, unwilling to be burdened by the children in battle.

As they crunched up over a pumice stone beach ridge and into the thick grass beyond, Ani noticed people were suddenly ducking and dropping into the grass. Some were grunting and others crying out.

'Get down!' Ani hissed to Purdu, but he was unsure why everyone was dropping so suddenly. They must be trying to avoid being seen, he thought. But then he realized what was happening. Dark streaks were whizzing through the grass at high speed and sailing over their heads. Arrows!

'Lie down!' he said to Purdu as an arrow whizzed only inches above their heads. 'They've seen us!'

They both thrust their faces into the dark sandy earth, trying to cling to the ground so closely as to be invisible to the defenders on the walls.

'Get up!' the captain yelled at them harshly, wading through the tall grass behind them.

Ani felt the stabbing pain of a spear point in his bare leg. It took no further inducement to get him back on his feet. He cast a quick glance over his shoulder and saw the captain's spear was already red and dripping. He pulled Purdu up next to him and they both broke into a stooped run towards the wall.

They passed someone writhing in agony in the grass, an arrow shaft through his leg. Bright red blood was smeared on the crushed green grass where he thrashed. It turned Ani's stomach to see it. Others also lay still, crumpled in the grass.

The grass ended abruptly and now they were in front of the wall, exposed and at the mercy of the archers leaning out over it, killing anyone and everyone in sight.

They were in a waking nightmare. Screams, bodies, and blood seemed to be everywhere. Ani desperately searched the line of terrified recruits flattened against the wall and cowering beneath their shields, trying vainly to avoid the deadly hail of arrows fired down at them from above.

At last, he saw them. The Gal Meshedi and his men were running along the base of the wall. They were already a long way away and were heading for a forest and a break in the wall. He took Purdu's hand and pulled her out from the wall.

'What are you doing?' she shrieked as he brought them straight back into the line of fire from the archers above. Arrows began to thud into the ground around them.

'We have to follow them! We won't survive here!'

'Who?'

'The Gal Meshedi!'

Ani felt her hand go slack, and her body grow rigid. He looked back. She had come to a dead halt. An arrow grazed her head as she stood motionless, a look of horror fixed on her face. Blood began to run down her forehead as she stood motionless. 'No!' she said.

'Come on!' he yelled and dragged her along the line of blubbering recruits. The captains of ten were yelling at their groups, trying to get them moving along the base of the wall, but the recruits were dropping like flies. One of the ship's crew was lighting arrows tied with rags using the brazier of coals they had brought aboard the landing boats. He was handing the burning arrows out to his fellow crew who were dashing out from under the shields and firing them over the walls and into the town.

'You two!' they suddenly heard a deep voice cry from under a shield. Ani felt a firm grip on his arm. Spinning around in alarm, fearing their captain had spotted them running off, he saw Mezarus, looking extremely anxious. 'Where are you going?' He held his shield out over them, exposing himself in the process.

'The Gal Meshedi and his men are here. We need to go with them if we want to survive.'

'What, how?' Mezarus looked totally confused.

'I won't go with that murderer!' Purdu cried.

Mezarus looked unsure.

'Do you want to die?' Ani screamed at them both. 'It's our only chance!'

Purdu and Mezarus stared disbelievingly at Ani. Then several arrows struck the shield above their heads and a woman to their left dropped to the ground with a scream.

A moment later and they were all running beside Ani, giving tacit approval to his plan.

'How did they get here?' Purdu cried miserably.

'I don't know, but if we stay behind them, we may have a chance.'

'He'll kill us if he sees us.'

'So, we don't let him see us!'

They followed the path the Meshedi had taken around a bend in the wall. A closed gate stood around the corner in a narrow ravine formed by the stone wall on one side and a sheer rockface on the other. A guard tower stood above the narrow entryway and a pile of bodies lay in front of the gates. Arrows stood up everywhere in the ground like stalks of ripe wheat.

A large group of recruits and crew were huddled behind trees above the entranceway, shooting arrows at the defenders on the walls and in the tower. A deadly rain of arrows whined back at them in reply.

They tore up the gravelly slope to a clump of trees and rocks that offered the only available cover. Others began fleeing the base of the walls following behind them, trying to reach the same meagre cover. Many fell as they ran.

From his position behind a rock, Ani spotted the group of Meshedi at the rear of the huddle atop higher ground opposite the gateway. They were crouched down behind their shields, seemingly making some kind of plan. Then, as one, the Meshedi broke away from the group and disappeared silently into the trees.

'We have to follow them,' Ani whispered. Mezarus and Purdu nodded their agreement. They edged out from behind the rocks and scrambled from tree to tree, hoping the archers would not find them in the scattered woods, while trying to work out which way the Meshedi had gone.

As they ran, they passed several recruits hiding in the woods. Ani slowed as he recognized a woman huddled behind a tree in terror, muttering loudly to herself. It was the house slave - his sparring partner - looking deranged with fear. She jumped as they passed, obviously frightened that her desertion had been discovered by one of the crew, but she looked away as soon as she saw Ani, as if too ashamed to look him in the eye.

They soon spied the group of Meshedi climbing the steep hills that ran behind the town, keeping among the trees and rocks to remain hidden. They appeared to be heading for a road that ran steeply down the hillside to the rear of the town. Mist still clung to the hilltops where the Gal Meshedi had led his men.

'They'll be trying to find a rear entrance,' Mezarus whispered from where they huddled behind a boulder.

Ani nodded his agreement. 'Then we will too!'

They waited until the Meshedi once more crept out from behind rocks and trees and advanced rapidly down the steep road to the rear of the walled town. Inside the town, they could hear shouts of alarm, children crying and frenzied attempts to organize a defence.

The Meshedi disappeared behind the wall. Ani stopped and watched. Within seconds they saw a flash of movement as one of the Meshedi slipped silently over the wall and into the town. Another followed, and then another.

'Not long now and the gates will be open,' Mezarus said quietly.

Ani adjusted his position as if about to run a race, ready to make a sprint for the gates as soon as they were open.

Startled shouts and screams erupted from near where the road must enter the rear of the town.

'Now,' Mezarus hissed, and they sprinted across the open hillside and around the curving wall to where the rear entrance must lie. They paused when they reached the wall and looked carefully around the corner. The gates stood open, but there was no sign of anyone.

They stalked to the gateway. The road was very steep here as it descended through many stone terraces and into a kind of stone-walled courtyard in front of the rear gates. Ducking his head quickly around the door, Ani could see several bodies lying on the road within. He nodded to the others and they all slipped silently in through the gates.

They heard sounds of battle ahead as they strode quietly along the narrow road, fringed by low stone houses with thatched roofs. They could now see the devastating effect the raider's fire arrows were having on these houses, as a cloud of thick smoke rose from many further in.

They hurried along, eager to catch up to the Meshedi lest they get cut off. There was the sound of fighting ahead and the cries of the wounded and dying. Unwilling to go further, they found a barn full of cows beside the road. Mezarus led them inside. The cows looked up in curiosity but did not stop chewing their straw.

A loud shout went up from the other end of town. There was the heavy thump of sword on shield and many men shouting. People ran past the barn, fleeing the battle now raging at the front gate, while others seemed to be hurrying towards it, carrying water and weapons.

Ani, Purdu, and Mezarus hid themselves behind the manger, their heads almost touching the stomachs of the cows munching away in front of them and tried not to listen to the terrible sounds outside. Soon they heard an almighty shout, and the sound of the main gates being thrown open. The clamouring, shouting and clash of weapons continued for many minutes, then suddenly, it ceased. In its place, they heard cheering.

They ran to the barn door and peered into the roadway outside. There were bodies everywhere, including those of women and children. Ani's heart sank. This new world was deeply depressing, and he longed to be far away from it, somewhere quiet and peaceful.

'We'd better not be found here,' Mezarus whispered, bringing Ani back to his senses. Mezarus picked up his shield and found a sword lying beside a dead man. We'd best look like we were fighting like the others.'

He led them from the barn, found more swords and dipped the blades in a pool of congealing blood beside a fallen warrior. 'Here, take these,' he said and handed them their new swords. 'You look convincing,' he said, eyeing the fresh blood from the arrow wound dribbling down Purdu's face and onto her armor. 'But we need to do something about you, Ani. What's it to be, a smear of someone else's blood, or a real punch on the nose?'

'Neither,' Ani said, stepping away in disgust.

'Come on lad, they're going to think you hid in a barn or something. You need some battle wounds.' With that, he reached over and wiped his hand across Purdu's forehead.

'Ow!' she cried and jerked her head back in pain.

'There!' Mezarus said as he wiped a streak of thick blood across Ani's cheeks, then turned and led them down the narrow lane towards the front gates.

5.

'Michael?' the voice repeated.

'Yes,' Michael rasped back in disbelief.

'Come, we must hurry!' the voice behind the torch said quickly.

A strong hand grabbed his arm and helped him off the bed. His vision was slowly adjusting, and he made out shadows on the wall and the image of a tall, well-built man, dark-skinned with a wary face and a worried expression.

'This way,' he said in his thick accent and helped Michael through the cell door.

It was different outside the cell to how he remembered it. It was a brightly lit corridor with many doors when they had brought him in, but now it was completely dark. The torchlight briefly passed across a body lying in a pool of blood in front of his cell door. He could distinctly hear loud banging coming from elsewhere within the building, and the all-too-familiar gurgling and wailing.

They moved off down the corridor, the large man leading him with a tight grip on his arm. As to where they were going, Michael could not tell. He had only seen the interior of the building once briefly when he had been escorted silently through a maze of corridors and security doors before being dumped in his cell.

'What's happening? What are those sounds?'

'Don't worry about them. Just lean on me and go quickly.'

'Who are you? Are you MIT or police?'

'No!'

'So how did you get in here then?'

'With much difficulty.'

Michael struggled to comprehend what was going on. The man was clearly Turkish, but apparently not one of those who had arrested him. Why was he helping him?

'Where is everyone? Why is it dark in here?'

'You have been in here some time, Michael. Things have changed… In many ways, you might have been better off staying in your cell.'

'Nothing could be worse than that,' Michael said hoarsely, struggling to keep up. He could barely take another step he was so weak.

'You might soon change your mind.' The man stopped suddenly. 'I think I am going to carry you.'

'It's OK, I can walk,' Michael wheezed, then almost immediately buckled at the knee. He felt himself being lifted onto the man's back in a fireman's carry hold. He realized now how light he must have become!

'Please, tell me what's going on.'

The man was grunting under Michael's weight and was breathing hard now as he jogged along dark corridors, following the bouncing beam of torchlight in front of them. But the man was unable or unwilling to answer any questions at present.

There was a sudden flash of movement in front of them and the torch beam briefly caught a face darting out of the darkness towards them. It was contorted and shriveled, with bulging red eyes and a rabid look. The mouth opened to reveal protruding broken teeth and a bluish tongue. It lunged at them, its jaws opening wider as it let out a gurgling wail from its hideous gaping maw.

Michael shrieked and nearly fell off the man's back.

There was a deafening bang, a spray of blood, and the creature dropped with a thud. Then they were on the move again, faster now.

'You just shot someone!' Michael gasped in horror. 'Who was that?'

'What was it, you mean. You don't know?'

Michael struggled to assemble his thoughts. The last time he had seen something that horrific was in the HASAWA lab when they had been chased by INS victims intent on tearing them to pieces.

'No, it couldn't be… INS?'

'Yes.'

'But, how did it get in here?'

'It's everywhere. The thing we tried to prevent has happened.'

'Wait, the thing *you* tried to prevent? What…?'

Michael's question was cut short by two more dark shapes lurching at them out of the darkness with terrifying gurgling cries. The torchlight briefly landed on each disfigured face, followed by a loud bang and a spray of blood. The creatures dropped to the ground motionless.

'They're everywhere!' Michael gasped in horror.

'There are not so many. Soon you will see many, many!'

'What?' Michael said, disbelieving of what the man was saying.

The corridor was blocked by a heavy security door, dripping with the gore from the two INS victims that had just been dispatched.

'You're getting heavy,' the man groaned. 'I'm putting you down for a second.'

Michael lost his balance as his feet touched the floor and fell heavily against the wall.

'Sorry,' the man mumbled as he pulled back a bolt and yanked the heavy door open. 'No maglocks now,' he muttered as he turned and found Michael in the darkness and lifted him back over his shoulder.

They jogged along another corridor, then turned a corner and burst through another heavy door. This time the man did not stop, but simply rammed the door open with Michael still on his back, bruising Michael's shoulder quite badly in the process. Before Michael had any idea what was going on, there was another string of loud bangs and flashes as disfigured and gurgling figures dropped away into the shadows to left and right.

'Sit!' the man said once the shooting stopped and lowered Michael into an office chair. 'I have to call my friends.' He pulled a radio from the webbing Michael now noticed he was wearing and flew into rapid Turkish. An abrupt answer came back over the radio at once. 'Tamam,' he said and pocketed the radio. 'Let's go,' he said and lifted Michael onto his shoulder again with surprising ease.

'Where are my friends?' Michael could not help but ask. He had re-run the final moments on the rooftop through his head again and again while in his cell, trying to make sense of Nathan's actions and their consequences. 'Is Nathan alive?' He had never had a chance to find out as the MIT had dragged him from the roof at gunpoint. Even now he was surprised he himself had survived.

The man grunted. 'You come with me now!' he said gruffly, his mood suddenly changed at the mention of Nathan.

The man shoved open a fire escape door and heaved Michael down the stairs quickly, each step jarring Michael's ribs painfully.

There was the sound of a heavy vehicle outside, a truck perhaps, screeching to a halt. The man threw open the fire stair door and they ran out into a bright lobby fronted with glass doors opposite a large empty and untidy front desk. Daylight was streaming in through the front doors, causing Michael to squint painfully. The front doors flew open as three men in black fatigues, webbing and helmets and carrying assault weapons, rushed into the lobby. A black armored truck had mounted the curb threateningly outside the building, it's huge engine rumbling noisily.

To his horror, Michael noticed dozens of figures, disheveled and ragged and covered in sores and dry blood, running towards the vehicle with talon-like fingers outstretched and mouths gaping. A terrible gurgling wail filled the street outside.

After a quick exchange in Turkish, the men retreated back through the doors with Michael in tow. At once they broke into rapid firing at the crowd of shambling figures descending rapidly on the armored car.

'In the back!' the man cried as he nonchalantly shoved his pistol in the face of a crazed old man only a foot or so away and pulled the trigger, leaving a shattered mess on the pavement.

Michael, paralyzed with fear, immobilized from starvation, and sick to his stomach at the violence around him, stood shakily gaping at the scene before him. At last, one of the men holstered his weapon and dragged Michael into the back of the truck. The doors slammed shut and the vehicle screamed away from the building.

'Welcome to the Ankara Meshedi,' his rescuer said with a faint smile and held out a blood-stained hand for Michael to shake.

6.

It had been several hours and still no word from Ariel. Arla was pacing the room frantically, pulling her hair out with worry about him, and about James. She flicked back and forth between TV channels, then switched it off as the horrifying scenes of mayhem and carnage in cities around the world were repeated on every channel. For once in its life, Israel seemed a peaceful oasis amid a sea of chaos. But for how long would it last?

Arla knew it was down to the efforts of the likes of Ariel and the network of watchers, listeners, and fixers that he belonged to that meant Israel remained standing - that, and nature's gift of an ocean on one side and a desert on the other as formidable barriers to undesirable incursions.

She had contacted Ariel as soon as they had arrived in the hospital in Ankara, and he had wasted no time in taking action. The country had activated its tried and tested national emergency system to mobilize its army reserves, close the borders and remain on alert. But now Ariel had left the safety of Israel, she worried about his safety.

She poured another cup of coffee, hoping it would clear her mind and help her find what James had seen in the text. What was it he had realized? Why could she not see it? Was it something to do with how it all ended, or how to combat the disease?

She scanned her notes again. She had jotted down several key observations. She went over these again in her mind as she abandoned the notepad and strode onto the balcony to stare out over the forest of apartment blocks, a hot wind blowing in her face. In the distance, the call to prayer began and was taken up almost immediately by all the mosques of the Old City and the Muslim side of the city. It was a constant reminder of the tensions that underlay the fragile, often shattered, peace.

She pondered her list once more.

First, the 'demons', as the scribe had called them, sought their victims through sight, sound, and smell. Nothing new there.

Second, they traveled in packs, east to west, following the sun it seemed. Interesting, but not very useful.

Third, they could not be killed except by decapitation. She knew this already, or more specifically, she knew it was all about destroying the brain stem.

Fourth, the scribe and his band had observed the corpses of INS sufferers who had expired from starvation and dehydration. The scribe had described them as 'emaciated and mummified by the sun'. Could be useful, she thought, since it proved the creatures eventually died. But such an ending would also require there being no victims left to feed on. Not a good outcome.

Fifth… She could not think of a fifth. 'Damn it!' she swore and banged the railing. At that moment she caught a glimpse of someone on the street below. He was watching her, she was sure of it. The moment she caught his eye, he disappeared into the crowd. Great! Now she was being followed as well!

She stormed back inside, instinctively picked up her phone again, then tossed it on the bed in disgust as she saw there were no new messages.

She returned to her notes, trying to force her fractious mind to focus and think. But all she could think about was the calamity that was closing in around them, and about James. She knew she had to act fast if she was to help him, but everything was taking too long! Ariel had dragged her back to Israel, the government and military had interviewed her endlessly, and now she didn't even know where James was! Ariel had said it was already too late, that he was most likely already 'terminated', but she refused to believe that. Maybe Gökman's super drug could still be found? But the chances of getting hold of it, even with Michael's help, seemed very slim now that it was locked away in some top-secret lab under the watchful eye of characters like Mr Thompson.

She was deep in these troubled thoughts when there came a quiet knock on the door. She checked the time - 11:58 am. She was not expecting anyone. She was sure it must by government, police, health and military advisors seeking yet more information about the disease and what to do about it. She couldn't stand it anymore! She had told them everything she knew. She just wanted them to leave her alone so she could do what was now most important to her.

She walked silently into the hallway, then snuck a peek through the peephole. It was the man from the street! The man who had been watching her! He was a young man, clean-shaven and neatly dressed. He looked anxious. Now that she thought about it, she realized she might have seen this guy with Ariel once in the past.

Against her better judgment, she unlooked the door and opened it a little, leaving the catch on. 'Hello?' she asked cautiously.

'You're Arla right?'

'Yes.'

'I thought so. You look like Ariel. Well, not exactly the same,' he said a little nervously and looked away.

'Well? Do I know you?' she pressed.

'No, not exactly. I know you, sort of. I have been keeping an eye on you,' he suddenly swallowed, 'I think you saw me. It's on Ariel's orders,' he quickly added as she began to bristle.

'I see,' she said, unsurprised, but nevertheless irritated by this invasion of her privacy. Deep down she knew Ariel was being protective - perhaps over-protective – but that did not make her any happier about having someone spying on her. 'Well, can I help you or have you come to tell me I've left the iron on or something?'

'Sorry, no, nothing like that,' he coughed nervously. 'It's just that I've been trying to contact Ariel for quite some time, and he's not answering his phone or email or anything.'

'I can relate to that. Do you need him for some reason?'

'Well, yes. That is, the department does. They are quite angry that he's disappeared.'

'And you're getting some of the heat?'

'Erm, well, yes. He's my partner'

'You'd better come in. What's your name anyway?'

'Yosef.'

Arla led Yosef into the small sitting room and motioned for him to take a seat on the sofa.

'I'm usually quite tidy,' she said apologetically and swept aside notes and a pile of newspapers reporting the unfolding global disaster.

Yosef sat rather awkwardly on the sofa and looked around the apartment.

'Look familiar?' she said frostily.

'Sorry,' he said again. 'I'm not staring at you all day if that's what you think. It's the people coming and going that are my main concern. You have enemies remember.'

Arla sighed. She felt bad. 'I'm sorry. I'm not myself at present. I've been quite rude. Would you like a drink?'

'No thank you. Look, the reason I came is to talk to you about Ariel. You see I do know where he is.'

She stared at him for a moment, unsure if he was genuine or trying to lure information from her. She decided to go with her instincts and trust him. She sighed and nodded. 'OK, so why are you here?'

'I think we both know this has something to do with you and what happened in Turkey.'

'Yes, well, perhaps…'

'Well, I received a text from him this morning.'

'You did? That little creep. Couldn't he have messaged me? I've been worried sick about him.'

'Arla, it wasn't that kind of text. I think he is in trouble. A lot of trouble.'

'Why? He's not doing anything illegal going back to Turkey is he?'

'Not that. I think he's been abducted.'

'Shit! By whom?'

'It just said *Meshedi*.'

'Oh god! But they had disappeared! Nathan killed the Gal Meshedi! No one's heard of them since.'

'Well, now we have. Why did he go there Arla?'

'To find Michael, to get the cure.'

'Michael?'

'The guy the CIA and the Centre for Bioterrorism were working with. He was arrested after Nathan did what he did, you know, with the helicopter. He knows about this drug, this possible cure for INS. I asked Ariel to find him. I need it, I mean *we* need the cure. I didn't think he would actually go back there.' She sighed worriedly. 'He always has to be such a hero.'

'Yes, well he is known for that, and decorated for it too.'

'So where is he?'

'I was hoping you could tell me. He is effectively AWOL. I've been ordered to go and get him. I was supposed to leave immediately, but I wanted to talk to you first.'

'I'm coming too.'

'What? No, you're not…'

'Don't you dare,' she said, holding a fist up to Yosef's face. 'He's my brother! He went there for me! I'm going!'

Yosef gave her a sober look and lowered her fist gently from his face. 'This will be very dangerous.'

'So what! The whole world's about to end. Now, what the hell are we waiting for? Let's go!'

7.

The sack of the town had been brutal and bloody. Ani and Purdu were deeply traumatized by the bloodshed, the merciless slaughter of innocents and the wanton destruction. The theft of food and belongings had been total. The able-bodied who were not butchered were rounded up and marched to the beach, while the few infirm survivors were left bereaved and destitute in their burnt outhouses.

They had lost sight of the Gal Meshedi and his men in the confusion of the sacking, as everywhere there was smoke, crazed destruction, and unbridled slaughter. The apprehensive recruits, previously certain of their own demise and seemingly unwilling to kill, had been transformed into the basest of animals. Mortal fear had turned to bloodlust and greed.

Mezarus had led them quickly out of the town gates and back to the beach. There they had found many wounded strewn about by the landing boats. No one tended to their wounds, and some had already succumbed. They quickly got to work, pulling out arrows and tearing up any loose clothing with which to bind wounds.

As they worked, they soon saw the bands of recruits and crew returning, blood-soaked and humping large bundles on their backs, or roughly leading groups of bound prisoners along behind them.

'To think we survived the demons only to fall in with such creatures!' Mezarus spat in distaste as the first of the victorious men and women dumped their piles of spoils into the boats. Several captains of ten reappeared by the boats and began yelling commands.

Ani heard a familiar voice behind him. He looked around and saw Troan, bloody and bruised, leaning against the neighboring boat, a bow, and quiver of arrows hanging over his shoulder. Ani had not even noticed him when they landed.

'You see, I warned what would happen if the world were in the hands of slaves. Just look at their handiwork. They are worse than animals. This would never have happened if those of higher birth were in charge.' Then he changed to a whisper, 'It could still be so again, If…'

His next words were cut short by the loud orders of a captain of ten who marched along the beach in front of their boat. 'All spoils in the boats!' he was shouting. 'The Captain owns it, not you! He decides who gets what. Anyone found keeping spoils will be dealt with harshly.'

The groups of ten slowly reassembled at their boats. Ani saw now how many had not returned. Only around half of the original band now sat in their boat.

'Where is everyone?' Purdu asked as she looked around the half-empty boat.

The captain of ten guffawed loudly. 'Lost or dead! What are you still doing here anyway? I thought you runts would have been trampled to death by now. Hide somewhere did you?'

'They fought like everyone else!' Mezarus retorted angrily.

The captain snorted in disdain but turned his attention to the prisoners now being loaded into the boats. They were prodded and jabbed forwards as they climbed or fell into the bows of each boat, their arms tied unnaturally at the elbows behind their heads. Any conversation between prisoners was cruelly silenced by hard blows.

Ani noticed they were shoving off the beach, but the wounded still lay on the sand. 'Sir!' he cried, tugging at the captain of ten's armored sleeve, 'you've forgotten the wounded!'

'And so will you if you know what's good for you,' he returned coldly.

Ani, Mezarus, and Purdu exchanged horrified looks.

'You can't leave them! They fought hard like everyone. They deserve to be taken back aboard!' Mezarus cried.

'Are you offering your place aboard?' the captain said, swiveling around with a look of malice. 'No wounded!' he added cruelly, then spun around again to deliver a hard blow to one of the prisoners who had dared to whisper.

As they drew away from the beach, Ani saw the Gal Meshedi and his men climbing into their boat and shoving off, a bundle of weapons in their arms.

*

The captain with his horned helmet and huge beard looked approvingly at the massive pile of spoils heaped beside the mast. The number aboard was greatly reduced, but those present seemed to wear grim though satisfied expressions. The master-at-arms stood silently beside the captain, running his eyes over each of them in turn as if trying to gauge their worthiness as future warriors.

'You have done well! Very well!' the captain bellowed in his thick accent. 'Those of you that have survived have earned your right to eat and to be one of us.

This is how we live on the sea. You may feel sorry for those people. Perhaps you feel like you have done a bad thing. Well, wake up! We fight, we steal, we survive! You have proven yourselves, so take what is rightfully yours!' he said and waved his log-like arm dramatically over the pile of food and goods.

The crew stepped forward and began to dole out the large quantity of food and wine that had been brought aboard. Ani and Purdu also ate their share, though they had lost some of their appetites remembering how it had been acquired.

'I can't go through that again,' Mezarus whispered forlornly as he chewed a piece of bread. 'I won't do it. I'd rather be stabbed in the back than slaughter innocent people.'

Ani nodded. Instinctively, he cast a glance towards Troan, who seemed to be looking meaningfully back at him as he gulped down a large mouthful of wine. He was sitting next to a fine-boned woman with fair skin that Ani knew at once must also be of noble birth. He did not believe in Troan's view of the world since he knew that goodness had nothing to do with one's status, but he did agree that a scene such as that witnessed today must never be allowed to happen again. He knew Mezarus and Purdu felt the same way.

*

They endured the blazing heat of the sun by day, fully exposed to its intensity, then slept on the cool open deck under the stars by night. For several days they lived off the food they had captured, supplemented by fresh fish caught by the crew. As the horrific memories of the raid faded, the journey through the open ocean towards an endless horizon had almost begun to numb Ani's ever-present grief at the past and his anxiety about the future. The other ships in their fleet always remained in sight, and occasionally they drew near one another as signals were exchanged with smoke or flags.

Each day of their journey they scrubbed the decks and were taught more about how to crew the ship. The captain it seemed had taken a dislike to Troan, and Ani noticed he was often given the most undesirable jobs around the ship.

Their daily fighting practice also continued. Ani was aware at once that his old sparring partner had never returned from the raid, but whether she had fled, died in battle, or suffered at the end of a captain's spear, he could only guess. Now he sparred mainly with Mezarus, which was both good and bad. Mezarus never intentionally hurt him, as others sometimes did, but he also did not pull his blows, knowing that Ani must learn to fight in earnest to survive, even if that meant a painful blow to the head or body. Ani soon learned to use his smaller size to his advantage against a much bigger opponent, ducking and weaving and avoiding the blows altogether, rather than attempting to parry them with sword or shield, both of which ended in painful bruises. He also had grown much more accustomed to wearing armor, and some skillful adjustments by the master-at-arms had made his suit much less uncomfortable.

Purdu, on the other hand, was making little progress at weapons training. Her heart simply was not in it, and although she adequately performed the maneuvers she was taught, it was clear she was mentally remote during the training.

'Purdu,' Ani said one afternoon after a long training session. 'I don't want to fight either, but you have to try harder. Whoever we face next will not take pity on us. We have to survive.'

'You sound like one of them when you say that,' she said despondently.

'That's not what I mean.'

'Killing demons was different, Ani. I could do that if I had to. I just can't kill people. I don't think Amuurana and Sidani would have either.'

Ani felt a sharp pang of grief at the mention of their names. He also thought of poor Duskzi who he missed very much. They had not spoken at all of what had happened in the fort after Ani had left. He did not want to hear it, and Purdu and Mezarus also seemed unwilling to relive it.

Late that same afternoon, Troan sidled up to Ani as he leaned over the rail and watched the foam hiss and boil out from under the stern below the rear castle. 'You make good progress young lord,' he said quietly, almost mockingly. Ani guessed his meaning. 'Keep practicing. We will need you soon,' he whispered and was gone.

*

The next morning saw a change of atmosphere on board. The crew seemed tense, obviously aware of something that the recruits were not. They still slept apart, and the crew had been informed of something imminent that had made them silent and brooding. Then as the morning drew on, it became apparent what this was. Land! A buzz ran through the ship as land was sighted off the port side. Rumors raced through the recruits about another possible raid, the picking up of more refugees, and even the occasional mention of demons.

'This is our chance to escape,' Mezarus whispered. 'I don't want to stay with these butchers any longer.'

Ani nodded, but he was worried by what Mezarus had in mind. They had found it easy enough last time to slip away in the heat of battle, but it may not be so easy a second time without feeling a spear or arrow in the back.

Purdu tightened Ani's straps on his armor as the preparation for landing began, and he did the same for her. She looked very striking with her long black wavy hair, her pretty face and slender body. He thought she looked how a warrior princess might look, if such a thing existed, for she was much stronger now, and there was a fierceness in her eye that had not existed in former days.

As the sun dipped further in the sky, they saw what Ani thought must be their next objective. It was another walled town, high on a cliff overlooking the ocean. It was inhabited by the looks of the smoke lifting from the rooftops.

They were called to attention by the master-at-arms and formed up in lines on the deck. The bearded captain walked among them, swishing his whip, instructing and threatening the captives from the previous raid. He looked much surer of his command over the survivors of the previous raid, and he gave Ani, Purdu, and Mezarus no trouble at all.

'We attack tonight!' he cried jubilantly. 'We have no surprise like last time, and the assault will be uphill and more difficult. Our entire fleet will attack at once from three sides to weaken their defense. The same rules apply – fight or die! Obtain as much food and loot as you can and return with it to the ship to be shared among all. Any attempt to keep it for yourselves will result in your immediate death. We are all one now. We rely on each other. Look to the person beside you. Protect them and they will protect you. We will attack in groups of ten again. And there is one more thing…,' He looked the group up and down gravely, 'there may be flesh-eaters! So be careful.'

A worried murmur spread through the ship.

'That's right! We are attacking the mainland, as no islands are to be found for many days from here and our food will not last that long. We must conquer this town to fill our bellies. It is a simple task, though dangerous. May the gods give you strength and courage, for you will need both!' With that, he strode off to the rear castle and conferred with the master-at-arms and the captains of ten. A signaler was busily relaying messages between ships.

A somber mood now fell over the recruits as the crew began to hand out the newly acquired weaponry and organize people into their groups of ten, with a captain and an original crew member in each group. The new captives were added to the groups to make up the numbers lost in the previous raid. It was clear that these men and women would be closely watched by the crew, and that they would be killed on the spot if they tried to run.

*

'We will charge the main gate,' the captain said as the crashing of waves on the dark beach became audible. 'Use your shields and do not stupidly throw away your lives. Our goal is to keep the defenders busy at the main gates while the second and third groups attack from behind. You will form a shield wall in front of the gates but beyond the true aim of the archers. We will stand fast there until the battle is joined from behind. Do not stop until you reach the top. Remember, stragglers will be treated like deserters! Now go!'

Everyone lurched forward as the boat ground to a halt upon the shelly beach, foam spilling over the sides as the waves surged in over the top of the boat.

Ani found Purdu's hand, and they jumped together into the waist-deep water and waded through the foam, trying not to topple as the waves crashed over them.

The group of ten quickly assembled on the beach, then broke into a run towards the twinkling lights on the clifftop above.

Ani scrambled up the gravelly slope. The extra weight of armor, and this time a sword and shield, made his legs burn. Purdu puffed loudly along beside him. He could sense the mortal threat of the captain with his long spear behind them as they hurried up the cliffside.

They came to a halt when they reached those already drawn up in a shield wall around fifty yards from the walls. Ani and Purdu linked their circular shields with the men and women beside them and stood in line, waiting for orders. As they had been warned, there was no element of surprise, and flaming arrows were already appearing high in the air above them, dropping to the ground around them to provide light for the archers on the walls to find their mark.

'Keep your shields locked and do not lift them over your heads!' the captains barked as people instinctively tried to protect themselves against the burning arrows dropping among them. There was a scream as a burning arrow plowed into the line, but Ani also saw what happened when someone lifted their shield – at least a dozen arrows quickly found the unprotected soul. The line closed in around them as they fell.

Ani huddled behind his shield, close beside Purdu, terrified by the sound of arrows whizzing overhead or thunking into shields or the dirt in front of them.

Soon there came the sound of horns blaring from the other side of the town.

'Advance!' the captains cried shrilly, banging their shields with their long bronze swords as they urged the line forwards.

Ani took tentative steps in keeping with those beside him. He could not really see where he was going behind his shield.

Suddenly there was a hiss from behind him. He spun around fearing a demon had crept upon them, as they had been warned might happen. But it was only Troan. He was looking cautiously over the top of his shield, ducking as arrows flew close overhead.

'What is it?' Ani hissed back.

'You don't want to go up there. That way lies the end. Come with me.'

'Where? What if we're caught? They'll think we're running away!'

'We are! But not to hide. I have a better plan.'

Ani looked over at Purdu who had also fallen just out of the line. The captains had not yet noticed them in the din of the advancing line and the bashing of weapon on shield.

They scurried back down the slope behind Troan, quickly finding cover behind some bushes to avoid the watchful eye of the captains.

'I've some people I want you to meet,' Troan whispered as they continued their rapid, slip-sliding descent down the gravelly slope.

Ani had a sudden sense that he and Purdu were being drawn into something that he liked perhaps even less than raiding towns.

On the beach, they could see the faint lights of many ships bobbing in the distance, out beyond the breakwater. They also heard voices talking in the dark.

'Wait here!' Troan said and trudged off down the dark beach. Only his dark silhouette could be seen in the starlight, which was now bright and clear in the night sky.

A minute later, many dark shapes appeared out of the night and surrounded them.

'These two?' someone said scornfully, apparently disappointed by the sight of Ani and Purdu.

'They're useless to us. They can't fight,' another said dismissively.

'They're just kids,' said another.

'They are nobles like us, and anyway, the boy is strong and the girl is smart. Now do not argue. They will be of use to us. Now into the boats.'

'What are we doing?' Ani asked, fearful of the answer.

'Taking back what is rightfully ours,' he sneered. 'Don't worry, it will be an easy fight. Your job is to keep watch and warn us if any of the other ships notice what's going on. There are two at anchor close by and we don't want them lending a hand. Got it?'

'But who are we fighting? What about the raid?' Purdu said worriedly.

'Come on kid, grow up! How long until you're killed in one of these stupid raids? How long until all of us are dead? It's madness! We're just cattle sent to slaughter, sacrificed to fetch food to fill their bellies. They don't care about us or anyone! Look at how few came back from the last raid. Half was it, maybe less? And the wounded all left on the beach to die! It was a disgrace! I won't be ruled by these barbarians. We're setting things right. Those born to rule will rule again. I was robbed of my birth rite by those foul demons. Now I'm taking it back. This getting out on the ocean thing was a great idea, but we need proper leadership, not foreign scum pushing us around and leading us on suicidal missions! You're part of the solution now. You're of high birth, like us. You were meant to rule over slaves and commoners. We'll show them what's what. They'll soon remember their place. Now climb in and help row.'

Ani and Purdu exchanged worried looks but did as they were told. Troan was right that the Sea Peoples were barbaric, but Ani also did not agree with what Troan had in mind. He was also worried about Mezarus, as he was still up on the cliffs with the others. An orange glow now outlined the summit where fires were spreading within the town. But the sounds of battle were absent, lost in the rhythmic crash of waves and the squeak of oars.

'I can't believe there's not even a rearguard on the beach,' one of the rowers beside Ani scoffed. 'What fools! They deserve to die!'

'Not enough people left for one after they abandoned the wounded to die. Well, they'll soon be avenged,' someone rasped bitterly.

Ani grew more and more worried by this talk of violence and vengeance.

'I don't think we should hurt anyone,' Purdu spoke up, sounding distressed. 'That's not what you're planning is it?'

There were sniggers and mocking laughter in the boat.

'Just do as I tell you,' Troan said, reassuringly, perhaps even protectively. 'Just stay in the boat and keep watch. You don't have to do anything else.'

The boat bumped against the side of the ship, more noisily than was perhaps intended.

'Who goes there?' a voice called down from the deck.

'We return from the raid victorious!' Troan called back.

In a moment a rope ladder dangled down over the edge and the men were out of the boat and hurrying up over the side. There was a startled gasp and then a thump as a body dropped to the deck.

Troan glanced back down over the edge at them. 'Row around the ship and keep watch!'

Ani and Purdu picked up the oars and began tentatively rowing alongside the ship. There was a sudden huge splash beside the boat as a body landed in the water nearby, then another. Then the sounds of furious battle ensued on deck.

'I don't like this!' Purdu cried, looking panicked. 'What are they doing?'

'They're killing anyone left on board of course. They're taking over the ship!'

'Let's get out of here Ani! Let's row to shore, find Mezarus and run away.'

In silent agreement, Ani began at once to steer the boat away from the ship, but at that moment he noticed a large shape emerging out of the darkness. It was another landing craft, but whether it came from the beach or one of the other ships he could not tell.

'You there!' someone on board called out to them. 'What's going on!'

Ani froze, unsure what to do, but Purdu acted quickly. She pulled hard on one of the oars and changed their course rapidly away from the approaching boat. 'Row!' she hissed at Ani.

He pulled with all his might, increasing speed, but the boat was turning too, following them. Then loud cries aboard the ship seemed to draw the boat away. Ani and Purdu slipped silently away into the darkness and rowed for shore.

8.

'What on earth's going on?' Michael wheezed as he shook hands with the giant that was his rescuer. He was passed a bottle of water by someone in the back, which he skulled in one long gulp.

'World's gone to shit, that's what!' the man said bluntly. 'And it's because of you.'

'Me? What?' Michael cried, choking on the water. He could make no sense of the chaos and carnage happening around him. He could see through the small bulletproof glass windows of the armored truck - the exact same model as the one they had escaped in during the siege - that the world had indeed 'gone to shit', as he put it. People were colliding off the windows leaving bloody streaks. Their rapid collisions gave him just the briefest glimpse of gnashing teeth and claw-like hands grasping and champing at the glass. He became aware that the vehicle was bumping and bouncing violently over bodies, crushing them beneath its wheels as it raced through the streets of downtown Ankara, swerving around empty cars and other debris in the streets. They passed a square with a large fountain in the middle, still pouring out water. The whole place was full of motionless figures, staring into space, their arms limp by their sides. As soon as they perceived the roar of the engines they immediately turned and began running towards the vehicle.

'Oh god, is this really happening?' Michael said as he instinctively jerked his head away from the glass as another tormented face glanced bloodily off the window beside his head. 'How did it come to this?'

'I told you that you would wish you were still in your cell. This is what we have tried to stop for so long. This is what our great leader said would happen. This is what you caused.'

'*Me*? Why do you keep saying *me*? How have I got anything to do with it? I'm a victim too!'

'Because you and your friend killed our leader and stole the cure.'

'I didn't kill him! That was Nathan! I would have stopped him if I'd known what he was going to do! I only wanted to talk to him. And I didn't steal it!'

The man looked over at his companions and grunted something in Turkish that could only be an obscenity.

'So if you hate me so much, why did you rescue me?'

'You are going to help us. You are the only person like us that knows what is happening. And you know how to make the cure. Gökmen showed you.'

'No, no, no! You've got it all wrong! Gökman made the cure while I was there, but I have no idea what he was doing! I'm not a nanotechnologist!'

'We have footage. You saw what he did. You make the formula or we kill you!'

'Is this a sick joke? I can't do it! I just can't! From what I gather it's so advanced he was way out in front. Even the other nanotechnologists at the CBT couldn't work it out. Besides,' he said glumly, his outrage melting into despair, 'it doesn't work.'

'Of course not. Gökmen was paranoid shit. He fooled you! He gave you a dud! He was just trying to escape. He was a devious little shit.'

'What?' Michael nearly fell out of his seat at this revelation. 'You're saying Gökmen never even gave me the real drug?'

The man shrugged, pulled a face and nodded.

'The bastard! He cost me…' he couldn't say it. His eyes stung and his aching head drooped onto his chest as he thought of Corinne and his failed attempt to save her. Now he was glad Gökmen had died in the brutal way he did.

'He cheated us. But his cure was good.'

'The man he cured in the video?' Michael said, looking up in shock. 'You mean that was for real?'

'Yes. Our brothers in USA say it worked. They have recovered the notes and have sent to us.'

'Recovered them? How? They were behind fifteen frigging feet of concrete walls in a bunker that would survive an all out nuclear war. They were locked away in the CBT vaults.' He paused, considering how unlikely this was. 'I doubt they have them.' He shook his head, disbelievingly.

'CBT no longer exist. Nothing exists! Look out the window.'

Michael didn't need to look out the window. In any case, the blood was so thick on the glass now that there was nothing left to see.

'But…' he was speechless for a moment. 'They were synthesizing it from the notes. I gave them the vials of FAVE Best. Mr Thompson said they had nearly cracked it.'

'You trust that shit?'

'Well, no, but I thought they would crack it in time, before it got out of control.'

'No. The USA is shit, just like here. There are compounds, survivors, people hiding. The rest is toilet. The same in US. The end is here now Michael. Now we look to you - little shit - to get us out of toilet you have created.'

Michael's jaw practically hit his collarbone. How could they possibly blame him for this? How could any of this be his fault?

There was a sudden deafening bang and a flash of light. Everyone flew forwards out of their seats as the vehicle plowed to a sudden halt. There was rapid excited chatter among the Meshedi in the truck as they tried to work out what had happened. Smoke began to fill the cabin.

'Out!' the man yelled at Michael as everyone grabbed their guns and made a leap for the rear doors.

Michael screamed inside at the thought of getting out of the truck in his condition into the hell that was waiting outside. He was barely able to sit upright in his seat let alone run for his life. The day was just getting worse and worse! 'What's happening?' he asked the man as the doors were flung open.

'Explosion. Can't get through,' he replied in alarm as he dragged Michael out the back doors with one hand, a sub-machine gun held in the other.

The Meshedi spilled out behind them. They were in a narrow lane sandwiched between tall apartment blocks. A wall had collapsed onto the road blocking their path ahead. Scorch marks on the walls and road around told of an explosion that had brought the wall down in their path. Around them was a swarm of INS victims, wailing and gurgling as they staggered around the armored truck, eager to tear into them. Smoke was pouring out of the front of the truck.

There was a sudden blaze of noise as the Meshedi opened fire on the encircling crowd. Everywhere Michael looked heads vanished in red puffs as the Meshedi quickly and efficiently carried out their brutal and practiced work. Within seconds the vehicle was clear, but there was no way through, and more shambling figures were staggering up the street behind them. The only escape from the lane was by entering the buildings that flanked the street or backtracking several blocks.

The Meshedi broke into a hurried discussion as the drivers of the vehicle joined them. They were pointing up, explaining the explosion had come from above.

Michael was woozy now and felt like he might fall to his knees at any moment. As he began to wobble he heard the distinct throb of a helicopter, approaching fast.

The Meshedi instantly dispersed and flattened themselves into the doorways and shop fronts along the street. Michael staggered after them, trying to work out which way to run.

'Here, shithead!' the man called to him, and reached out and yanked him into an alcove beside him.

Michael fell to his knees as he slammed roughly into the metal shutter that covered the doorway.

'Someone is trying to kill us!' he muttered as he scanned the narrow slash of sky above.

The Meshedi seemed suddenly to catch a glimpse of something above him and he raised his gun as if about to fire. But he fired no shot! Instead, he sagged silently to the ground next to Michael. Michael looked over in surprise. With horror, he saw a large red hole in the middle of the Meshedi's forehead and a deep crimson pool spreading around his body.

'Oh, Jesus!' Michael cried and scrambled back away from the body in shock. He heard the helicopter roar again as it made another sudden pass overhead. He saw another Meshedi drop to the ground on the other side of the street.

He looked up, fearful he also was in sight of the gunman above. He heard the helicopter approaching again, coming around for another pass. He shrank into the alcove in terror, hardly believing he had been rescued only a short time before to be killed in some random assault from above. Who were these madmen picking them off one by one?

He remained hunched in the doorway for what felt like a long time, unwilling to look up lest it be his turn next. But nothing happened. The helicopter was gone!

A moment later he saw a pair of boots appear before him. A command was barked at him in Turkish. He looked up. A very angry looking Meshedi was staring down at him. He felt the boot strike his chin. He reeled in agony and fell to the ground again, grasping his chin and spluttering, the taste of blood in his mouth. The same order was barked at him again. He knew now what he was being commanded to do. He crawled to his knees, then shakily stood up.

The Meshedi grabbed him roughly by the arm and pulled him into a slow jog down the street.

9.

It was immediately obvious that something was very, very wrong on the ground. The airports around Ankara were not responding to the pilot's hails as they circled the city, looking for somewhere to land. Not even a military jet had appeared to challenge them.

'Why aren't they responding?' Arla asked worriedly.

Yosef shook his head. 'Where are all the planes? There's nothing down there! It's as I feared!'

Arla stared out of the window. He was right. Usually busy tarmacs, hangars, and bustling terminals lay ghostly quiet and empty. Her eyes widened as they passed over the international airport and she noticed the charred tail of an airbus protruding from a gaping hole in the front of the passenger terminal. Bodies lay on the tarmac surrounding the plane, charred or skeletonized.

'We can't land here!' she called to the pilot as he brought them in for a low pass over the runway.

The pilot pulled up at once as hundreds of shambling, off-balance figures came running out of one of the terminals, their hands reaching into the air as if praying to the sun.

'Well, I need a runway! I can't just land anywhere!' he replied sharply.

'What about an empty road?' Yosef asked. 'If we get further out of town, maybe you can land and we can find an empty car. There seems to be plenty of them down there.'

Arla had noticed it too. Cars were abandoned everywhere - in the streets, on main roads, and at intersections. It was like a photograph of a huge, chaotic traffic jam where nothing was moving and all was quiet. INS victims were everywhere. A city of them! They walked aimlessly through the streets in groups, or stood still, staring up at them with their arms raised and hands outstretched as they passed low overhead.

'My god,' Arla whispered, 'this is so much worse than when I left. 'There's nothing but infected down there now.' She sat staring in disbelief at the ghastly scene below, a deep sadness washing over her as she watched.

Yosef was silent too.

Arla came to her senses. 'Ariel!' she said in a sudden panic, looking up at Yosef.

He nodded but said nothing.

They had banked away from the city now and were heading south when the pilot pointed to the ground ahead. 'My maps say there is an old aerodrome out here and I think I've found it!' He was pointing to an empty airstrip sitting on its own in the heavily farmed countryside. A rusty hangar sat beside the tarmac but there was no sign of anyone on the ground. They flew low over the airstrip once before turning sharply and bringing the small jet back around and into a landing approach. A moment later the wheels screeched and the jet skidded to a halt at the end of the hot tarmac.

Yosef immediately unstrapped and hurried into the main cabin to where their equipment was stored among the passenger seating. Arla followed suit.

'I don't think it's safe for me to wait here,' the pilot said, following them out of the cockpit.

Yosef was already donning the protective Kevlar overalls they had brought to guard against bites and scratches.

'That's right,' Yosef replied and tossed the pilot a pair of overalls and boots. 'You're coming too!'

The pilot nodded and started pulling on the protective clothing.

They loaded packs filled with water and other supplies, pulled on riot helmets with face shields, then slung the standard-issue IDF Tavor submachine guns over their shoulders.

'Remember your basic training?' Yosef said with an anxious smile as he cocked his gun.

'Some of it,' she replied, unamused. She did not feel at all ready for what they were about to face.

'Just stay close to me.'

Arla rolled her eyes a little but said nothing.

Yosef relayed their position and immediate plans via sat phone, then waited for a reply. Once the OK was received he packed the phone away and hauled on his pack. 'How far out of the city do you think we are?' he asked the pilot as they climbed out onto the baking hot tarmac.

'About ten miles. It's going to take a while to walk in. I hope we have enough water.'

'It'll have to do. We've been instructed not to drink the water here. I'm sure we'll soon find a car.'

They jogged out onto the access road that joined the northern end of the tarmac and followed it through wheat fields and rolling hills towards the city. Small towns began to appear on hilltops around them and soon tall buildings began to dominate the horizon.

They rounded a corner when Arla suddenly became aware of a flash of light on a hilltop close by. It looked like sunlight reflected on glass. 'I think someone's watching us,' she said, pulling Yosef instinctively to the edge of the road and into a crouch.

'How do you know?'

'I think I caught a flash from binoculars. Up there!' She pointed to the location.

Yosef ferreted in his pack for his own binoculars and zoomed in on the spot. He shook his head. 'Nothing there. They probably realized you'd seen them.'

'Who do you think it is?'

'Could be anyone. I guess a jet landing out here draws some attention nowadays.'

They carried on along the road, more cautiously now, and kept to the edge and among the long grass whenever possible. Before long they heard the sound of large engines ahead. A heavy vehicle was approaching.

'Should we hide?' the pilot said, a little panicked. He glanced around the barren hills edging the road for a place to conceal himself.

'Perhaps,' Yosef replied, looking uncertain.

'Yes, of course we should,' Arla insisted and began to lead them quickly from the road towards the only cover, a gully full of dry shrubs some distance away. But at that moment an armored personnel carrier with military insignia came tearing over the crest of the hill nearest the gully they were heading for and plowed through the wheat fields towards them, kicking up a cloud of dust as it came. It skidded to a halt in front of them, enveloping them in a choking cloud. A machine gun turret swiveled onto their position, a helmeted soldier peering down the gun sights at them coolly.

'Drop your weapons!' Arla hissed to her companions.

They unslung their guns and tossed them to the ground in front of them, raising their hands in the air.

The back doors of the armored car flew open and three soldiers jumped out, immediately scanning the surrounding area before training their weapons on Arla, Yosef and the pilot.

The pilot hailed the soldiers in Turkish as they advanced. 'I told them we're just passing through,' he relayed to Arla and Yosef.

'Hmm, that's convincing. No doubt they'll just let us go,' Arla muttered sarcastically.

'Tell them we're here on behalf of the Israeli government,' Yosef added.

The pilot called out again, but the advancing soldiers did not answer. Two of them stopped around ten meters away, guns raised, while the third advanced cautiously. He spoke to the pilot for a moment then radioed back to the truck.

'He wants to know why we're armed and why the Israeli government has sent people here. He wants to know why they have not been informed.'

'Tell them we can prove our identity as government agents searching for a missing person, and that we can put them in touch with our superior officers in Israel if they wish. Tell them also that we tried to communicate with the authorities here, but no one answered our calls.'

There was another exchange between the pilot and soldiers, at which point the lead soldier picked up the dropped weapons and motioned for them to follow him back to the truck.

An officer jumped out of the back of the truck as they approached. 'You have landed illegally in Turkey, and must come with us,' he said in good English. 'We cannot speak here,' he said, pointing over their shoulders. 'We must go somewhere safe!'

Arla looked over her shoulder and saw a pack of around twenty INS victims lurching over a hill towards them. She climbed into the back of the truck alongside the other soldiers and her companions and they sped off through the wheat fields.

*

'Strange to see Israeli's here now after help was denied for so long,' the clean-shaven officer said as he looked them up and down and examined their passports. They had been taken into a barbed wire compound on the outskirts of Ankara, patrolled by guard towers and full of demountables. The place seemed well organized and well-provisioned, with perhaps a thousand residents consisting of civilians and soldiers. Led inside one of the buildings, they now faced another officer of high rank by the looks of his decorations, who seemed genuinely intrigued by their appearance before him. However, his expression darkened when he saw their passports.

'Israel sat idly by and watched Turkey die, along with all its neighbors. What makes you think coming here now was a good idea? Hmm? As government representatives no less – the first we have seen in quite some time. I would have thought it unwise for you to come here. You might be held accountable. Some would like to see you punished.'

No one had anything to say. Arla did feel ashamed that her government had done nothing to help. But then, what could they have done? Whole cities had been overcome with INS in only a few days with no way to control the outbreak or its horrendous consequences. Instead, Israel had chosen to prevent such a thing from happening within its own borders.

'So why are you here exactly?' the high ranking officer asked.

'We have come to find my brother,' Arla spoke again. 'He works for the embassy and he came to look for someone. He was looking for them for me,' she felt tears begin to come, but she forced them down.

'Oh, and who is this someone that is worth your brother's life?'

'He is someone that could change things.'

'Change things? Go on.'

'I'm not at liberty to say.'

The officer stifled a cynical laugh. 'I see. We will see how you feel about that shortly.'

The officer now turned to Yosef. 'And who are you?'

'My name is Yosef Benzekri. I am her brother's assistant. I came to help her find him.'

'Assistant?'

'OK, partner. I work for Mossad, but that has nothing to do with why I'm here. I came here to find Ariel and make sure he gets home.'

'I see. And him?'

'He is our pilot. He is Turkish.'

'A Jew?'

'Of course. We are all Jews.'

'You must think you are truly the chosen people to have survived when so few others have.'

'I am a man of reason, not some religious zealot. I know this is a deadly disease and not some divine plague sent to punish the gentile or Muslim. I am here to try and help put a stop to it, that is all.'

'Noble actions indeed!' he said mockingly. 'If only Israel had been so magnanimous when we needed your help.'

'I'm sorry,' Arla said, growing tired of the slurs. 'I'm sorry for what has happened here, we are not the government of Israel. We are not personally responsible. What could we have done?'

'Well since we are being so frank, the truth is that we don't want you here. We have limited resources and keeping you alive would only jeopardize the wellbeing of others. You see, we have the same philosophy now! You have made a mistake coming here. We have no choice but to dispose of you since you have nothing of benefit to offer us, and are *not at liberty* to say why you are here. We're not going to hold you prisoner. We don't have enough food. So it's off to the flesh pit with you.' He nodded to the soldiers that stood at the ready behind him and they moved forward, their guns raised.

'Wait!' Arla said as one of the soldiers grabbed her arm and pulled her roughly towards the exit. 'Wait!' she repeated.

The officer cocked his head slightly as if expecting a confession, but when none came, followed silently along behind as they were dragged struggling down a short hallway and out into the heat and light. They were forced along a gravelly path at gunpoint, then turned hard left into a concrete bay built against the barbed wire fence. At the end of the bay was a metal trap door. Below this, they saw a blood-stained chute that passed under the fence and down a dusty slope. Skeletons and refuse lay bare and fly-blown in the dust below. INS victims stood silently in the distance, gazing into space, their hands working by their sides. They looked slowly up with vacant expressions, then started slowly ambling towards the fence, gurgling harshly as they came.

'Don't do this,' Arla said angrily, her fists clenching as she was dragged towards the chute at gunpoint. 'We're looking for something,' she spat at last, as her toes curled instinctively over the edge of the concrete and locked in place.

A soldier who had been walking alongside the officer now walked to the edge of the fence and pulled back the metal cover over the chute with a loud, metallic screech.

'Something…,' the officer said with disinterest, picking his ear. 'Well, everybody's looking for something, as the Eurythmics song goes.' He nodded towards the soldiers again. 'At least now you won't have to look any longer.' He lifted a finger and the soldiers grabbed tightly onto Arla and Yosef's shoulders and began forcing them forwards towards the chute.

Yosef did not make a sound she noticed but seemed to be carefully studying the lay of the land beyond the fence.

Arla could see an INS victim below, staring up the chute at her. Its tongue rolled behind torn blue lips and broken teeth, the scabby face contorting and grimacing as it snarled up at her expectantly.

'No!' she screamed as she lost her footing and nearly tumbled down the chute. 'Something important! Something you want! Something you need!'

The officer sighed as if he was disappointed she had finally decided to talk. 'Oh, and what is that?'

'A cure! There is a cure. I know where it is. We were going there.'

The officer laughed sarcastically. 'Just accept your fate. It will be over soon.'

'Don't be a fool! I know there is a cure and I can take you to it. It was developed in the US, but they brought it here. There is someone in town who has it.'

The officer stayed the soldiers with a raised hand. They stopped shoving them forwards but did not let go. 'What is it and where is it?' he asked matter-of-factly.

'What, so you can throw us in and go and get it?' Arla seethed.

'OK then,' he waived the soldiers off them. 'Hmm?'

'We can take you there, but we're not just going to tell you where it is. We're not stupid! And I will only take you there if we agree to split it. I have someone I need to help.'

'You drive a hard bargain for someone about to be torn apart. What is it?'

'It's very advanced. It's a nanoviricide developed by a brilliant scientist. The man we have come to rescue knows about it. He got it from Gökman, the scientist.'

'He was Turkish?'

'Yes, I think so, a Turkish American.'

The officer snorted dismissively.

'So do you want the fucking drug or not?' Arla practically shrieked as she looked down the chute at the grotesque snarling crowd that had gathered there now. She closed her eyes, trying not to think what was coming if the officer rejected her plea.

The officer regarded them for a long while before answering. 'If they had a cure, why didn't they use it?'

Arla wasn't expecting this question and it caught her unprepared. She hesitated. 'By the time they had perfected it, it was already too late. But it exists, here in Ankara!' She was horrified at the sound of her own words. She hadn't lied this badly since she was a kid trying to avoid a belting, but all she could think of was getting out of this situation at any cost. 'All we have to do is go and get it… and find my brother.'

'Your brother?' the officer repeated disinterestedly, sounding suddenly put off. 'And who is he?'

'A spy, like Yosef told you. He came to find the drug and the guy that has it. If we can find him he will take us straight to Michael and the cure.'

'Aren't all Israeli's spies?'

'Don't be stupid. Of course not.'

'This cure… how does it work? Can anyone be cured? Will it cure them?' he pointed with disgust at the moaning, gurgling crowd in the chute, clawing at the air, impatient for her flesh.

'Yes, anyone!' She said almost jubilantly. She groaned inside at her outrageous lies, but the officer seemed to be falling for it.

'I have a daughter,' he said quietly. 'Will it cure her?'

'Yes, yes, definitely!' she insisted. Now she just felt sad. There were so many that would want this cure she was so freely offering - a cure she had no proof existed at all, and certainly not in Ankara.

The officer seemed to battle his own emotions for a moment, then spoke to the soldier beside the fence. The cover was pulled back on.

'Come with me!' the officer said and turned sharply on his heel.

10.

The boat churned through the foam as a fat wave came spilling in over the side, pushing Ani off his seat and into the bottom of the boat, where he gulped in copious quantities of seawater. Choking and spluttering, he hauled himself in his heavy armor back onto the narrow wooden bench, trying to regain his composure while steering the boat in against the beach with the heavy oars.

'Hold on!' Purdu cried over the crash of another wave as they plowed up onto the beach again.

Ani could not see where they were going in the dark, but he hoped they had landed far away from the main assault landing. His hopes were soon dashed, however, when he saw the silhouettes of large groups of people hurrying down the beach towards the rows of boats drawn up nearby.

'What do we do?' Purdu called, turning around to face her brother.

Ani surveyed the beach. It was obvious they could not turn around now. Several silhouettes came running down to the boat and dragged it up higher onto the beach. Ani found his shield in the pool of water swishing in the bottom of the boat and climbed out.

He could hear orders being shouted over the din of the crowd and the crash of the waves.

'What's happened?' Ani asked one of the men who had helped with the boat.

'Flesheaters! Millions of them! We've got to get out of here!'

Ani shot a worried look at Purdu. He was thinking of Mezarus.

Hundreds of people were dashing down the beach, jumping into boats and trying to push them off the beach and back into the waves.

Captains were screaming at their troops, trying to rally them into a defensive retreat, but everywhere was panic.

Ani was knocked into the water as a man dashed past him, wailing with fear as he ran.

Purdu pulled him up. 'We've got to find Mezarus!' she cried over the tumultuous sea.

The boats were leaving quickly, many half-empty, while the captains and crew began to take drastic action, cutting down those that tried to flee past them for the boats. 'Form a shield wall!' they kept crying in vain.

Ani could hear the terrifying snarling, barking, and gurgling of the demons hot on the heels of the retreating raiders, along with the screams of those unlucky enough to be caught in flight. The press of men and women down to the boats was unstoppable, and soon even the captains and crew abandoned any hope of order and fled for the boats.

Ani took Purdu's hand and dragged her along the beach at a run.

'Mezarus!' he called again and again as they ran.

A strong hand suddenly grabbed Ani by the arm and brought him to a dead stop. Purdu drew up beside him.

'Mezarus!' Ani sighed in relief, much relieved to see him alive and safe. He stepped forward to hug him, but the figure did not reply and stepped back.

'What did you say?' a deep, familiar voice said in the darkness.

'Mezarus… Is that you?' Ani said uncertainly, straining his eyes to see the face more clearly.

'That name. It is the name of the High Smith's apprentice. How do you know this man? Is he here?'

Ani felt the grip tighten on his arm as the figure stooped down to look him in the face.

To Ani's horror, he realized he was staring into the eyes of the Gal Meshedi.

Ani inhaled sharply and tried to pull away. He heard Purdu gasp as well.

'Answer the question!' the deep, callous voice commanded.

Ani felt a shiver to hear that voice and he remembered all the suffering it had caused. 'I, uh…' Ani stammered.

'Mezarus you said. Where is he?'

'I don't know who you mean. You must be mistaken,' Ani lied, not wanting to give anything away to this evil man.

'Do not lie to me boy!' the Gal Meshedi said, his voice dangerous now. Ani felt the strong hand leave his shoulder and close around his throat.

'Leave him alone you brute! You evil man!' Purdu cried from behind Ani. 'Get your hands off him!'

There was silence for a moment as the Gal Meshedi seemed taken aback by

Purdu's savage tone. 'I know you two,' he said at last, realization dawning in his voice. 'You are the children of Amuurana!' He seemed genuinely shocked for a moment, then in a flash of movement, Ani realized a dagger was now held at his throat. 'Where is Amuurana?' the Gal Meshedi asked with pure malice in his voice.

Ani could not answer. His throat was constricted and he was beginning to struggle for air. He also refused to tell this man anything.

'He's dead, and so is Sidani thanks to you!' Purdu cried, suddenly bursting into tears. She thumped the Gal Meshedi hard in the chest several times, then fell to her knees in the sand and balled.

Ani felt the Gal Meshedi's grip loosen around his neck, and he gasped for air. 'Is this true boy? Is Sidani dead?' he said, his voice changed now, almost regretful.

'Yes, they both are,' Ani rasped. He felt hot tears begin to sting his own cheeks as he thought of them.

'You were there?'

'Yes. And Purdu.'

'So you are Purdu?' the Gal Meshedi said, letting go of Ani and effortlessly dragging Purdu to her feet. He looked into her face in the starlight. 'And you are Amuurana's daughter!'

'No. He adopted us.'

'I see. I thought there was something strange about you two! And what of Mezarus. Is he here?'

'What's it to you?' Ani retorted defiantly.

'Answer the question or I'll have you flayed alive, boy!' All remorse had left his voice now and he sounded venomous again.

'We're not yours to command or punish anymore,' he cried, anger and hatred welling up in him. 'You're just another of the Sea Peoples now like all of us. I don't have to answer your questions or listen to your threats anymore.'

'Oh, we'll see about that you little guttersnipe!'

'You can insult us all you like, but we don't owe you anything, and it's you who ought to pay for Amuurana and Sidani's death. You forced her to leave Hattusha, and in the end, they sacrificed themselves for us!'

'I dare say that was a waste. I haven't forgotten your sentence of treason, or your ridiculous attempts to free Amuurana. How did a pair of rats like you get away anyway?'

'Lelwan!' Purdu shouted through her tears. 'He was a good man. He saved us! Many times.'

'Ah, our fallen captain. How sweet! And is he here as well?'

'No, he's dead too! Now leave us alone you horrid man! You should feel ashamed of how you treated Sidani, your own niece! You made her run into the wilds, and now she's dead! They're all dead!'

There was a sudden shout from further down the beach and the sound of heavy feet on the wet sand. Ani looked over his shoulder. A large man was running up the beach towards them carrying a long sword. Ani could see it was Mezarus from his huge torso and unusual ivory helmet. 'Ani, Purdu!' he yelled as he drew nearer to them.

When they looked back, the Gal Meshedi was gone.

Ani threw his arms around Mezarus when he arrived.

'Who was that?' Mezarus asked worriedly.

'No one,' Ani replied, but he could hear the fear in his own voice.

'We have to go! There are demons everywhere! They've taken half the raiding force!'

'Where did they come from?'

'Teshub only knows! There's thousands of them and they're damned hungry.'

They tore down the beach to where a large group of retreating raiders was jostling for places aboard the last boat. A fight broke out amongst them, and the boat was overturned, sinking into the waves and foam and was lost.

A shield wall had finally formed behind them, fending off the rabid attack as best it could, but it was clear it would not last much longer. It seemed they were going to be trapped between the demons and the sea.

A moment later the shield wall broke. It crumpled back in on itself, then toppled as half-naked demons in rags surged over the top of the fallen warriors and fell upon the hapless defenders behind.

Ani fell to his knees in terror as hundreds of demons erupted through the last of the defenses, tearing chunks out of people as they came, or latching onto throats and tearing with their bare teeth. The savage slashing of short swords did nothing to halt the onslaught that came crashing in upon those trapped on the beach. Suddenly something occurred to Ani – something he had seen once before.

'Follow me!' he yelled to Purdu and Mezarus and anyone else standing nearby. He waded quickly out into the crashing surf, until he was at least chest deep, jumping waves and struggling to stay upright.

Sure enough, others followed, until a long line of raiders stood chest-deep, battling the force of the waves. As they stood looking back onto the beach at the corpses being devoured by the hungry pack, Ani noticed not one of the demons entered the water. They drew up, shuffling, sniffing thc air, standing at the uppermost edge of the approaching and receding sheets of foamy water, then turned around and shuffled away, back to the bodies lying on the beach and in the dunes behind.

Suddenly new boats appeared out of the darkness, cutting through the surf.

'Here! Here! Come aboard!' a man standing in the bows called to those in the deep water. Ani realized it was one of the men who had accompanied Troan back to the ships.

Ani, Purdu, and Mezarus were pulled aboard. Others piled in after them, including a captain of ten. In a few moments, the boat was out beyond the breakers, and the terrible sounds were lost in the distance beyond the crashing waves. The terrible scenes on the beach were replaced by clear starlight, the rhythmic splash of oars, and the panting of the terrified escapees.

No one spoke as they rowed towards the dark shapes that bobbed a little further out. Ani knew that things would be different once they arrived, but in what way exactly he could not guess.

As they drew nearer, they saw the faint glow of lamps aboard the ships. They stood at anchor very close together and he heard faint noises aboard.

At that moment, the man Ani recognized from Troan's party stood up. Several of his accomplices who were with him on the boat also stood. He stepped over Ani to the back of the boat where the captain of ten was staring worriedly at the ships ahead. Suddenly there came a flash of bronze in the starlight and a startled cry. The captain slumped forwards with a mortal groan and lay still. Troan's accomplices all unsheathed their swords at once. They were the long kind as originally worn by the crew. They glinted menacingly in the starlight. There was a cry among those on board, then a fear-filled silence.

Ani threw his arms around Purdu protectively, but she shrugged him off. He could see she was clutching her short-sword in the bottom of the boat.

'No one moves a muscle!' the swordsman cried as he yanked his blade from the captain's chest with a spurt of blood. 'Things have changed. We are in control now. We have taken over the fleet and we are restoring things to their proper order. Any resistance will be crushed immediately.'

Ani could tell now what the commotion was on some of the ships they were approaching. There was obviously a struggle going on between the usurpers and the original crew.

The man who had killed the captain looked down at Ani and Purdu and winked. 'Things will be a whole lot different soon, for you and for them.' He cast a disdainful look at the others in the boat who Ani guessed, like them, were of low birth. 'Troan will be happy to see you both.' He reached down and pulled a small bone-handled dagger from the belt of the dead captain and handed it to Ani. 'Take this, you may need it soon!'

11.

Michael looked briefly down at the chair in which he was being ordered to sit at gunpoint. The Meshedi's initial hospitality had expired along with his English-speaking rescuer. His new captor had all the niceties of an octopus meeting a rather plump prawn after missing lunch.

They had run through back streets for many blocks, Michael being dragged and kicked along. His inability to run or even walk at anything like a decent pace had infuriated the Meshedi. More frightening than the kicks and abuse he had received was the reappearance of the helicopter strafing them overhead. The anger with which the Meshedi greeted its presence was mostly directed at him, and at one point they had seemed ready to dispose of him there and then. At the last second, one of their number had pushed the gun away from his temple, picked him up and carried him the last few blocks to what was apparently their bunker.

They had entered through a large double door in the side of a traffic tunnel and followed an underground service tunnel until they finally reached a series of underground rooms, heavily barred with gates and steel doors. How long it had been their base Michael could not tell, but the place looked well stocked with food, medical equipment, and unbelievably to Michael, nanoreactor equipment.

He fell back in the chair as instructed. Opposite him was a stainless-steel table, on top of which lay a thick spiral-bound book of photocopied handwritten notes.

'Gökmen!' he barked and flicked a few pages over irritably. Then he poked Michael in the chest, slammed his fist on the open page, picked up a pen and pretended to write, then pointed meaningfully at the nanotechnology equipment, all the while grimacing homicidally at Michael like he intended to gauge his spine out with the ballpoint pen he was holding. The other Meshedi looked on doubtfully.

'So no one here speaks English?' Michael asked hopefully.

Michael copped a slap in the face for that remark, not that he imagined his tormentor had understood what he had said. The Meshedi slapped the open pages again, then rather comically in Michael's somewhat deranged view, pretended to study the notes closely. Then he pointed once more at the nanotechnology equipment.

'Yes, I understand,' he said nodding, exaggerating it in a similar pantomime-like style.

The Meshedi turned and spoke to his comrades for a moment. One of them suggested the word 'make'.

'Make!' his captor shouted at him fifty times louder than necessary.

'OK, no problem. I take it you don't mind waiting six or seven years while I get up to speed on nanotechnology, learn how to use these machines, oh, and decipher this scrawl, which I might add is written in Turkish, a language I don't understand!'

For that, he took a right hook to the eye socket, again, not because his aggressor had likely understood a single word, but for daring to speak at all.

Michael grasped his blazing cheek, his brain throbbing painfully and threatening to blackout. He decided against further speech and just nodded.

The Meshedi watched him expectantly. At last, Michael summoned the strength to stand on his quivering legs and begin to inspect the huge ream of notes. This brought a faint smile to the lips of the Meshedi, and the mood in the room suddenly became far less hostile. A glass of water materialized before him and even some sujuk sausage and bread. Michael stared at the food warily, trying to remember how to eat, then devoured the meal in several large gulps. More food was brought while he perused the book, nodding sagely as he pretended to understand what it said. It only took a moment to see the notes had in fact already been translated in a crabbed hand under each line or in the margin, leaving Michael wishing for his reading glasses. Knowing as he did that these notes had somehow been lifted from the CBT, he deduced it was they that must have translated them.

After some time the food began to take effect, and Michael actually began to take some notice of what he was reading. His mind slowly began to clear, only to realize that the terminology was completely foreign to him.

'I can't understand this!' he said at last, hesitantly, expecting a savage blow of some kind. 'I need a dictionary or the internet at the very least, though I suppose that no longer exists. Better still would be research papers that explain what these processes are and what they mean. The notes are meaningless to me otherwise.'

'Make!' the Meshedi reiterated, slapping one hand into another. 'Make!'

'Yes, I know that! I would truly like to make this drug but I don't know how! I need more information.'

The Meshedi looked puzzled. Michael attempted to mime his puzzlement at the notes and what they meant. At last, the Meshedi nodded enthusiastically and left the room. He returned, wheeling a TV monitor and video player into the room. He held up a labeled video cassette and pushed it into the video knowingly. A moment later the screen flickered, then grainy CCTV footage of Gökmen in the funeral parlor lab appeared on the screen, with himself looking anxious and twitchy in the background, clearly holding a pistol pointed at Gökmen through his jacket pocket while Gökmen worked.

'Make!' the Meshedi repeated, slapping the screen, then broke into what appeared to be a long string of obscenities under his breath.

Michael nodded, then patiently watched the video through. Gökmen was going back and forth from shelves, fridges full of vials, centrifuges, supercooling units and other devices in what was an unfathomable dance that Michael quickly realized he had as much hope of understanding or replicating as the intricate dance of a honey bee instructing its cohort to the location of a good flower patch. His heart sank as he watched. How long could he stall them? What was the point of stalling them anyway? How would this all end? He thought he could guess.

Having watched the video, his captors watched him expectantly. He rewound it and played it again, then limped from machine to machine while it played, trying to work out which ones matched those in the video and the sequence in which they were used. At last, he collapsed in his chair in front of the screen. 'I'm going to need help. I need someone to help me. Do you have anyone who can help me?' Blank stares greeted him. 'Helper!' he said at last, very slowly.

There was a short argument among the Meshedi in the room. At last one of them left. Michael sat for a long time staring at the video again, unable to work out what on earth was going on. At last, there was the faint squeak of wheels entering the room. What have they brought me now, he wondered in despair. He turned wearily around, expecting to see another unidentified machine brought for his amusement. But there, slumped and half-conscious, heavily bandaged, and possibly drooling a little, sat Nathan in a wheelchair. He looked up sleepily, noticed Michael in front of the monitor, then murmured so quietly that Michael could barely hear him. 'Don't bother. TV's crap here.'

12.

'I already told you, Ariel had found someone who knew where to find Michael. Then I lost contact with my brother. We need to find Ariel or the person he met with. That will lead us to Michael.'

'I received a message from Ariel two days ago. We think he's been captured by the Meshedi,' Yosef added.

'So, you think these Meshedi want the cure as well?'

'Yes, they developed it, Michael and Nathan stole it, and now they want it back.'

'It's a bit late isn't it?'

'Is it? It's not too late for a lot of people we love and want to save. We all have people like that don't we?' she looked knowingly at the officer.

He looked away. 'If I can help you find your brother and this Michael, and we find the cure, you said you would share it. How much is there and how do we use it?'

Arla had never seen the cure. She had no idea how much there might be, whether there was any in Ankara at all, or how to administer it. 'I'm not sure of all the details, but Michael will know. I believe he knew the mastermind behind the drug.' She also remembered him saying it did not work.

'Why was it developed in the USA and not here? Gökmen was Turkish, and the first outbreak was here.'

'Here? Are you sure? I thought it was in the US. That's what Michael told us.'

'Our scientists studied the disease for a short time before the final days.' He pulled a folded newspaper from a drawer in his desk and pushed it slowly, almost mournfully, across the table. The front page showed mass chaos and carnage in the streets of Ankara. 'As you can see, it was sudden and swift when it came, but before that, there were earlier cases. Military scientists were working on a drug, but I don't know what became of it, or the scientists for that matter. I imagine they all died since no cure ever came.'

'Can you help us find Michael?' she replied hopefully, pushing the broadsheet with its distressing images away from her. 'It is the only hope for us all, all of us remaining. All of us still with a chance.'

'Perhaps. But what's to stop your people taking it from us once we get it? How can I be sure you won't call your dogs on us?'

'We are not 'dogs',' Arla replied patiently, 'but yes, that is a legitimate concern. If you can get us back across the border with our share, I will ensure you are left alone.'

Yosef nodded in response to the officer's glance in his direction. 'I can guarantee that.'

'Guarantee?' he replied mockingly. 'I do not take Israeli guarantees seriously. But, I have little choice but to accept your noble assurances,' he added sarcastically. 'We survive on little here. There are few of us left, and we badly need many things, most of all this drug. There are many I would save – many that still need help. You would not be alive otherwise. Remember that!'

'I will! Now time is short. We must move quickly. By the way, you never introduced yourself.'

'Major Demir.' The officer reluctantly held out a hand to shake with each of them in turn. 'We will have news of Michael and your brother soon. We have one or two MIT here who may still be able to find them.'

Arla nodded with relief, but she felt her concern for her brother increase.

*

Arla and Yosef climbed into the heavily armed helicopter sitting in the center of the compound some distance from a haphazard collection of military vehicles, a huge water tank, and stacked shipping containers. Missiles were mounted menacingly on either side of the chopper. A number of military personnel were already inside. Arla looked them over slowly. One was obviously a sniper and held a long and very powerful looking rifle with a large telescopic sight. The other two looked ready to deal out lethal fire from large-caliber machine guns suspended on either side of the central doorway. The fourth, a woman in black MIT uniform, was sitting with a laptop open on her knees.

The pilot finished his checks and fired up the rotors as Arla and Yosef took their seats beside Major Demir and pulled on their headsets.

'Where are we going?' she asked him over the intercom.

'Captain Karan has information about your brother,' Major Demir replied, casting a glance at the woman typing on the laptop. 'He made contact with MIT in the last days before Orion's Belt was launched.'

Arla frowned enquiringly.

'It was an old plan hatched by the military to retreat to strategic locations around major cities in the event of a nuclear or chemical attack. Things did not go to plan, but this compound was one location intended for such use. We tried to carry out the plan and to bring important people here, both military and civilian, but it was not easy to retrieve them. Very few compounds succeeded.' He paused for a moment as if deliberately emptying his mind of recent trauma. 'To return to your question, your colleague is correct,' he said, tilting his head towards Yosef. 'It seems your brother was kidnapped shortly after coming to Ankara. Captain Karan is sure your suspicions of Meshedi involvement are correct.'

Arla turned to the captain. 'You know about them, these Meshedi?' she asked, feeling vaguely encouraged that someone had at least some notion of what was going on.

'Yes,' she answered. 'You were at the attack at the Governor's mansion right?'

'Governor's mansion was it? I didn't know that, but yes I was,' Arla felt her pulse quicken at the thought of it. Meshedi blood ran deep it seemed if even the governor was involved. 'These people do not muck around. They are killers.'

The captain nodded. 'Your brother made contact with my superior officer. He found the Meshedi cell in Ankara and was watching them. He knew where to find the person Ariel was looking for - this Michael Fotheringham.'

'So your superior officer can take us to him?'

'Alas no. He did not survive the outbreak.'

'But you know where Michael is?'

'Yes. I know exactly where he is. We are going there now.'

'But what about Ariel?'

'I'm sorry. Perhaps finding Michael will lead us to him.'

Arla started to detect the unpleasant odor of betrayal. If they knew where Michael was, and he was the one with the cure, they would obviously bypass Ariel and go straight for him. 'It is imperative that we find Ariel first!' she insisted.

'That is not possible,' Major Demir cut in abruptly. 'As she says, we have no idea where Ariel is now, we only know that he was probably kidnapped. Michael is our best bet.'

Arla bit her lip. She wanted to protest further, but she knew there was little hope of swaying the situation now. Perhaps Michael could lead them to Ariel. Or perhaps she and Yosef would have to find him for themselves after all.

The chopper was now flying low and fast over wheat fields and small towns towards the line of buildings in the distance. Arla could see the devastation all around the outskirts of the city; abandoned cars, crashed planes, burnt-out apartment blocks, decayed corpses, and the endless shuffling victims.

'Where is Michael then?' Arla asked at last as they headed in over the choked but motionless highways towards the old kale, or castle, on the hill that overlooked central Ankara.

'MIT headquarters. Michael was taken there. As far as we know, he is still there. No one else is though,' she added under her breath.

'But how can he be there alone?'

'He was… incarcerated.'

'You mean he's been locked in a cell all this time? With no one to look after him?'

'I'm afraid so!'

'But he could be dead!'

'Yes, I'm afraid that is also possible.'

Arla gaped at Yosef.

He shook his head in disbelief.

They were now skimming the tops of the taller buildings in downtown Ankara, with Karan directing the pilot through the city to MIT headquarters. Finally, they slowed and hovered for a few moments over a square with a fountain, packed with INS victims. They all looked up and reached in vain for the chopper hovering overhead, drawn by the noise and desperate to reach the soldiers hanging out the side silently training their machine guns on the crowd as if impatient to let loose.

'We are close now,' Captain Karan said as the chopper accelerated forwards again and gained altitude. At last, they set down on the rooftop of a tall building overlooking a narrow lane below.

'Come on, we'll take a look before we do anything,' Major Demir said, and climbed out of the chopper with binoculars in hand. He strode to the edge of the building, then lent over the wall and stared into the street below. Arla and Yosef followed with Karan and the sniper by their side.

'Is that MIT headquarters?' Yosef asked, sounding unimpressed by the drab entrance.

'Yes, the back entrance. It will be safer to enter this way. The front opens onto a square that will be crowded with those things.'

Arla leaned out over the edge as well. She briefly caught a glimpse of the street below before Demir suddenly pushed her back from the edge and crouched down. The others followed suit.

'What is it?' Arla whispered.

'Listen!' he hissed.

The sound of an approaching truck became audible. Major Demir motioned the pilot to cut the engines. The large truck stopped in front of the MIT building and there was the sound of a heavy door opening and closing. Then the vehicle roared off down the street. Demir quickly stole another glance over the edge with binoculars as the vehicle turned a corner. A moment later there was a loud bang and he again jumped up and scanned the streetscape below with his binoculars.

'Who is it?' Arla asked, just as Karan asked the same thing in Turkish.

'I don't know, but they are heavily armed and they just entered the building.'

'What?' Arla said in distress. She stared at Demir and Karan in bafflement. 'Well, what do we do?'

'We must wait,' Demir said. He handed the binoculars to Arla, then ran back to the helicopter.

Arla searched the street below. It was covered in refuse and decayed bodies. There was no sign of anyone. Demir returned and took back the binoculars and continued to monitor the street below. Minutes passed, then, at last, the massive truck returned to the street below. Now all of them peered cautiously over the edge.

'It's a Marauder!' Yosef announced.

'It's the same type of armored car the Meshedi used at the Governor's House,' Arla said in shock. 'They're here! They've come for Michael, and beaten us to it!'

The huge armored car ground to a halt in front of the rear entrance and the back doors flew open. Several men in black fatigues and holding assault rifles jumped out of the back of the truck and stormed the building. They returned seconds later with another man dressed the same way. He was helping a limping man out of the building. This man was gaunt and pathetic looking in comparison to the well-built man assisting him. Instantly there was gunfire in the street below as many INS victims descended ravenously on them.

The gaunt man seemed to crumple under his own weight as the firing began. He staggered back away from the carnage towards the back doors of the vehicle.

Acting on instinct, Arla seized the binoculars from Demir and trained them on the skeletal man who seemed unable to bear his own weight. She knew at once who she was looking at. It was Michael! He looked terrible; emaciated and clearly very week. She tried to zoom on him in some more when he was suddenly yanked into the back of the vehicle as the group of gunmen finished their grisly work and jumped in after him. The engines roared into life again and Marauder carved a path through the staggering crowd down the road and out of sight.

Major Demir spun around and gestured to the pilot. The engine immediately whined and the rotors began to spin. 'We must follow them!'

There was a rapid conversation in Turkish as they lifted off. The chopper swiveled around as it rose, then dropped its nose and plunged over the edge between the tall buildings in hot pursuit of the receding Marauder.

'What are you going to do?' Arla asked, fearing Michael could be injured in an attempt to stop the truck.

'We will block its path!' Demir said.

'How?' Arla puzzled aloud, but she did not need to wait for an answer. There was a loud, roaring, fizzing sound from either side of the cockpit, and two smoking trails became visible out of the side of the chopper as two rockets hurtled like flaming arrows towards the truck below.

'No!' Arla cried, outraged that they could risk harming Michael like this.

In a second the rockets hit their target. A huge boom and plume of smoke and rubble rose from the street below. The helicopter veered suddenly away, and Arla lost all sight of the street, the explosion, and the armored truck.

'You've killed Michael!' Arla shrieked.

'No!' the co-pilot said in a thick accent, jerking his head briefly back to face Arla. 'Roadblock!'

She nodded, but her pulse was racing and her knuckles whitened. If Michael was seriously injured, all hope of finding a cure, and of helping James, would be lost forever!

The chopper described a tight arc and wheeled back around to cross the street above where the plume of dust was rising between the buildings. Arla noticed the sniper had taken Karan's position by the door and was leaning out the opening, training his telescopic sights on the ground below.

'Be careful!' she cried, grabbing his arm. 'Do not hit Michael!'

He pulled away from the scope and looked up at her in irritation, but nodded faintly.

The chopper passed quickly over the street then turned and wheeled back again. On its next pass, the sniper began taking shots at targets she could not see.

Arla lent over the sniper, trying to see what he was shooting at and to prevent him firing at Michael if necessary. His high powered scope obviously gave him a clear view of the ground, but she could see next to nothing over his shoulder. The sniper shrugged her off and barked at her in Turkish.

The helicopter made two more passes, then suddenly veered away and hurried from the scene.

'Where are we going?' Arla cried at the co-pilot. 'We'll lose them now they're on foot!'

'Out of petrol!' he called back.

Arla gaped in disbelief.

'Our petrol supply is very low,' Demir explained, also looking deeply annoyed and more than a little embarrassed. 'We did not have enough to fill up before we left.'

The pilot dipped the nose of the helicopter and directed it at full speed away from their target and toward the outer edge of the city.

'We're going to lose them!' Arla cried in desperation.

'We'll find them again. There is petrol nearby. Don't worry!' Demir replied, though he too sounded worried.

Arla collapsed back into her seat, furious. The thought of losing Michael now they were so close was dementing.

They dropped out of the sky into a wired-off compound ringed by oak trees and full of demountables and rusty shipping containers. There was no one there to greet them. The place was deserted.

'This is one of the compounds that was never set up,' Demir explained as the two side gunners jumped out of the chopper and dashed across the open ground to a petrol tanker parked at the edge of the flat concrete area on which they had landed. In moments they were back, hauling a heavy hose that they attached to the side of the chopper and began pumping hundreds of gallons of avgas into the thirsty machine.

Arla was painfully aware of time passing as the huge fuel tanks slowly filled. She forced herself to think instead about how to find Ariel.

Yosef seemed to be consumed with the same thoughts. 'I don't see how Michael can lead us to Ariel,' he stated as the refilling operation seemed to come to a close. 'I mean, if he has been in prison this whole time, how could he know anything about Ariel's whereabouts?'

Arla nodded gravely. It was clear Major Demir and Captain Karan had no intention of finding Ariel now. 'If the Meshedi has him we'll find him soon enough. If Ariel had gone to rescue Michael, and they were watching the place, they may have caught him. I hope to god they're both OK.'

Yosef nodded. 'Me too! For all our sakes!'

Finally, the chopper shuddered back into life. It lifted off out of the disused compound and turned sluggishly back towards the city. The acceleration was slower as they headed back towards their last point of contact with the fleeing Meshedi, but before long they were roaring along at full speed.

The spot where they had last encountered the Meshedi was now deserted except for two bodies; food for a pack of hungry and disheveled INS victims.

Some quick chatter followed between Demir, Karan and the pilot as they circled the surrounding area slowly, searching every back street and park for the Meshedi.

'They've gone to ground!' Yosef muttered bitterly.

There came a sudden excited shout from one of the side gunners. The helicopter dived to the left and turned, and there, clear as day, running and ducking between cars, trees and buildings were the five Meshedi with Michael in tow. Arla could see he was in a very bad way. He was limping badly, hunched over and bleeding from the nose. He was being pushed and kicked along and seemed to look imploringly up at the helicopter, clearly hopeful of rescue. A large group of INS victims ran along behind them or burst out of laneways in front of them, drawn by the noise of the helicopter above. The Meshedi dispatched them effortlessly, their pace hardly slowing at all.

The sniper leaned further out of the chopper when a shot suddenly presented itself. Alra could see his sights were trained on the man kicking Michael along in front of him. Instinctively, she knocked the barrel of the rifle to one side. 'Don't shoot!' she cried. 'You could hit Michael!'

The sniper turned and yelled at her savagely. He swore under his breath and appealed angrily to Demir.

Demir only shook his head.

The sniper removed his finger from the trigger with a loud sigh but kept the Meshedi in his sights.

Turning the corner, the Meshedi and Michael suddenly disappeared into a traffic tunnel that delved beneath a once wealthy boulevard. The chopper hovered overhead for a long time, waiting for them to re-emerge at the other end, but they did not emerge as long as the chopper waited. Minutes passed as the chopper circled the spot. At last, Demir gave a command and they banked away, heading north out of the city.

13.

Ani climbed nimbly over the side of the ship but almost fell back at the sight that greeted him on board. The entire deck was washed in blood. Headless bodies were arranged in rows in the middle, while many severed heads hung from the yardarm. In the center of the ship, propped against the mast, was the headless body of the captain himself, illuminated by a burning torch hanging from the mast. The head hung grey and dripping from a hook driven into the mast, its lifeless eyes staring out over the decapitated crew arranged before it.

Troan stood proud and jubilant in the rear castle, smiling triumphantly. He was wearing the captain's horned helmet and armor and held aloft the long gold hilted sword that the captain had once worn. A line of his cronies, also now wearing the helmets and armour of the former crew, stood in front of the castle and lined the sides of the ship. Some were injured and clutched bleeding wounds, but they looked fierce and determined. There were at least twenty of them on board.

Ani cast a glance over the side toward the other ships that stood close by. They seemed calm now, and Ani saw bodies aboard these too. Beyond that, several ships were burning. He felt Purdu's hand slip into his. He looked down and saw fear in her eyes. He squeezed her hand and nodded reassuringly. Mezarus too put his strong hands on their shoulders and whispered to them to stay calm, and that Troan would not hurt them.

'Welcome aboard, my subjects!' Troan cried with elation as each boatload from the beaches climbed up over the side.

Ani noticed with sudden alarm that the Gal Meshedi and his men had also come aboard this ship. They were looking around in wide-eyed dismay at the slaughter, and at the usurpers that now took possession of the ship. They did nothing, however, but their hands hovered close to their sword hilts and they looked ready to fight.

Ani felt the steely, sneering gaze of the Gal Meshedi fall upon him. He refused to return the look and fixed his gaze on Troan instead.

'As you can see, things have changed, and for the better!' Troan was announcing to all aboard. 'The true and ancient order of our society has been restored! The barbarian horde has been cast down and their brutal use of us has ended. Your true lords rule once more, and the old order shall take root anew in the world we will create for ourselves here on the sea, or in a new land, far from the destruction of our Hatti lands. I am Troan, your new King!'

A murmur of surprise ran through the restless crowd as all wondered who this young man was that dared to pronounce himself king.

'If you doubt my right to such a title, let me assure you, I am of the highest noble birth and that my family is descended from the line of kings. I am nephew to the fallen king of the Hittite Empire, and thus I claim the right to the throne and begin anew an empire that will stretch from east to west, north to south, from shore to shore in this great ocean. You, my subjects, shall be safe and prosperous so long as you follow me unwaveringly and swear your fealty to me! Now kneel before me, and swear your loyalty, or pay the price of a traitor!'

Ani noticed the Gal Meshedi shaking his head slowly, a look of contempt on his face. His men also looked outraged by Troan's proclamation and seemed keen to take him down there and then. But just as before, they kneeled along with everyone else on board.

'Each has his place in the world,' Troan continued conceitedly. 'Some of you are slaves, convicts, and foreigners. As is your place, you will follow the orders of your betters. We know who you are. Slaves, while we offer you a degree of freedom compared to what you may have experienced before, you remain our chattels and are not free from your bondage. You must earn your freedom according to the old Hittite laws. Any attempt to assert your freedom without a pardon from me will result in your immediate death! Foreigners, you are not welcome, but neither are you free to leave. You must serve me, your new king. You live or die at my command. You are not slaves, but if you displease me in any way, or fail to fight as mercenaries, then you shall be banished or executed. Nobles, I restore your titles and welcome you back into the bosom of my court.'

Ani heard the Gal Meshedi snort derisively at that comment. Troan seemed to hear it also. 'My great uncle, the illustrious Gal Meshedi, please come forward.' Troan beckoned for the Gal Meshedi to come to him.

The Gal Meshedi looked for a second like he was deciding whether to approach the king or take back the ship, but at last, he strode forward and knelt before the new king. Touching the king was forbidden, Ani knew, and so he touched only the ground in front of Troan. Surprisingly, the Gal Meshedi even offered a prayer for Teshub's protection of the new king and a very long and prosperous reign. Troan seemed very pleased and beckoned for him to rise. He did so and took his place beside the king.

'And to my two young noble companions, who like myself, were cut off from their birthright and forced to toil like slaves, come forward Ani and Purdu and stand beside me. Your assistance in the struggle against the vile captain and his foreign crew is to be rewarded.'

Ani and Purdu moved tentatively forward from the group, across the bloody deck past the grisly bodies, and up to the rear castle. Ani felt a kind of shame at being singled out for special treatment like this. Purdu hung her head as she walked.

'Now, approach, and swear your fealty,' Troan said to them more quietly as they climbed the short ladder to the rear castle. Ani kneeled reluctantly, feeling ashamed to have supported a murderer and usurper. Purdu knelt beside him and shot him a worried glance.

Troan dictated an oath to them, which they repeated, promising unwavering loyalty and service for the term of their natural life on pain of death. They rose and found themselves standing next to the Gal Meshedi. He did not look at them, but they felt his menace. Instead, he continued to watch the deck warily.

'Finally,' Troan announced, turning his attention once more to the surviving crew. 'I call upon Mezarus, Master Smith of Hattusha to come forth!'

Ani audibly sucked in his breath. He knew now the Gal Meshedi could have no remaining doubts as to who Mezarus was. Ani sensed the Gal Meshedi straighten slightly, and looking up, saw a malicious smile on his face. What did he have in mind for Mezarus, he wondered.

'As one of high birth, you are of course already welcome in my court, but doubly so for your immense skill. We will have much need of the fine blades you make in the coming time.' Troan stood haughtily, chin raised, as Mezarus climbed the ladder and knelt before him.

'Gods spare us,' Ani heard Mezarus whisper under his breath as Troan regally accepted his fealty and made another short speech.

With a nod to those who had killed the original crew, the restored nobles leaped from their positions by the rail and roughly sorted the remaining recruits into commoners, slaves and foreigners. Any protest was quickly silenced by hard blows with short clubs.

Ani looked on in disgust as the old order was imposed on these wretched survivors of a horror beyond imagining. Now they were once more to be treated as beasts of burden, despised and mistreated, shunned and abused. Ani dropped his head to his chest, ashamed to see the mistreatment and denigration of those with whom he had fought shoulder to shoulder only hours before. To his horror, he saw some of Troan's soldiers take bronze chains from chests beneath the rear castle and fasten them around the wrists and ankles of the slaves.

'You must be taught your place once more,' Troan was shouting over the bustle and clatter of the chains. 'You have no doubt acquired erroneous ideas and assumptions during your recent period of unnatural liberty, but now you must know and bow to your proper masters. Any insubordination or attempts at escape will be punished as treason.'

Ani could not believe the docility with which the slaves allowed themselves to be put in chains. It was as though they truly believed in their own worthlessness, and that the liberty they had experienced - if it could be called that - had been a fleeting fancy, a dream and a mere figment of their imagination. He was sickened to see the expressions of dejection and hopelessness that he had seen on slaves before, quickly reappear on the faces of those otherwise beautiful, fit, suntanned people that were now worth less than nothing.

The slaves were chained in a group around the mast, and while they could move quite freely, they had no hope of escaping en masse with the mast to prevent them from moving more than a few feet in any direction.

'Please,' Troan said, turning to Ani and Purdu and clearly elated at how well things had gone, 'take food with me this morning. It will give our new, or should I say, old slaves something to do.' He laughed cruelly as he said it.

Ani said nothing, and Mezarus knocked him lightly on the shoulder. Troan looked crestfallen for a moment, noticing Ani's hesitation.

'Yes, thank you, it would be our great pleasure!' Ani forced from his mouth.

'Good!' Troan said with obvious hurt, and turned to Purdu and smiled.

For some reason, Ani did not like the look he gave her. He had seen Troan watching her a lot of late with that strange and almost leering expression, and now a protective urge rose up inside him. He knew Purdu was changing, and she looked very womanly in her armor, but she was still a girl! Whatever trust or faith he may have had in Troan vanished in that instant.

14.

'But...,' Michael was speechless. 'You were dead! I saw your lifeless body as they dragged me away!'

'I don't remember,' Nathan replied faintly.

'Well I do, and I could have sworn you were dead. They must have shot you ten times! How the hell did you even get here?'

'Dunno! Bulletproof vest helped, I guess. I just woke up here. Where are we anyway? Who are these guys? MIT?'

'No! Do you really not know?'

'Nup! I woke up on a stretcher bed in a hot room a few days ago. Only one guy spoke English, and he had amongst the worst potty mouth of anyone native or foreign I've ever met. Took a lot of the joy out of the conversation. Otherwise not bad I s'pose, given the state of things.' He looked down at his heavily bandaged body. 'Where is the English-speaking guy anyway?' he looked around the room as if seeing it for the first time, wincing in pain as he did so.

'He's dead.'

'The disease?'

'No. Look things might seem safe and pleasant to you, but we're actually up to our chins in a river of shit with our mouth's wide open.'

'Did you get that expression from him?'

'Huh? No! I mean these guys are not MIT. They're Meshedi, and we're here as hostages to make the cure for them. They could kill us at any moment.'

Nathan looked dazed for a second. 'Hang on...' he continued to look concussed. 'Ok, say that all again.'

'We are captives! We were hunted on the way here after my rescue by some trigger-happy clowns in a helicopter. They killed the foul-mouthed guy and a few others. They nearly killed me too. The Meshedi are furious about it, and I'd say we haven't got much time to make their cure. We've been followed here. They may come soon.'

'Who are they?'

'I have no idea. It was a military chopper, I think. Maybe it's the MIT still hunting them.'

'So, what do they want us to do? We don't know how to make that bloody drug. Gökmen made it, didn't he? You've never done it have you?'

'No, of course not. I have no idea how to make it. They think because I was there with Gökmen when he made it that I must be his assistant or something. They have some footage of me there while Gökmen made it at the funeral parlor. I was just pointing a gun at him. I don't know what on earth he was doing. But the whole thing is on video - no sound of course. There was a CCTV camera in the safe that captured it all. Plus, they've got his original notes here. They somehow got them from the CBT back home before or after it imploded.'

'Imploded?'

'Yeah, apparently things are quite a mess back home now.' Michael suddenly thought of his sister. He had thought a lot about her while in prison, and he longed now to know where she was and that she was safe. It was his deepest regret that he had not warned her of what was coming. But then, he had had no idea really what was coming.

'What about here? Are we safe here?'

Michael realized Nathan knew nothing of what was going on. 'Surely the English speaking Meshedi told you something?'

'Nope. He kept saying I had done something bad. This might seem like a stupid question, but what did I do?'

'You don't remember anything?'

'Nothing. Only running out onto the roof with you.'

'You killed the Gal Meshedi!' Michael said in all seriousness, then suddenly felt a little tickle of laughter inside, then broke into crazed laughter for several seconds.

'Steady on there old chap,' Nathan said worriedly.

'You killed the fucking Gal Meshedi Nathan! You shoved a grenade in his face!'

Nathan looked very confused. 'Did I?' he said after a moment, suddenly looking quite chuffed with himself.

'You blew his helicopter and all its nasty little Meshedi passengers to kingdom come. I can't believe you don't' remember it! It was the bravest, craziest, most epic thing I've ever seen! But you were…'

Suddenly Nathan's face became ashen. He twitched and suddenly a strange expression crossed his face and he hunched forward in his wheelchair as if reliving the whole experience.

'You remember it now?' Michael asked, kneeling down beside him.

'Yes. I remember it now. And you… I remember you calling my name.'

'Make!' came a sudden harsh command from behind.

Michael felt shooting pain in his back as he realized he'd been used as a football again.

'OK, goddamn it!' Michael cried, jumping to his feet and spinning around angrily to confront his abuser. He stepped back suddenly and dropped his aggressive stance when he saw the Meshedi was pointing a pistol at his head. 'OK, OK,' he said passively and backed away.

The Meshedi slowly lowered the pistol. 'Make!' he repeated less harshly now.

'So, what are we going to do now?' Nathan said, rolling himself forwards towards the table on which the thickly bound notebook sat.

'Fake it and hope someone rescues us soon!' Michael said, quickly flicking through several pages of the book. 'Can you turn on the machines? Make it look like you know what you're doing would be my advice.'

'Since when have I ever taken your advice.' Nathan wheeled himself over to the nearest machine and began examining the back of it, looking for a power cord. 'I've been wondering, what happened to you and the others after I was shot?'

'Oh yes, naturally, MIT had no idea what was going on and thought I'd killed the minister. They hauled me off to prison and I was rotting in that cell for a week or more while Ankara turned into a stinking zombie-infested hellhole.'

'Is it that bad?'

'You have no idea. Potty mouth who rescued me said I'd regret leaving my cell, and he was right. It is…,' he could find no words to describe it.

'That bad, eh?' Nathan said somberly. 'What about Arla and James?'

'I don't know. They were taken to the hospital remember, as James was in a bad way. I hope they made it!'

'Yeah. They were cool. Arla was a force to be reckoned with. I think she was on her own personal mission to destroy the Meshedi after what they did to those diggers up in the mountains.'

'Yes, well she did get a few. How are you going with those machines?' A beep and a grinding whirring noise sounded just as Michael asked the question, confirming Nathan had successfully switched on the first machine. Michael shot a look over his shoulder and saw Nathan wheeling over to the next machine, a Meshedi following along behind him and watching closely.

'They have no idea that we haven't a clue what we're doing. They think you're my assistant. Hah!' Michael broke into an unhinged cackle once again.

'Easy there mate. Don't give away your insanity just yet. So, you don't think we can make it? I mean, you are a pharmacist.'

Michael noticed Nathan was giving him one of his rare hard stares.

Michael sighed, 'Sorry Nathan, I really wish I could, believe me! But this is totally beyond me! I've got about as much chance of successfully making this drug as I would building an operational intercontinental ballistic missile with a thermonuclear warhead on that TV show Scrapheap Challenge in under two days.'

'I thought you said there was a video. Surely with these notes and the video you could work it out? I reckon these Meshedi aren't so stupid as they look. I reckon you can do it. With my help of course. A bit of internet help on nanotechnology and …'

'Sorry Nathan, you're going to find this very, very hard to take, harder perhaps than anything that's happened so far.'

Nathan shook his head dumbly.

'There's no internet anymore.'

'Oh, I wouldn't be so sure of that. The whole time we've been talking I've been thinking about this exact problem. What we need is not a local connection, as the servers and lines are probably all down, not to mention most computers. What we need is satellite feed that will take me to the one computer that is sure to be still active, and which has a near-complete map of the web stored in its data banks.'

Michael looked at Nathan in surprise. 'Yes?'

'The DISA mainframe. I'm certain it would still be operational on emergency power, even if everyone was gone. I'm confident I can hack it again. And satellites will also still be transmitting as they're always switched on and out of range of all the craziness down here on earth.'

'You're a brilliant man, Nathan Videc! But we'd need a computer and a satphone at a minimum I guess – neither of which we have.'

'Oh, don't be so hasty my friend. You've only just arrived. Barely had time to take in the scenery. There is a big computer lab here, they just don't know what to do with it. I, on the other hand, do! I'll have a DIY step by step guide on how to make nanodrugs up and ready for your pleasure in no time. That combined with the video of Gökmen actually making it and we should be home and hosed.'

'There's one crucial problem, Nathan.'

'What's that?'

'Gökmen's drug doesn't actually work, remember?'

'Are you so sure?'

Michael suddenly remembered what the Meshedi had told him soon after he had been rescued – that the drug did work, but that Gökmen had been deceptive and had made sure it was ineffective for Michael and almost everyone else too.

'Not entirely.' Michael stared hard at Nathan. 'Damn it, you're right, it is worth a go! We need to get you on those computers, and I need to read these damned notes.’

15.

Arla was furious. For some reason, just as they had tracked Michael and the Meshedi to their underground location, they had turned and left the city. Again, she felt the sharp sting of betrayal. They had found what they wanted, and now they had no intention of taking her and Yosef there.

'What are you doing? Why are we leaving?' she shouted into the intercom.

'We have to conserve fuel. They are not coming out. We cannot wait here any longer,' Major Demir replied impatiently.

Arla saw what could only be deceit in his eyes. 'We should leave an observer. What if they leave once we're gone?'

'It is too dangerous. We cannot leave anyone behind in the city.'

'But… we'll lose them! We'll never find them again! Do you really think they'll just sit there waiting for us to come back?'

'We have no choice.' Demir was losing his cool now. 'We need a plan and many more soldiers. Do you think we can just walk in there? How do you think they've survived all this time? It will be like a fortress!'

Arla fumed. She knew he was right about having more soldiers, but she was angry all the same. To have come this far and then lose Michael was infuriating. But it was clear they would need to come prepared for a fight. Either that or they planned to dump her and Yosef and go after Michael on their own.

Arla noticed Major Demir watching her closely for the remainder of the flight back to the compound. She avoided making eye contact and stared at the floor trying not to see the depressing scenes outside.

'We start back early in the morning, but we will talk more soon.' Demir said as they climbed out of the chopper upon arriving back in the compound.

'The morning is too long. We need to discuss a plan now.'

'Yes, after dinner. Rest now.'

*

'I'm surprised you trust these people,' Yosef commented as they lay on their stiff military bunks in a demountable provided for them among shipping containers and water towers that loomed overhead. It was dirty and riddled with cockroaches but looked never to have been used.

'Trust is a strong word,' she replied. 'I don't see that we have a choice though, do you?'

'No! You were very clever.'

'What do you mean?'

'Telling them Michael has a cure. You saved our lives. I thought we were going to have to dash through that crowd of horrors to save our lives. Is it true? Does he really have a cure?' he asked so quietly she could hardly hear him.

'No. At least I don't think so. It was all I could think of at the time. But I think he knows where one is.'

Yosef sat back, looking deflated. 'Well we're dead the second they find that out.'

Arla nodded wearily. 'I guess I hadn't really thought that far ahead. What do you think we should do?'

'Well, I came for Ariel, not Michael, but since you both want him so badly, I think we have no choice but to rescue him too.'

'Perhaps the one will lead to the other?'

'Yes, maybe. I also think any help here will evaporate once they find out the truth. I'd rather go it alone now we know where to look. I fear a bullet in the back of the head the moment we have outlived our usefulness.'

She nodded again.

Yosef looked warily at the silhouette of the guard walking slowly back and forth in front of their quarters.

'So, we escape tonight and go on alone?' Arla asked quietly.

'It will be risky, but yes, I think we have no choice. We go into Ankara tonight and get Michael. Hopefully, we will find Ariel at the same time.'

'Seems straight forward enough. What about the getting out, surviving the hoards of zombies, breaking into the Meshedi's lair and rescuing Michael, and the not getting killed bits?'

'Yes, well, therein lies the rub. Got any ideas?'

'None.'

'Me neither.'

*

The stroll to dinner under armed guard gave Arla and Yosef a look at another part of the compound. They saw yet more stacks of shipping crates and long lines of demountables housing the dejected survivors of Ankara along with its many military personnel. They were a skinny, downcast and depressed looking lot. No laughter was heard. People ate their meager rations cheerlessly, then departed the mess immediately. All the while an incessant gurgling, moaning and barking came from the perimeter of the compound keeping everyone permanently on edge.

They found Mati the pilot in the long queue.

'We're getting out of here tonight,' Yosef whispered in the pilot's ear as they lined up for rice served with a thin-looking gruel and bread.

He nodded subtly in reply.

'Can you fly a chopper?'

The pilot nodded. 'You mean that badass Heuy parked out there? Of course!'

'Then be ready at midnight.'

During dinner, Arla noticed Yosef slip a sharp knife into his boot as he bent down to pick up a piece of bread that he had no doubt dropped deliberately.

They returned to their quarters, noting which was the pilot's room along the way.

*

'Why did you ask Mati if he could fly the chopper?'

'You need to ask?' Yosef replied in surprise. 'How else are we going to get out of here?'

'Are you serious? Don't we need keys or something? How long is it going to take to start that thing?'

'I don't know exactly. You can ask him when we get there.'

Arla frowned and felt a knot growing in her stomach. Slipping under the fence through the chute was terrifying enough but attempting to steal the helicopter from under their noses was quite another. It seemed suicidal. 'I think you could have discussed this plan with me first.'

'It only just occurred to me while we were in the mess. Don't you think it could work? The Blackhawk would give us firepower and a way to get back to Israel with

Ariel.'

'I thought there was no fuel?'

'Yes, that could be a problem. I don't believe that was the reason, though do you?'

'No, I don't. I'm sure they plan to go back there without us. What about James? I want to find James.'

'What? Who's that? You've never mentioned him before.'

'He's the reason I want Michael. He's the reason for it all.'

Yosef stared disbelievingly at Arla for a moment. 'You are a dark horse, Arla. I thought we were here for Ariel and Michael, but it turns out you really came for someone else entirely? Who is he?'

'He's someone who needs my help. I left him here before, and it was the stupidest thing I have ever done. I'm not leaving him a second time.'

Yosef shook his head worriedly. 'Can he help us? Can he help Israel?'

She stared at him, unsure what to say. 'Let's say it wouldn't hurt to have someone to test the drug on when we get it.'

Yosef's eyes widened. 'You want me to help you find an INS victim and cure him? Arla, we are here on borrowed time. I don't think you realize how much Israel…,'

'I don't care about any of that and I don't want any patriotic speeches, thank you. I am not going home without James. You can leave me here if you want. I will do it on my own if I have to.'

'OK, OK, calm down. Can we just focus on Michael and Ariel first, please? Then we'll take stock of the situation. Does Ariel know about James?'

'Yes.'

'How does he feel about it?'

'I don't know. It makes no difference. I'm going to find him one way or the other.'

Yosef shook his head. 'Now I can see where Ariel gets it from. Stubborn and more than a bit crazy.'

She smiled. She liked Yosef. 'How do we get the chopper then? I don't want to hurt anyone if we can avoid it.'

'You mean, create a diversion?'

'Yes.'

'Well, that won't work. We'll end up alerting everyone, the place will go mad and it will be much harder to slip away. I think we have to take out the guards and rush the chopper. Don't forget they were about to throw us down that chute. They intend to betray us Arla!'

She nodded, but she was uneasy all the same. In a world where only a few were destined to survive, it seemed wrong to take any more lives.

*

There was a muffled cry and a gurgle as the soldier sagged to the ground at Yosef's feet. Yosef kept his hand over the man's mouth until he was still, then quickly cleaned the knife and unslung the battle rifle from around the young man's neck.

Arla looked away. She was not happy about this part of the plan at all, but Yosef had insisted it was necessary. She thought only of their need to escape before all was lost.

'Come on!' Yosef hissed, and darted to the next closest shipping container, keeping low as he ran.

Arla followed in a similar fashion, hunched and running as quietly as possible.

They wove their way through the lines of stacked containers, searching in the dark for Mati's demountable. A few more turns and they arrived at the long line of double-story buildings. A guard sat wearily on an empty oil barrel opposite Mati's room, smoking and humming to himself.

'Walk across to Mati's room,' Yosef whispered. 'Catch his attention while I jump him from behind.'

Arla sighed but did as she was asked. She walked quickly and silently across the dark open space towards Mati's door, unwilling to see the soldier's face. A moment later there was a muffled gurgle, then silence.

She stood at Mati's door, waiting. Yosef joined her a second later. He nodded and handed her a rifle. His hands were bloody and were shaking. She took it and slung it over her shoulder without a word.

The door opened even before they had time to touch the door handle.

'I thought it would be you,' Mati said, and slipped silently through the doorway to join them outside, his eyes falling briefly on the slumped body beside the oil drum. 'Any guards at the chopper?'

'We haven't been there yet. Let's go. Silently now!'

Again, Yosef led the way through the dark and silent camp. There was a faint glow from a light here and there, but overall, the dark camp was easy to move through unseen.

They came to a stockpile of drums on the edge of the vehicle parking lot and helipad. A single floodlight lit up a guard absentmindedly pacing the tarmac.

'How are we going to do this?' Mati whispered worriedly.

'With god's help,' Yosef muttered, scanning the guard towers on the perimeter fence that stood some distance away but overlooked the helipad. 'That's where the trouble will come from. They have machine guns up there.' He pointed to the two guard towers around fifty meters away in which the glow of cigarettes could be faintly seen.

'There are gatlings on the sides of the Huey,' Mati said softly. 'I suggest you use them! It's going to take a while to spin up and things could get pretty dicey.'

'Do you need keys or access codes or something?' Arla asked, worried they would find themselves stranded inside the chopper.

'Let's hope not.'

They waited until the guards had circled the compound and were out of sight before Yosef broke into a crouched run and dived beneath the fuselage of the huge helicopter. Before long the guard returned on his circuit, but Yosef remained hidden in the deep darkness beneath the machine. Arla and Mati remained hidden while they waited for the guard to disappear again. As soon as he stepped out of sight, they too dashed across the open tarmac and crawled under the fuselage. A moment later and they were climbing in through the open pilot door and into the chopper.

'Fire it up Mati!' Yosef cried jubilantly.

'OK, it's going to take a second. I haven't flown one of these in a while. And it's bloody dark in here!'

'Here come the guards!' Arla called anxiously as she saw the first of the guards round the corner and stroll nonchalantly towards them, sucking hard on a cigarette.

'OK, get down and stay quiet,' Yosef whispered.

Arla crouched beneath the gatling gun next to the little window through which it projected. She could hear Mati rustling around in the cabin. Suddenly the lights flicked on inside the chopper and there was the loud whining of engines engaging and then the roar of the twin turboprop engines coming to life.

'Sorry! I didn't mean to do that! Looks like our cover's blown!'

Arla jumped up. The guard next to the chopper had nearly jumped out of his skin in fright as fiery blasts had suddenly erupted out of the twin turboprop engines atop the helicopter. He ducked and ran for cover.

Arla squeezed the trigger of the gatling, not aiming at anything in particular, but keen to send a message in case anyone tried to storm the helicopter. More soldiers appeared at the edge of the tarmac as a stream of tracers spewed out of the spinning barrels.

'Cool!' she muttered to herself as sparks flew off steel poles, ripped holes in shipping containers and shattered glass on the vehicles parked around the compound.

Yosef's guns were blazing too. 'OK, stop!' he cried, spinning around to look at Arla. 'Save the ammunition. Are you nearly ready to get us out of here Mati?' he called up to the cockpit.

Mati was in the right-hand pilot's seat, furiously fiddling with dials while trying to control the throttle and lift. Sweat was pouring off him.

Arla nearly fell backward as the chopper suddenly jerked and lurched off the helipad and nearly nose-dived into the tarmac.

'For god's sake, do you know what you're doing?' Arla screamed. 'You're going to kill us all!'

'Like I said, it's been a while. Hold on!'

Arla noticed that Major Demir had appeared at the edge of the tarmac with a squad of soldiers. He was yelling at them, red-faced and furious. At once, they opened fire and Arla heard bullets smack into the fuselage and ricochet noisily off the steel struts. She ducked for cover and instinctively squeezed the trigger again. A thundering shudder erupted in her hands as the gatling gun sprayed its lethal fire across the compound, but she was not looking where she was firing.

There was a loud click and sliding noise, and all the cacophony of the engines and rotors came rushing in as the side door suddenly slid open. Someone flung something inside then jumped in after it.

The chopper was rising rapidly now, and bullets were clanging and sparking off the metal around her. She turned in dread to face whoever had jumped in. Yosef also spun around, bringing his pistol to bear on their unwelcome stowaway. Arla expected guns to be blazing and felt herself counting her last moments, but instead, she blinked in sudden recognition. Lying panting in the eerie green light of the instrument panels was the last person she expected to see at that moment.

'Don't shoot,' the man cried in Hebrew, throwing his arms in the air as Yosef seemed about to pull the trigger.

It was Ariel!

16.

Ani and Purdu crouched on the bloodstained deck, huddling in the shade of the sail along with most of the other recruits. Fortunately, they had all learned enough in the last few weeks to understand the basics of sailing, but Ani still wondered if they knew enough to handle the ship in rough seas or enter and leave a narrow harbor without dashing her on the rocks.

Another reason for huddling together at one end of the deck was to stay out of the way of a huge row that was now going on inside the little cabin beneath the Fighting Castle that Troan had made his lair. Ani could hear it all too clearly through the narrow windows.

'I have tolerated your little charade, but I am growing tired of it. What makes you think you have the right to seize command and appoint yourself king? You're a jumped-up little squirt with no right to the throne at all! I am the King's brother. How dare you think you have a claim over me!' The Gal Meshedi roared at Troan.

Troan's stooges stood shoulder to shoulder in front of the door to the little cabin in a tense face-off with the Gal Meshedi's men on the other side of the deck. Neither moved but simply stood with hands to sword hilts watching each other intently.

'Uncle do not be so mad with me,' Troan said whiningly, sounding a little frightened. 'My intention was only to take back what is ours and to free ourselves of the yoke of foreign rulers. Is that not our royal birthright?'

'Do not talk of royalty to me boy. I barely know you. You grew up in southern lands and are hardly kingly material. You are a pretender! You should be hung from the yardarm for this outrageous usurpation. Never have I seen such impudence! I have a good mind to part your head from your shoulders this instant, just as you did to that captain and all his men. Do you really think these misfits, slaves, and children out there are ready to sail this fleet or fight an action at sea? Do you really think you can suppress a rebellion if they choose to rise against you with your handful of scribes, altar boys and mother's brats? You have mistimed and misjudged the situation appallingly. Did you not consider that I might attempt a similar coup d'état at the right time once we were trained and ready? Now we are a floating circus - a troop of clumsy and unskilled buffoons barely capable of hoisting a sail, let alone navigating these treacherous waters and ensuring our own survival. It's a farce! The whole thing makes a mockery of your ancestry and of our once-great Empire! What have you to say for yourself?'

There was an awkward silence. Ani now imagined Troan as a naughty child being scolded, but this did not last long.

'I could have you executed for speaking to me like this,' he replied tentatively, his voice trembling in a mix of fear and rage.

'Try it, I dare you!'

The opposing lines of men in front of the cabin stiffened at these words and looked ready to slice each other to pieces.

'Uncle,' Troan said soothingly after a long pause.

'Do not uncle me! I told you, I barely know you.'

'Then let us not quarrel. If you desire the kingship you shall have it. I will abdicate to you.'

'I do not desire it! In any case, it is not to be given or taken so lightly. The king is divine. No man can simply take such a thing. It must be his birthright and his divinity bestowed upon him by the gods. You have neither birthright nor divinity. For all we know the king still lives. What then?'

'Well, he is the king of the Hittites. I am king of the Sea Peoples... and you have sworn allegiance to me.'

There was a stifled gurgle from inside the cabin and Troan's men shifted worriedly on their feet. Finally, there came the sound of gasping and deep reviving breaths. Ani moved a little closer along the deck, straining his ears to hear the conversation inside.

'This is what I will do for you, my nephew - if indeed you are that - in exchange for your life,' the Gal Meshedi uttered in a quiet but lethal tone. 'I will take charge of your protection, as I did for my brother. I will maintain your ridiculous charade, as galling as it is to me whose right towers over yours like the Taurus Mountains over a pine tree. And when I give you advice, you will take it. I will make important decisions on your behalf; you will agree to them. In exchange, you may lead the life of care-free luxury and vice you so obviously desire. I will ensure that for you. But, if you show one sign of disobeying me, or of undermining me, I will have you castrated and dangling from a pole by your stump of manhood before you can cry for your mother. Do you understand?'

There was a long pause before the Gal Meshedi continued, having obviously secured Troan's reluctant agreement to his terms. 'Now you and I must visit the other ships. I'll wager your… *kingship*,' he spat the word, 'hangs by a thread. You'd best make an appearance before your skinny retainers are butchered and thrown overboard. Come!'

The Gal Meshedi burst out of the cabin. He looked authoritative and very pleased with himself as he stepped into the sunlight, practically dragging Troan through the door after him. Troan did not look so pleased; he was bent, rubbing his throat, and wore a resentful sneer on his lips as he followed after the Gal Meshedi.

'Those three,' The Gal Meshedi said, stopping suddenly and pointing at Ani, Purdu and Mezarus with a gloved hand. 'They come with us.'

*

A long line of ships spread out across the broad expanse of water, their billowing sails and dark hulls resembling a line of snails moving imperceptibly over wet grey stones. Ani counted at least twenty ships. Many appeared to be struggling to maintain their course and were drifting off or inexpertly tacking to try and stay with the fleet. He did not know how many of the crew must have perished in Troan's coup, but the consequences were clear to see. It was chaos!

Ani was unsure why they had been selected by the Gal Meshedi to accompany Troan and his men on his debut visit to the other ships. It seemed a potentially hazardous journey. What if the coup had been unsuccessful on some ships? What if the new crew rejected Troan as king? Perhaps someone would make an attempt on their lives and wrest control from Troan? Ani did not know what to expect, but he felt a sense of dread as they approached the first ship.

Their small boat rowed in alongside. A rope was thrown down and their boat tied alongside the long, low ship with its high bow and stern fighting castle. It was an identical ship to their own. The occupants hung over the edge in an unruly manner and watched first the Meshedi bodyguard climb the rope ladder and go aboard, followed by the Gal Meshedi, Troan, and last of all, Ani, Purdu and Mezarus.

'What's he got us here for?' Mezarus whispered as he hauled himself up the ladder behind Ani.

'I don't know. Maybe he plans to kill us?'

Ani climbed over the rail and gasped at the scene before him. It was even more grisly than that on their own ship. Dismembered bodies lay on the deck. Seabirds sat on the mast, waiting for their chance to peck at the slowly putrefying flesh. A handful of men and women surrounded the grisly remains of the former crew. The rest of the recruits kept their distance and watched warily as Troan and the others came aboard. Ani noticed several of the group had fiery red scratches and bite marks on their arms and faces and looked pale and feverish. Some were coughing and had streaming noses.

'You have done well!' Troan announced loudly as he tiptoed through the gore and embraced a woman who was obviously the leader of this group on board the ship. Ani recognized her now as the noblewoman he had seen Troan whispering conspiratorially with these last weeks. 'How many did you lose?' he asked, looking around the central throng of men and women clutching their long swords.

'None!'

'Then you did very well indeed. Let me introduce you to the Gal Meshedi and his men.'

The woman did not bow at first. 'What's he doing here?' she asked, clearly upset by the Gal Meshedi's presence.

'He is my personal bodyguard. You should bow to him,' Troan added quietly but insistently.

The woman bowed reluctantly.

'Who do I have the pleasure of meeting,' the Gal Meshedi replied testily.

'This is Mastigga. She is a Hassawa from Kisuwatna. She is a holy woman of some fame in those parts,' Troan answered, almost reverently.

The Gal Meshedi grunted in reply but showed no further interest. He strolled off and wandered around the ship, assaying the worth of each man or woman as well as the likelihood of rebellion.

'So, you are now king then?' Mastigga asked Troan quietly, smiling happily as she did so.

'Yes, thanks to you. Your prayers and rituals have made it come to pass.'

'Not I, it is the gods who favor you. So, what now?'

'I wish you to remain here and ensure there is no dissent. I will send for you soon. We will head south. I have heard it said there is great wealth in the land of Canaan. A land of milk and honey they say.'

She nodded and embraced him again.

The Gal Meshedi returned from his stroll around the deck and nodded. With this, Troan repeated his speech from the previous night and the slaves and foreigners were separated. The slaves were put in chains around the mast as before. They left the ship soon afterward and rowed to the next ship and then the next, each showing signs of recent slaughter and each held by a few of Troan's men and women until they had visited all twenty ships. The sun was setting when they finally returned to their own ship. Troan looked exhausted from a long and tense day, but he was also clearly very pleased with himself.

The Gal Meshedi had said nothing to them all day, nor had he even acknowledged their presence. Ani was surprised by this. He was sure The Gal Meshedi had some dreadful punishment in store for them. At various times he spoke privately with Troan, but Ani had not been able to overhear these conversations. Once, Ani noticed Troan looking over at them with a puzzled expression as the Gal Meshedi spoke.

'He's poisoning Troan against us,' Ani said later once back on board their own ship.

'Who?'

'The Gal Meshedi. I think he told Troan we are not nobles.'

Purdu gave Ani a worried look. 'Troan gives me the creeps,' she said looking away.

'He gives everyone the creeps. I can't believe what he did to the captain and crew. He's a monster!'

'I know, but I mean he makes me feel uneasy in a different way. I can't really explain it.'

Ani did not reply, but he knew what she meant. The way Troan kept looking at her was making Ani feel very uncomfortable.

'If he tries anything, anything a bit strange, you call out. I'll be right there.'

Purdu gave him a puzzled look. 'What do you mean? What would he try?'

Ani shook his head. 'I don't know. Don't worry. I'm just saying I'm right here, OK!'

'Yes, I know that. Thanks.' Purdu looked worried and confused and went off to find Mezarus who was helping direct the repacking of stores arriving from other ships.

*

Several days passed without incident. The slaves were unchained and forced to sail the ship and perform all duties. Their first was to scrub the decks until all the bloodstains were removed. Thus, the new order was imposed and the subjugation of those that had previously been treated as equals, albeit under the strict command of the captain, was now complete. In those few days, Ani noticed the fleet also improving its maneuvers, such that now they traveled in a relatively neat pack rather than the dispersed swarm of previous days. Boats rowed back and forth between the ships carrying orders and a constant flow of what appeared to be special stores for Troan's personal use.

Ani, Purdu and Mezarus were freed from even the lightest of duties. Most nobles assumed a guard role or else luxuriated on deck. Ani began to feel bored, wandering around the baking deck by day as the slaves worked hard. He did little besides eat and sleep and practice his fighting. The slaves and foreign recruits were not obviated from fighting practice, but Ani noticed that they were badly treated. They were scolded if they scored hits on nobles and were often treated to heavy blows that they were powerless to avoid.

Ani also heard rumors that fever had been spreading throughout the fleet after the demon attack at their last raid. The chilling story was that Troan had ordered anyone with fever thrown overboard for fear that they might turn into flesh-eaters. Ani was both horrified and relieved.

The Gal Meshedi had seemed almost to forget about Ani and Purdu over this time, paying them no heed at all. However, he had frequently kept council with Mezarus. Mezarus seemed pleased with this but did not discuss their conversations with Ani and Purdu.

Several times they had dined with Troan over these few quiet days. His cabin was cramped and smelled faintly of musty stores and bilge water, but the food was much better than the standard fare prepared by the slaves. After each meal, Ani had been dismissed, but Purdu had been asked to remain. Ani had been reluctant to leave, but in the end, he been escorted out by one of Troan's guards. Each time, Purdu had left the cabin later looking happy with a trinket or special treat that Troan had given her, but Ani could tell she was becoming increasingly uncomfortable.

'What do you talk about after I am asked to leave?' Ani asked suspiciously after the latest of these sessions.

'Nothing much,' she answered a little shiftily.

Ani stared at his sister but said no more.

'When are we leaving?' she said after a long silence.

'Leaving? What do you mean? Where would we go?' he said, glancing to the horizon as if to make his point.

'I don't feel safe here, Ani,' she said turning to him and looking very upset.

'Has he done something?'

'No. Not really. But I don't feel safe with him anymore.'

Ani felt a cold feeling invade his chest. He felt something was not right with Troan. He wanted these meetings to end. He wanted Troan gone!

He paced over to his nest of things tucked behind sacks at the front of the ship and fished out the bone-handled dagger Troan's man had given him in the boat on the night of the coup. 'I want you to keep this with you at all times,' he said, returning to his place beside her.

She looked at the dagger, confused. 'Why?'

'I don't trust Troan. Use it if you have to.'

She frowned then nodded, took the small dagger hesitantly and hid it in her dress.

17.

After the excitement and the sense of possibility had come sleep. Nathan had somehow communicated the necessity to conduct internet research to their captors and had been escorted away under armed guard to whatever computer facilities they possessed. Michael, on the other hand, had gestured for food and sleep, and both had been granted.

He had awoken many hours later, rested but crowded in by gloomy thoughts. In the stillness and silence, he questioned his ability to make the drug, or do anything much of worth. He replayed Gökmen's last hours in the lab in his mind, trying to reconstruct his memories. He soon realized his mind was simply vamping what he had seen on the CCTV footage and that there was nothing of substance in what he could remember. He was so tired and emotional at the time that he resurfaced little more than feelings of fear and panic and a deep sense of loss over Corinne.

His gloomy thoughts were suddenly interrupted by the bedroom door banging open and a wheelchair clumsily bumping its way into the room. The Australian wore a victorious grin. 'Yes!' Nathan cried.

'What is it?' Michael replied excitedly, pulling himself reluctantly up from the bed, suddenly filled with hope.

'Got it!'

'Got what?'

'The instructions on how to operate the machines, grind and mix nanoparticles, blah blah blah.' Nathan was clearly very excited.

'Oh!' Michael said, instantly deflating. 'Look, sorry, but I think it's pretty much pointless. It's not like mixing a few powders and squishing them into a tablet. That's my trade, Nathan, not retro engineering the most complex nanoworm ever made. We don't even have a source of fresh prions.'

'Prions? Are you crazy? Look outside mate! How many billion frigging fresh prions do you want?'

'Well, I suppose so, but that's not really the point.'

'Come on Michael. Listen to yourself, mate. You've got a lab to yourself–OK, apart from the deranged goons with guns. You've got detailed instructions, Gökmen's notes, all the machines and ingredients you need. We've even got the 'cooking with Gökmen' video. What more do you want?'

Michael forced a faint smile. Nathan made it sound so easy and his unwavering positivity was infectious. He took a deep breath. 'If we're going to try – and I mean try - I will need more time to study Gökmen's notes. I was in no state to make head nor tail of them last night. It could take days or even weeks to make some sense of them, assuming I ever can.'

'Well, I've found loads of helpful stuff. You'll be alright! Anyway, we don't have a choice, right?'

As if to make Nathan's point, two agitated looking Meshedi paced down the hallway and yelled something at them.

'Looks like it's time to start work!' Nathan said as he spun his wheelchair around. 'We'll do it together!'

*

'So, you've searched the web then?' Michael asked as they entered the lab and returned to the heavy tome sitting on the table.

'Yes, for many hours. Some networks are still up, but there's no sign of recent maintenance or posts.'

'So how bad is it?' Michael asked, not looking up from the table.

'I take it you are asking is it a full-scale apocalypse or just a local outbreak in a few unlucky cities?'

Michael nodded.

'Do you really want to know?' Nathan fixed his gaze on Michael with another of his rare hard stares.

Michael nodded again but feared the answer.

'It's full-scale,' Nathan answered quietly. 'Civilisation has basically shat itself. The news stopped a few days ago, but it was pretty harrowing stuff up until that point. You don't ever want to read those stories, believe me. What beggars me is just how the bloody thing spread so quickly. It was like lightning. Just a few days and it was suddenly everywhere. What we saw at the CBT was just the very beginning. It got out of control as soon as we came here. People wandering the streets in great packs tearing each other to pieces. Governments just evaporated and the army was devoured from within. It's like INS slipped in under ever door and windowsill, through every water pipe and air duct in every city on earth.' Nathan was silent for a minute. 'Maybe there's a tribe in the Amazon that hasn't heard of it yet, but everywhere else is pretty much screwed! Israel was about the only place still free of it when the news stopped. The Holy Land! Maybe God's hand is still at work there after all!' Nathan snorted cynically to himself as he said this. 'Sorry it's not what you wanted to hear is it?' he added with a deep sigh.

Michael could not answer. He felt sick at what Nathan had just told him. He knew it was true, but somehow, he had not quite been able to bring himself to believe it. Deep, irrational parts of his brain clung to the hope that if they could just escape and get home, everything would be alright. Everything would be normal again. Maybe he could even go back to his old job and continue life as it once had been. Meanwhile, the rational part laughed mockingly at these foolish and deluded notions. His rational brain had always won in the end, and now it crushed and flattened his last hopes under its hard-soled jackboot like an over-ripe tomato. Tears rolled down his cheeks at the thought of it. His sister, his friends, his workmates. Everything was gone!

'I know,' Nathan said quietly, staring into his lap. 'It sucks! I thought you knew.'

'Yes, I suppose I did, or I guessed it at least. It's still hard to hear. No cure, no rallying of humanity, no big international fight. Just death and collapse, quick and simple. It's so depressing.'

Nathan sighed. 'But there's still hope. You're holding it in your hands, mate. So, get to work. I'm not giving up until we've given it a bloody good go.'

Michael looked down at the book on the table and wiped the damp fog from his eyes. 'Maybe so. Pray that God in his Holy Land is still with us then.'

'Speaking of which, I contacted the Israelis,' Nathan whispered.

Michael lifted his eyes but did not look up. 'What?' he hissed.

'I found an emergency contact site on a survivor's webpage that was set up in the hours before the end. It was the Israelis. If they're still out there listening and watching, then maybe someone in the Holy Land knows we're here. It would be good to give them a reason to come and get us don't you think? Now get reading!'

*

'You know, the principle behind this is very simple,' Michael muttered as he added ferrous particles to the mix of components outlined in detail in Gökmen's notes. Nathan's research had proved indispensable. He had read out basic procedures and found definitions of key terms that made Gökmen's notes and recipes come to life.

'It's self-assembly, so the whole thing is meant to come together without external direction. All we have to do is ensure precision in our measurements, follow his steps to the letter, and introduce the materials to nanoassembly unit in the right sequence, and hey presto, we should have a serum to which we can add prions.'

Nathan was resting in the wheelchair nearby. Michael had been glad of his company and regular encouragement, but the truth was he been unable to help for some time. Michael occasionally sent him back to look something up or find details on a procedure, but that had long passed. It was probably just as well, as Nathan was far from recovered from his many wounds and clearly needed rest.

Meanwhile, Michael had gone through the steps in Gökmen's notes, again and again, reading, then watching Gökmen perform each step on the CCTV footage, then trying it for himself. Then he would observe his results under the tunneling microscope that occupied one half of the large bunker-cum-laboratory.

It had taken most of the first few hours to simply work out which instrument was which and its role in the process. Then Michael had had to learn the basic procedures and which ingredients to use in what order. Luckily this was well explained in Gökmen's notes. Luckily also, the CCTV footage showed Gökmen carrying out each step, which proved invaluable in accurately following the sequence and timing of each procedure.

A day and night passed without sleep, not that there was any natural light to go by, and finally, exhausted, Michael attempted his first full run through. As he spoke, he transferred the ingredients to the micro-assembly unit, just as Gökmen had done.

'This is it, my friend!' he said to Nathan with a mix of pride and amazement.

'That was way simpler than I thought it was going to be,' Nathan said, stifling a yawn.

Michael yawned also. 'From where you're sitting maybe. I would not have described that as simple.'

'OK, quicker then.'

'Agreed. It was much quicker than expected. The man was a genius.' Michael set the timer for the micro-assembly unit to 'grow' the nanoworms. 'Now we wait!'

A group of Meshedi had gathered in the room over the last hour, watching Michael as he worked furiously towards the final assembly. They had chattered excitedly at times, but now they were silent and watched expectantly for the results. Michael feared what would happen if the drug failed, as he was sure it would.

At last, he flopped into a chair beside Nathan, his body twitching with nervous excitement.

Nathan leveled his gaze at Michael. He was serious for a record third time that day. 'Will it work?' he asked gravely.

'Probably not, but we're getting closer.'

Nathan yawned and closed his eyes. 'Wake me up when it does.'

*

Michael opened the unit and retrieved the twelve little vials, placing them immediately into the freezer. He knew the serum lacked the vital ingredient for self-assembly – prions! He hadn't really thought about this step at all. He had not wanted to. He never wanted to see an INS victim again, but he knew now he had no choice, and perhaps little time. He spun on his heel. The Meshedi looked up, every eye now turned on him. He kicked Nathan gently, who grunted and woke up.

'Is it ready?' Nathan asked groggily.

'Yes, the serum is ready, but we still need prions.'

'Oh, that.'

'We need to explain to our violent friends here that we need a fresh INS victim from which to extract the prions.'

'I can do that. Google translate should still work if I can find an active server.' He turned his wheelchair and bumped his way out of the crowded lab to the door, then waved a Meshedi to follow.

*

Michael stood at the entrance to the tunnel beneath the overpass, the cavernous space now gathering a huge pile of wind-blown rubbish. He half-expected to hear a helicopter buzzing overhead, but there was nothing but silence. The air was cold and there came the sound of an open door or shutter banging in the breeze in the distance.

The Meshedi stood in a protective huddle around him, bristling with guns and wearing body armor. The leader, a lean brutal-looking man who had often assaulted Michael for speaking out of turn, nodded, and they filed out of the tunnel. Michael noticed cameras fixed to the walls of the tunnel entrance, and further along the street beneath the overpass. No one was getting inside without the Meshedi knowing about it!

They ran to the edge of the overpass, where the deep shadows gave way to brilliant sunlight. The scene was confronting, as it had been the previous time, he had seen it. The streets were filled with debris, a chaos of jumbled cars, and an eerie silence hung over the city. Michael felt his stomach tighten and his legs go wobbly as his eyes fell on the still, bedraggled figures that stood in groups in the middle of the road, staring up into space, their hands working at their sides. The shutter continued to bang noisily on the side of the building closest to the group, holding their attention. It only took a few moments for them to notice Michael and the Meshedi approaching quickly from doorway to doorway. Almost as one, they turned and began to stagger towards them.

The lead Meshedi barked an order and the group dropped to their knees in front of Michael and opened fire. A young man with a torn face was singled out and allowed to approach – the rest were downed before they got within a few meters of their position. The young man staggered forwards, gurgling loudly, talon-like fingers outstretched. Two Meshedi stood and took hold of him as he lurched into the group, jaws snapping as he reached out for one of the Meshedi.

Michael held the syringe ready in his trembling hands as the young man was forced to the ground. Another two Meshedi dived on top of him, his exceptional strength forcing them to pin him with all their might.

'Şimdi yap, hızlıca!' the leader cried, glaring at Michael.

Michael stabbed the syringe deep into the man's chest and withdrew the dark red blood up into the syringe. 'Got it!' he cried in disgust as he pulled the syringe out with a spurt of blood from the writhing body, quickly checking it was full.

The lead Meshedi leaned down, placed his pistol to the back of the man's head and pulled the trigger. The writhing ceased as the gunshot echoed down the empty street.

'Haydi gidelim!' the leader cried, and the heavily armed group turned and retreated to the tunnel.

19.

'They were right!' the pilot cried, glancing down at the fuel gauge. 'There's little more than a whiff of petrol left in this beast.'

They were now cruising out over the black void that surrounded the compound.

'Where are we headed?' the pilot asked.

'Just get us back to the airstrip,' Yosef said, climbing out of the front seat and back to the cargo area. 'We need to check-in.'

Arla was still sitting beside the gatling gun, agog at the sight of her brother smiling back at her from the floor of the cargo bay.

'But…? Where…?' she could not find words.

Ariel nodded but kept smiling. 'Sorry to make such a commando entrance, but I had little choice.'

'But how on earth?'

'Yes, I know. Long story. The short version is I was there a while. They captured me, just like they captured you.'

'But they said they couldn't find you, that you had made contact but were still missing. They lied!'

Ariel gave her a knowing look. 'I'm afraid they do that at times like these. I'm glad you're OK!'

Arla jumped up and flung her arms around her brother. 'I was sure you were dead!' she said, a tear moistening her cheek. 'How did you get to us?'

'I saw you, but you didn't see me. I was in a second-story cell of sorts, under close guard. I had already found a way to escape but I was waiting for the right time. Then I saw Yosef with a gun outside, and I knew the time had come. I had to hoof it as you were already lifting off by the time I was clear.'

'But how did they catch you? What did they want with you?'

He shook his head. 'It was the very end. Everything just collapsed. The government and military fled. There was disorder and the streets began to fill with those things. It was Armageddon. I found an MIT agent after much hunting, and he grilled me hard about who I was and what I was doing there. I thought he was going to do me in there and then. But he got interested when I told him who I was looking for. He knew something but wouldn't let on. He arranged a rendezvous on the edge of town for later that evening. Bastards grabbed me and threw me in a truck. Either they really hate Jews, or they thought I knew something. Don't worry, they didn't get anything out of me,' Ariel added as Arla's eyes widened. 'But they tried, the bastards!'

As she sat close to her brother she noticed now in the dimness of the cockpit, lit only by small green lights on the roof, that he was wincing in pain. 'They beat you?'

'And then some!'

A long, guttural growl emanated from Arla that made Yosef, who had joined them, sit back in alarm. 'They'll pay for that!' she spat.

Ariel croaked out a pained laugh. 'It's all part of the job, Arla. Don't worry about me.'

Despite his protests, she lifted his shirt and saw the deep purple bruises in thick stripes across his back and arms. 'God in heaven!' she cried and sat back in horror. 'My poor little brother!'

Yosef was on his knees at once with a torch examining the bruises. 'That looks bad. I'm surprised you could move at all let alone combat roll into a moving helicopter! Who the hell are you, First Lieutenant Egozi or something?'

'Hardly,' Ariel chuckled, then groaned in pain. 'Now it's my turn, what on earth were you doing there? I thought I was seeing things.'

'She came for you, of course, you daft bugger. I told her about your SMS and she insisted on coming.'

'And you let her?' Ariel slapped Yosef on the forehead in a gesture of severe disapproval.

'You try saying no to her,' Yosef protested.

'Just as well that's true or you'd have a lot to answer for my friend. So how did they catch you?'

'They saw our plane land. It didn't take them long.'

'Figures. No air traffic control or air force?'

'None. Air traffic control is gone. It's as silent as the grave,' Yosef replied.

'So why were you not put in a cell, like me? I saw you go somewhere with them in a helicopter. What were you doing?'

'We've found Michael!' Arla said excitedly. 'The Meshedi have him. I told Demir he had a cure and he agreed to help us rescue him in exchange for a share of the drug. I know, I lied,' she said with some regret, 'but then, so did he! They told me they didn't know where you were.'

'Of course they did! I'd been there for days. Why didn't you rescue Michael then? Did something go wrong?'

'Yes. The Meshedi have some kind of underground bunker. They escaped with Michael and Demir thought it was too dangerous to go in after them.'

'Probably true,' Ariel nodded thoughtfully. 'Where is it?'

'In the center of town, beneath a traffic overpass. There must be a tunnel or something.'

'How many Meshedi were there?'

'We only saw seven or eight. Demir's sniper got a few, but they escaped with Michael. They want him for some reason.'

'It's obvious! Didn't you say the drug's what they've always wanted?'

Arla nodded. She stared at Ariel for a moment, unable to hold back the question she had wanted to ask since she first laid eyes on him. 'Did you find James?' she asked quietly, her voice charged with emotion.

'I'm sorry, Arla. The hospital was overrun. There was no one there except those *things*.'

She felt her last hope of finding James fading away, and with it, her resolve to carry on.

'But I found out one thing. I don't know what it means. There may be nothing in it. The MIT guy said the Americans came and took some people away. He didn't know if it was James or not.'

'The CIA?' Arla asked, suddenly filled with hope again.

'I don't know, Arla. Don't get your hopes up. He's probably gone. You know that. He was sick and he didn't have much time. I doubt they could have saved him even if they did take him home with them.'

'Home? God, I hadn't thought of that. He might be in America. He could be…'

'We're over the airfield now!' the pilot interrupted from the cockpit. 'Shall I land? We've only got a few minutes of gas left.'

Yosef climbed back into the cockpit. He donned the light intensifier goggles and searched the ground below. 'There's an armored car parked behind a building down there. Looks like they weren't keen on us leaving without their say so.'

'Take it out!' Ariel ordered angrily.

'What?' Yosef said, looking around at Ariel, a little shocked.

'Take it out I said. We've got armaments, use them! We don't want anyone spoiling things now.'

'But we don't know who they are!' Arla protested. 'It could be anyone!'

'I think we know who it is.'

'They've spotted us and are moving,' Yosef interjected. 'It might be hard to get a clear shot in a second. We've got rockets. What are we doing?'

Arla stared at Ariel, willing him not to give that order.

'Do it!' he said emphatically, staring defiantly back at her.

She glared at him. 'You are a cold-hearted bastard!' she said jumping up and leaning through the cockpit to where the pilot was giving Yosef instructions on how to target the rockets. 'Don't do it Yosef,' she said quietly.

'I don't think we have a choice Arla. I'm sorry,' he added. 'Think what they did to your brother and what they would have done to us. We have no choice. They'll just get in the way.' With that, he pulled the trigger.

There was a slight jolt as two bright lights streaked away from either side of the cockpit, arcing down into the inky blackness below. A moment later there came a huge flash, then a boom, audible even over the roar of the chopper engines. The chopper shuddered for a second as the shock wave washed over them. A moment later a fiery glow lit up the ground where the truck had been.

'Good man, Yosef!' Ariel said, patting Yosef on the back. 'Now that wasn't so hard was it, sis?' he whispered. 'And now we can land!' he announced to the pilot.

Arla said nothing, but she hated what they were doing. She also felt something she had felt many times before - a simultaneous love and hatred for her brother.

'We have unfriendlies,' Yosef called out again as they hovered for a moment above the airstrip, close to their plane, which glinted metallically in the chopper's landing lights. 'Can you get back on the minigun, Arla?'

Arla nodded wearily and resumed her place in the door gunner position and leveled the heavy minigun. She could see nothing in the darkness outside her little window. Then suddenly, as they began to set down, she saw four or five figures stagger quickly towards them out of the darkness, their contorted faces caught in the landing lights. A blinding flash erupted as she squeezed the trigger and the figures fell to pieces before her eyes.

Yosef appeared beside her as they set down. 'Good work!' he said soberly, then yanked open the door and made a run for the jet.

'What are we doing here?' Arla asked Ariel, unsure why they had returned to the jet.

'I'm not sure yet. I need to check-in and let them know we're alive. I'll probably cop hell for it, but I need intel and new orders.'

More staggering figures appeared out of the darkness and Arla cut them down again with disturbing efficiency. Then she let go of the weapon and climbed out after the others, the pilot jumping out after her.

The plane had obviously been ransacked. Lockers had been emptied, seats slashed, cargo bays opened, and every space turned over.

'They've taken all the fuel!' the pilot announced angrily from the cockpit once they had all climbed in and locked the door.

'I'm not surprised,' Yosef said. 'The radio's gone too! We'll have to use the main UHF. No encryption.' He jumped into the cockpit and fired up the radio and hailed Israeli airspace control. After a few short exchanges, Yosef was transferred, and he handed the headset over to Ariel.

Arla collapsed into a seat in the cabin. She was exhausted and still shaking from their terrifying ordeal. She could hear Ariel's one-sided conversation, talking quickly and exchanging information. She was barely able to concentrate on what he was saying she was so tired. She leaned her head against the window – something she always did when she flew. She wished she was sitting on an ordinary flight, heading to some exciting dig or long-overdue holiday instead of shaking with post-adrenaline fatigue and trying to force memories of death and terror from her mind.

'Does Michael have the drug?' Ariel shouted from the cockpit, interrupting her nostalgia.

'What?' she replied in surprise.

'The drug, does Michael have it?'

'Well no, I don't think so. I actually don't know. I suppose he could have. Maybe he does?'

'That's very helpful, thanks,' Ariel growled sarcastically.

Arla knew Michael knew things about the drug, things that obviously made him valuable enough for the Meshedi to rescue him, and to have placed him under the protection of the CIA and MIT before that. 'Perhaps he knows how to make it?' she ventured.

Ariel went back to his rapid-fire conversation and Arla drifted back into her dream, feeling the urgency of sleep descending on her.

'We'll give you co-ordinates soon,' Arla heard Ariel say before he signed off.

'Co-ordinates?' Arla perked up. 'What for?'

'The Meshedi bunker. They're sending in special forces. We're going to bust that place open!'

'But what about Michael? He could be killed! We can't just bomb it!'

'No one wants Michael dead, believe me. You've made a convincing case all along that we should get this guy out of there and back home. We're getting him out. It seems someone in Ankara by the name of Nathan posted last night that they've got a cure for INS. That sort of thing doesn't go unnoticed these days.'

'Did you say Nathan?' Arla couldn't believe her ears. A grin quickly spread across her weary face. 'That's them. He's alive! I don't believe it. Is he with Michael?'

'I don't know, but we'll soon find out!'

20.

'Ships!' came the cry from atop the mast.

Ani gazed up at the man atop the mast, a man called Jeemah who he knew well. Jeemah was very dark-skinned and had come as a child from a foreign land where he was captured and made a slave. This last week Troan had forbidden Ani to speak to him, or to any of the other slaves on board. Like all the slaves, Jeemah had worked tirelessly since Troan had seized command. He sweated great sheets of water in the hot sun by day, and froze in near nakedness by night, huddled close together with the rest of his kind.

Ani had felt intensely sorry for Jeemah and the others. To have been friends - equals even - only a week before, and now to be made to avoid them like pariahs while they toiled night and day for the good of others was unbearable and deeply unfair. It was the old order restored. Ani and Purdu had themselves kept slaves, but not like this. They had treated their slaves kindly, more like family, though they were of course required to work hard around the farm. This, on the other hand, was sheer brutality. Ani could detect the bitterness in the air, and noticed many hateful glances cast in the direction of Troan when his back was turned.

The cry of 'sails' created a sudden excitement on board. Ani heard the cry taken up by other vessels nearby. At once Troan climbed into the fighting castle and was soon joined by the Gal Meshedi. Ani sheathed the sword he had been practicing with and scurried to the bow and peered out through the narrow gap between the steering oar and the sternpost.

'Who could it be?' Ani heard Troan wonder anxiously.

'How should I know?' the Gal Meshedi answered in the same peevish tone he always used with Troan.

'Well, do you recognize the sails?'

'I am not a naval commander, as you would know if you had ever visited the capital.'

Purdu nestled in against the rail beside Ani. 'Who are they?'

Ani shook his head and nodded up to the castle to indicate he was listening in. She nodded, fell silent and cocked her head also.

'What should we do?' Troan asked worriedly. Despite his arrogance, Ani noticed he always asked the Gal Meshedi's advice, like a child taking council from his father.

'You need to organize the fleet.' There was a long pause in which Ani imagined the Gal Meshedi shaking his head worriedly. 'We are not prepared for a sea battle. Perhaps it would be better to try and outrun them. At least the ships are rather lighter these days,' he added scornfully, obviously referring to the recent murder of the original crew.

'Well, I suppose we could. But, no, I wish to see who they are first. Perhaps we can defeat them, and they may have food. My men could win a battle at sea, and I think it is time we tried. We must have a victory to unify the fleet under my command.'

The Gal Meshedi snorted derisively. 'You are joking, aren't you?'

'No!' Troan replied defensively. 'Why should I be?'

'Must I spell it out for you? We are not ready to fight a library full of scribes let alone an organized navy. Your people are raw. So, they have conquered a small town and repelled a few demons. So what! It is worth nothing! This is a matter of tactics and skills in naval combat, none of which we possess, nor are we even familiar with them thanks to your butchering the only sailors who could have taught us such things.'

'You do not know that this is an organized navy. It may be just a group of scruffy refugees armed with hoes and sickles for all we know.'

'Like us you mean!'

'No uncle.'

Ani could hear the Gal Meshedi inhale sharply at the use of this familial term which he seemed to hate above all things.

'We have already fought several battles, and my men and yours are hardened warriors. I'd say we can easily beat down a bunch of hungry vagabonds. Even Ani and Purdu can fight now, and Mezarus is worth five men.'

'Those brats! You have clearly lost your mind.'

'I say we should linger long enough to take their measure, and if they are weak, we will destroy them and capture their ships and provisions and enslave their crew. If they are strong, we shall flee as you would have us do. Yes, I have made up my mind. That is what we shall do.'

Ani could hear the Gal Meshedi growl in disapproval, but Troan had already turned to address the crew who waited expectantly for orders.

'We shall lower sails and allow these ships to approach. At my order, we either attack or make sail and head south with all speed to outrun them. Freemen arm yourselves and prepare fire arrows. Slaves, stand by your posts and await orders to make sail.'

Ani and Purdu made their way to their sea chests, stashed below deck beneath removable boards along with all the rest of the cargo. All the free men and women hurriedly pulled on armor and gathered weapons, shields, and arrows and began to organize braziers of burning coals on deck.

The Gal Meshedi strode through the chaos, shaking his head disapprovingly and looking very dubious. At last, he gathered his own men to him to one side of the ship and spoke to them quietly. Ani tried to sidle up and make out what was being said, but the Gal Meshedi was careful not to be overheard.

Troan had sent a slave to summon Purdu once she was equipped, and Ani had followed her to the door to the little cabin but had not been allowed to enter. He knew Purdu had little choice but to obey these summonses without complaint, and it had at least meant she had been able to secure food and some other comforts for her and her brother, such as furs for the cold night air. Nevertheless, Ani remained far from comfortable with the situation. Troan had a creepy way of looking at and talking to Purdu that made Ani want to slap him, or worse.

As he waited by the door, Ani could see the ships fast approaching. He also noticed that they were spread far and wide across the horizon, perhaps two dozen or more in number. He noted that their course was irregular and veered left and right, to the point where some ships almost collided or capsized. The breeze was stiff, as it had been for several days, and had allowed them to keep a true course for some time, bringing them now, it was thought, close to the shores of Canaan.

At some point, Ani became aware of Jeemah beside him. He was also staring at the ships with interest, a frown etched on his dark leathery face. 'Are they drunk, sir?' he asked, using the title that all slaves were now required to use when addressing nobles.

'Why do you say that?' Ani asked curiously, remembering now that he was not supposed to be talking to slaves.

'They sail recklessly, sir. Watch how they nearly collide with one another and heel over and nearly capsize.' He pointed far to the right were two ships narrowly missed each other as they passed by one another. 'They are fools, or they are drunk.' With that, he disappeared back to his post.

Ani watched the strange, chaotic veering of the ships for some time. Their own ships had slowly formed into a fairly tight group and were almost at a standstill, bobbing on the chop of the waves whipped up by the strong breeze. At Troan's orders, archers stood ready in the fighting castle of each ship with braziers of coals swinging in the rigging beside them. Troan was in the castle along with his signaler and the archers, ready to give the order to fire.

Ani took his place beside Mezarus and like every man and woman aboard, watched as the strangely meandering ships approached under full sail. The first of these vessels approached at speed, and on a course that seemed certain to end in a collision with their own ship. At the last minute, the racing ship veered suddenly away just as a panicked cry erupted from all aboard.

As the ship passed, Ani saw something on deck that made his heart stop. Instead of rows of soldiers standing by the rail ready to launch a deadly volley of arrows or leap aboard with swords drawn, the decks were almost empty. Here and there were figures, staggering and lurching about strangely on deck. They were blood-stained, covered in wounds, and their arms hung limply by their sides. As the ship drew briefly alongside, these horrific figures snarled and ran to the rail, lifted their arms and outstretched their talon-like fingers as they passed, their hollow eyes staring at those on deck with hunger, their mouths issuing dreadful cries of inhuman anguish. Their teeth champed violently, and their claw-like hands grasped at the air, reaching out in vain for healthy flesh as they glided past. Paralyzed with horror and sick at the sight of it, Ani saw with dreadful clarity the skeletonized corpses that littered the decks. He also saw that the steering oar had been loosely tied into position, allowing the ship to continue on its predestined course despite there being no one at the helm.

'Fire!' Troan cried, horror oozing from his voice.

At once, the archers touched their oil-soaked fire arrows to the burners and launched volley after volley of flaming arrows into the passing ship. Other ships were doing the same as the horrifying fleet passed by.

It took little time for the huge sails to catch alight. The flames ran down the rigging like rivulets of burning lava spilling over the side of a volcano, and soon the burning masts came crashing down onto the deck. As the ships continued their erratic course out into the open ocean, the flames shot higher and a thick black smoke curled behind, mixing with the wake. Silhouetted against the flames were human figures, hands still outstretched in a final desperate act before they too were consumed by the flames.

Many ships that had passed near to their fleet disappeared below the waves in this manner, but others were well beyond range and continued on, disappearing over the horizon on their unmanned voyage to some unlucky destination.

Ani watched as the last of the blazing ships slowly burned down to the water line and finally disappeared beneath the waves. At last, there was nothing to be seen but a blanket of swirling smoke driven on by the wind towards the veiled horizon.

21.

'How many batches is that now?' Nathan asked as he wheeled himself over to the super-cooling chest where Michael was smiling to himself as he withdrew the latest batch ready for the crucial next step of adding prions.

'Nine.' Michael spun slowly and carefully around with the tray of little vials in his thickly gloved hands. He opened the fridge behind him with his foot and leaned down into the glowing white cavity and carefully placed the tray onto the shelf beside the other primer batches he had made so far.

He was feeling exceedingly pleased with himself, and for the first time, he felt he may actually have done it. Not that he would know of course until he harvested the prions and tested the drug on an INS victim. He had spent a lot of time going over the notes with a fine-tooth comb, watching and re-watching the CCTV footage, and replicating every step in the sequence with pinpoint accuracy using the exact machines and constituents mentioned in Gökmen's notes and the descriptions and definitions Nathan had provided from his searches on the last remaining tatters of the web.

He stood and straightened his back, feeling the pain in his spine that had been an unwelcome companion for the last few days as he endlessly bent over the folder of notes, nano-grinders, microscopes, test tubes, and computer screens. The notes and research had taught him a vast amount about a science he had barely known existed, except in science fiction, and through those forward-looking science shows that made the future look implausibly near and problem-free. How wrong those shows had been!

'Are we ready to test?' Nathan asked expectantly.

Michael sighed. He had to accept that by making batch after batch, learning and improving his knowledge of the machines and the process, he had been putting off the moment of awful truth - the moment he must face sooner or later – when he would learn if the formula was, once more, a failure. 'I think I need to make one more batch.'

'Michael, no!'

Michael sighed and stared at the floor, wracked by indecision and self-doubt.

'Michael, look at me!'

Michael felt his gaze pulled forcefully toward Nathan as though caught in the Death Star's tractor beam. 'What?' he said, sensing Nathan's anger.

'This is it, Michael. You know it is. You've spent enough time on this. Doing it again isn't going to make any difference. Nine times! It's time to try! For all we know the first batch might have worked just fine. We don't have much more time. The Meshedi are looking more and more demented each day, that helicopter's probably still buzzing around out there waiting to gun us all down, and the world gets no closer to fixing its problem. Do it!'

'But I still don't…'

'No Michael, now! Do it now!'

Michael sighed again and stared at his friend, still crippled and looking like a once-proud ship that had run aground and half sunk into the sand upon which it was trapped.

'Can't we just….'

'No!' Nathan snapped loudly. 'I want to do it now!'

A Meshedi looked up menacingly from his nap in a chair at the other end of the lab and barked something in Turkish.

Nathan cleared his throat and spoke more softly. 'Let's see what we have, eh buddy? We'll soon know one way or the other, right?'

Reluctantly, Michael nodded. He was amply aware of the passing time, but he had not been satisfied by his attempts until now. This last batch had seemed to go just as Gökmen's had specified. The imaging had shown the right molecular bonds had formed in their correct concentrations. Now it was simply a matter of adding live prions and he should have vials filled with frenzied, destructive little viricidal maniacs ready to wipe out the accursed infection from whichever patient was lucky enough to receive it.

'OK. You're right,' Michael said, turning his back on Nathan to hide the anxiety he still felt.

'I know you're worried about it mate, but what chance do we have if we don't do it? I'm sure they'll top us soon if we don't get on with it.'

Michael nodded reluctantly. 'Who do we try it on?'

'I don't care, and it's not like they're gonna care either. Let's face it, it can't exactly do any more harm. I don't think the Hippocratic Oath even applies to zombies. I'm sure these creeps have got a legion of INS victims tied up out the back somewhere.'

'Yes, you're probably right.' Michael took a deep breath. He walked slowly to the fridge where the prions were stored in the syringe Michael had used to extract them. He pulled open the door and reached in and retrieved the syringe, holding it reverently beneath the bright fluorescent lamp on a nearby desk. The pink fluid glowed within beneath the condensation that quickly formed on the tube.

'You know, I've been reading a lot of the news from the last weeks while you've been working,' Nathan said, wheeling closer to watch what Michael was doing. 'There were these medico boffins in the UK who were working on it. They thought they'd made a breakthrough or something. They talked a bit about what prions are, describing them for the public. They were trying to ease panic by making it look like they were in control and would fix it soon.'

Michael snorted and shook his head. 'So, what did they say?'

'They called it a 'prion bloom'. They said lots of organisms including algae, bacteria, locusts and rats, and even certain weird things like prions that aren't really organisms as such but complex proteins, can suddenly massively increase in numbers if their preferred living conditions are just right, and they bloom to epic proportions.'

'Is that what this is, a bloom?'

'Yeah, so they reckoned. But, and here's the important bit, they also said that like all blooms, it should die down just as fast it rises.'

Michael looked up, suddenly intrigued by what Nathan was saying. It made perfect sense from a biological point of view. Throughout the evolution of life, some organisms have prospered, risen to plague proportions, then died off as fast as they rose as they overextended and consumed all their resources or conditions changed. It was classic Malthusian theory – one of the cornerstones of Darwin's theory of natural selection. Then Michael sagged. He realized that while this meant prions would almost certainly decline in frequency again, thus ending the epidemic, there was a bleak and poignant outcome to this as well. 'That's great, Nathan, but you know how that story must end don't you?'

'I'm hoping you're going to say, 'with us all living happily ever after', but I think I know your gloomy-ass nature too well for that.'

'It means that the bloom only ends when the resources on which it depends are entirely depleted, or conditions change. It means it won't end until humanity is no more, or in utter tatters; that is until there is nothing left for it to feed on.'

'Oh, but what about immunity? Haven't humans always survived nasty plagues, viruses, infections, and pestilence before? Sure, it knocks us down, but we always get back up again?'

'Yes, we do. Or at least, we have done until now. We obviously survived the last bloom at the end of the Bronze Age, and presumably many others before that.' Michael sighed. It was depressing to think that even should humanity survive, it would have to rebuild itself again from scratch. How many would have to die before the bloom petered out? How long would it take? James and Arla probably had a good idea from the past, or could find out, but were they even still alive?

'How many of us do you think are left?' Michael asked quietly, still staring at the pink liquid in the syringe.

'I have no idea. The papers were talking about mass death, unprecedented since the Spanish Flu and the Bubonic Plague, only made worse by the fact that the hunted become the hunters, driving the infection rate out of all proportion compared to normal epidemics. Still, I would be very surprised if there's not a lot of us still holed up in secure places out there, but I guess we won't know until we get out of here. Do you think this drug can actually reverse the disease? Can it bring people back?'

'I damn well hope so!' Michael couldn't help but think of Corinne. If only Gökmen had not cheated him, he could have saved her! Gökmen could have saved so many! 'Here goes!' Michael said as he took the caps off the vials in his most recent batch and inserted the tip of the syringe into the top of a vial. 'I'm not sure how much of this to add, and Gökmen's notes aren't clear on this, so I'll just have to experiment.'

A tiny bead of the pink liquid gathered at the tip of the needle, quivered momentarily as Michael's hands trembled, then detached and dropped into the frosty vial. He increased the number of drops in each vial successively, then deposited the syringe back in the fridge and sealed the vials.

'So, this is it, mate!' Nathan said with a nervous smile. 'Who you gonna jab?'

'Up until now, we've worked on the assumption that Missilli only managed to cure a very recently infected patient. We have no idea whether this will work on more developed cases. I guess that means we need a fresh victim.'

'That's a scary thought. Do we tell one of the Meshedi to stick his arm out the window and get a bite?'

Michael smiled and nodded absent-mindedly, thinking hard. 'I know, we'll…'

At that moment a huge explosion rocked the room, sending Michael reeling to the floor. Sparks and chunks of concrete flew across the room. The flying debris would have killed Michael if not for the large freezers in front of him. The lights were out and Michael found himself choking on a thick cloud of noxious smoke and dust. He hunched on the ground, stunned and trying hard to breathe. He could make no sense of what had just happened.

Shouts erupted from around the lab. Several beams of light flashed across the room. One fell momentarily on Nathan. Michael could see he was hunched over in his wheelchair, obviously unconscious. Blood was streaming down his face.

'Nathan!' Michael coughed in panic but received no reply. He reached up and pulled his limp body to the ground beside him.

Dark shapes emerged through clouds of dust and smoke out of a jagged circle of light where the wall had been. A loud throbbing sound filled the room. A second later all hell broke loose as massive gunfire erupted around the room. Michael pushed himself flat against the floor and crawled under a desk as tracers whizzed and ricocheted off walls and posts.

'Stay down!' someone shouted at Michael over the noise, in English. He knew that voice…

22.

'I hope they get here soon,' Yosef muttered miserably to himself as he shared out the last portion of food from the sole remaining box of supplies. It had been tucked at the back of one of the storage lockers on the jet and luckily the ransackers had missed it. Once they had found these few remaining supplies and contacted Ariel's controllers back in Israel, they had retired to the hot and stuffy safety of the helicopter with its bristling guns and its precious but minuscule remaining fuel.

Arla sat beside the gatling gun and stared out of the increasingly dusty window at the ever-present crowd of shambling, gurgling figures surrounding the chopper, occasionally scratching at the door or planting their face against the window with a terrifying suddenness that made Arla jump every time.

She sat forlornly nibbling her crumbs, wetting her lips from her nearly empty canteen and trying not to let her aching stomach override her rational mind. The chopper cabin became dangerously hot during the day, and there were only tiny windows that could be opened safely without uninvited guests getting inside. Every hour took all her mental strength not to throw open the door and let in some fresh air and find relief from nagging claustrophobia. Now the sun was rising once more and so too the temperature in the cabin. Like Yosef, she desperately hoped succor would come soon.

Arla's attempts to strike up hopeful conversations about a speedy rescue, finding the cure and returning with James had been met with gloomy silence from all of her companions.

Yosef's ceaseless humming, on the other hand, had nearly caused Arla to yank the gatling gun from its supports and whack him over the head with it. Instead, she turned her attention to reading the safety and operation manuals for the helicopter she found stashed in a locker. Her Turkish was non-existent, but she read them all the same.

Ariel had focused his attentions on the radio when he was not baiting Arla with brotherly chides and insults about her esoteric profession and her headstrong manner. When the radio's silence grew tedious, he would watch the hills for signs of their watchers.

They had seen dust trails in the hills around them these last few days, and distant lights at night. They knew they were being watched by Major Demir and his people, but they had not approached within range of the guns. Their pilot had stayed put in the cockpit as much as possible in case urgent escape became necessary, but he had explained they probably had no more than ten to twenty kilometers worth of fuel remaining. Ammunition was also low.

They had been able to pick up brief activity on the radio when they turned it on, but for the most part, it remained eerily crackly and devoid of human voices. The little bits they had heard Ariel had translated. It seemed there was a group in the hills that was trying to make contact with any nearby survivors who could help them. They were in need of food, water, and medical supplies. Sadly, no one replied, not even Demir's group, even though Arla was sure they were listening in too. She had wanted to make contact with them and find out what was happening, but Ariel had insisted they do no such thing.

'I'm not your little five-year-old sister anymore, you know,' she had retorted angrily. 'I can do things without your say-so.'

But Ariel had emphasized the danger that would place them in by giving away their location to who knows who, thereby jeopardizing the Israeli military operation that would soon descend on their position.

*

'How can they leave us here like this?' Yosef moaned again. 'Don't they know we've run out of food and water?'

'Can it, Yosef!' Ariel snapped, sounding shorter tempered than usual. 'Do you think they can just throw together a mission that quickly? It takes some planning. They will be here soon. Be patient! Anyway, we haven't run out of food. You've still got some in your hand you glutton!'

Yosef held his last tiny cube of energy bar up to the sunlight and inspected it, as if intending to make it last forever, then quickly stuffed it into his mouth and devoured it. 'Not anymore!'

'You idiot, you should have savored it. Now you are going to be hungry.' Ariel slapped Yosef on the top of the head as he often did, knocking over Yosef's carefully piled pyramid of empty ration boxes in the process. It was a gesture both brotherly and genuinely irritated.

'That's not true,' Yosef said smiling and pulled a long knife from his belt. 'If I get hungry, I'll start with your left leg, and then your…'

'Shush,' the pilot suddenly interrupted their banter. He leant over and adjusted one of the little windows above his head. 'Hear that?'

A low hum shattered the silence of a normally empty landscape. It was the first human sound from outside the chopper they had heard in days.

Arla jumped out of her seat and climbed into the front with the others, crushing Yosef's second stack of boxes in the process.

Ariel leaned over and switched on the radio which was already set to a pre-arranged channel.

A call sign crackled over the radio in Hebrew, 'Scion, do you copy? Over!'

Ariel seized the receiver excitedly and gave the agreed code in reply.

'We will be setting down in your position shortly. Do you have any hostile presence? Over.'

'We have observers on the hilltops, and we are surrounded by this human carrion. Over.'

'Copy that. Stay put and we'll deal with them.'

The hum was fast building into a thundering crescendo and Arla could now make out a swarm of tiny black dots emerging out of the heat shimmer.

'Scion?' Arla asked, amused.

'It's my operator name.'

'As in little twig, or offspring of the Dark Lord?'

'Both I guess.'

Even before the dots had enlarged enough to be identifiable, bright dots trailing banners of smoke screamed overhead, tearing the air apart. A moment later their helicopter shook as blasts erupted simultaneously along the hilltops around them, sending up huge plumes of black smoke and clouds of dirt.

Arla could not help but feel sorry for whatever poor wretches were up there. Demir maybe a duplicitous scumbag, but he had just as much reason to want the cure as them. Now that she knew Michael and Nathan were alive and in Ankara, and that they had posted their possession of a cure on the skeletal net, all bets were off. It would be a mad dash for it, and who wouldn't risk everything to get it? She could not help but worry that Demir may already have obtained it. In any case, Demir's people were paying the price for competing for what was now the most precious substance on earth - worth more than all the gold and diamonds ever mined.

Arla felt Ariel's presence beside her.

'Good riddance!' he spat with characteristic coldness, rubbing the black eye he still sported.

'I don't know how you can say that,' Arla said sadly. 'They are just people like us.'

'Were. Anyway, they were all going to turn sooner or later.'

She shook her head and sighed. It was deeply upsetting to have such a cold-hearted brother.

'Don't think for a second they wouldn't do the same to us… and they still may!' he added severely, giving her a reprimanding look for her soft-heartedness. 'We play for keeps now. The rules are clear.'

'Rules!' Arla shot back in disgust.

The thundering of engines engulfed them as the shadows of half a dozen Cobra attack helicopters swooped back and forth across the tarmac. A hail of bullets rained down on the half-naked and emaciated figures that were already staggering across the tarmac in the direction of the explosions, drawn by the sound. They fell this way and that in batches like bowling pins struck by an invisible ball as the helicopters strafed them and the lead tore up the tarmac. Now and then stray bullets ricocheted off the fuselage of the helicopter, and Arla found herself seeking refuge on the floor beneath a bulkhead.

Another message crackled over the radio. 'The runway is clear. What is your status?'

The pilot responded into his headset, telling them that they were out of fuel, then turned back to the others. 'We're bailing out!' he announced as he ripped off his headset.

'Thank god!' Yosef cried and dived for the big sliding door.

Arla picked herself up and climbed out after him.

It was ablaze with heat and light outside and the hovering Cobras created tornadoes if dust that spun across the tarmac and stung Arla's face and hands. A heavily armed Blackhawk descended slowly some distance away and a helmeted Israeli soldier leaned out of the cargo bay and waved them over.

The four of them hurried across the shimmering tarmac. Arla was relieved to have the use of her legs again after the tight confines of the helicopter. If only they had cold water, she thought, licking her parched lips. She would do almost anything for a glass of it right now.

They were pulled aboard the vibrating machine and the door immediately slammed closed. An officer in his late forties greeted them and motioned for them to strap in opposite him as they lifted off the ground.

'Lieutenant Grossman,' he said, saluting them formally. 'Welcome aboard.'

They saluted back, all except Arla who titled her head in acknowledgment. 'Thank you for getting us,' she said with real gratitude. 'I may be about to expire of thirst!'

'I'm sorry it took so long.' He waved to a nearby soldier and bottles of water appeared for them all. 'There are many who thought this a fool's errand. I hope you have something for us to prove them wrong, Major Ashinsky?'

Ariel nodded thoughtfully. 'So do I!'

*

They had set down and assembled in an empty park not far from the overpass. Arla noticed that Ankara looked even worse on the way in than on her last visit. The streets were emptier, save for the decomposing corpses that lay everywhere amongst the rubbish, and abandoned cars and detritus.

Lieutenant Grossman strolled over to Arla where she was rifling through equipment that would fit her.

'We do not know how many Meshedi are in there, or their defensive capability,' he said conversationally. 'They are dangerous customers by all accounts. I think it best that you stay here with the pickup team,' he said.

'Actually, I'm coming too,' she corrected the Lieutenant matter-of-factly, picking up a bulletproof vest and heaving it over her shoulders. 'I know Michael and Nathan well. You'll need me to identify them.'

'We have photos. The team knows who they are looking for.'

'Yes, I'm sure they do, but Michael and Nathan don't know who you are. They won't trust you. They might panic and do something stupid. In fact, knowing them, I'd say that's highly likely. I need to prevent that from happening.'

'I'm sorry miss, that's impossible. I…'

'Just do as she says,' Ariel interjected bluntly. 'She won't follow any orders of yours or mine.'

'Well, she'll just have to…'

'She's coming too!' Ariel stated firmly and threw her a helmet.

'Civilians are not permitted to take part in military operations,' the lieutenant insisted, looking taken aback.

'Please, miss,' he turned to Arla imploringly.

'It's Doctor actually.'

'My apologies. Please Dr Ashinsky, it's not safe. You could be harmed.'

'I've done my IDF training like anyone else, and I've seen action. Plus, I have a score of my own to settle. These bastards killed our dig crew, Safika, and Kasif, and they shot James, twice. I'm going in there and that's all there is to it.'

Grossman cast Ariel a worried look.

He shrugged, then nodded.

'OK, but I want you at the back. No settling scores. That's my final word on the matter.'

Arla smiled and pulled on her helmet. Grossman shook his head disapprovingly and wandered off to oversee final preparations.

'Thanks,' she said to Ariel.

He chuckled and picked up his weapon. 'Like I had any say in it. Anyway, I'm staying at the back too. Leave this to the professionals, I say. I just want to be sure we get that cure. That's what I came here for after all.'

'Oh, I thought you came to rescue James?' She cast her brother a scathing look.

'That too,' he winked and stalked off.

'I'm going to have to do it on my own, as usual,' she said despairingly to herself as she fastened her vest.

'No, you're not. I'll help you,' came a voice behind her. She looked around.

Yosef stood behind her, fully dressed for battle, his weapon strapped across his chest. He looked unrecognizable in his full kit, but also happier than she had seen him for days. There was something else in his eye as well as he gazed at her.

'Thank you, Yosef,' she said and hugged him warmly, awkwardly entangling herself in his straps in the process. Then she tried to step away. 'You know I love James don't you,' she said warily, wanting that out of the way immediately.

'Yes,' he laughed embarrassedly as he helped her free herself. 'Yes, I do,' but she could tell he was wounded.

*

The line of troops shuffled along the overpass in a disciplined fashion, keeping low and moving quickly. A ring of Cobras kept a watch on things from the sky, keeping in constant radio contact with those on the ground and warning them of approaching INS victims. The team was equipped with silencers so as to dispatch the ravening figures that staggered towards them in desperate hunger without alerting too many more to their presence.

Once in position above the tunnel, a drone descended over the edge to inspect the entranceway. The team then hooked repelling ropes onto the overpass rails and climbed to the edge while demolitions experts prepared a shaped charge to blow the door. Radio confirmation was received that the other teams surrounding the overpass were in position, and the order came to commence the operation. Smoke grenades were dropped into the tunnel below, and the demolitions team slipped silently down their ropes and into the expanding smoke cloud.

Arla was near the rear of the group, as agreed, but she knew she had to get closer. She felt it was her job to tell Michael and Nathan not to panic once they were inside, and to prevent them from panicking. Slowly she inched her way down the line of soldiers.

Suddenly she felt a hand on her shoulder, pulling her back. 'Where are you going, sis?' she heard Ariel whisper in her ear.

She glanced around and saw Ariel's look of warning and Yosef's look of alarm.

'Don't worry, I'll be careful. This is important!'

Ariel nodded resignedly and relaxed his grip. She turned and crawled forwards to where the demolitions team had disappeared over the edge. She had to admit, she had not felt this anxious or excited in quite a while, but she also knew they were all in very real danger. The front row troops noticed her presence but seemed nonplussed. Women were not out of the ordinary in the Israeli army, and for all they knew, she was a spook like her brother.

She could hear on her headset the demolitions team muttering quietly as they went through the motions of affixing the charges and setting the timer to blow the door. Then they started a countdown, and everyone braced themselves for the explosion. A second later the whole overpass shook violently as if an earthquake had suddenly let leash beneath their feet, and huge cracks appeared across the asphalt. A section of the roadway broke away and dropped several feet, leaving a long gash of layered tarmac and gravel that looked like a neatly sliced Bavarian cake. In an instant the troops were up and over the rail, gliding smoothly down their ropes to the ground below. Arla too was on her feet, hooked on and slid down after them.

A huge hole had been blown through a series of interior walls and smoke and dust belched out of the jagged opening. The soldiers were already filing into the opening in groups. Gunfire and streaks of tracer rattled noisily inside the building and beams of light from barrel mounted torches cut swathes through the choked air.

She flattened herself against the wall momentarily, then took a deep breath and dashed inside, throwing herself onto the piles of bricks behind a shattered wall. In front of her soldiers were pressed against the wall, firing determined bursts into the room and then pushing forward one at a time to take new cover, yelling and signaling to each as they did so.

'Where are Michael and Nathan?' she yelled into the ear of the soldier immediately in front of her.

'Don't know! Keep down!' he cried.

She flicked on her barrel torch, dove for an unoccupied section of a low wall and swept her beam across the room, searching for Michael and Nathan through her telescopic sight. She saw shadowy figures darting between doors and pillars, firing in their direction. She ducked back and waited a few seconds, then swung around with her torch again. This time it fell on a familiar face. It was Nathan. He was seated upright, but his head had lolled forward, his face covered in a large amount of blood. He was either dead or unconscious. She rolled back behind the wall as another heavy burst of automatic fire showered her in plaster and brick fragments. The soldier beside her began another heavy burst in return, and she slid out again and searched the room with her scope. There, beneath a desk, she saw Michael, reaching up to pull Nathan to the floor.

'Stay down!' she cried as loudly as she could over the noise. 'Michael, it's Arla! We're here to rescue you!'

23.

The coast had appeared suddenly one morning from under a veil of mist. The day had turned intensely hot and blue, and the water had shimmered with a vermillion greenness that some said meant they were over a sandy bottom.

Troan had once again taken council with the Gal Meshedi, and signalers were soon contacting the other boats with orders to sail down the coast until a settlement was spotted.

'I don't think putting into port is wise,' the Gal Meshedi offered patiently. Lately, Troan had seemed to do the exact opposite of whatever the Gal Meshedi had advised, despite the pact they had made some weeks ago.

'Then what are we to eat? Planks, sails and tar?'

'Fish, boy, fish.'

'Do not call me 'boy',' Troan hissed back.

'Fish, your lordship,' the Gal Meshedi returned sarcastically.

'But this is the land of milk and honey, as everyone knows. Why eat stinking fish when we may have roast lamb and wine?'

'Because if such things still exist, there will be those ashore to keep it from us. Our numbers are half what they were when we raided the islands. And on top of that, I fear sickness is spreading aboard your other ships. Have you not noticed the signs?'

'How could it spread? We have been miles from the land, and no one was brought aboard with the sickness.'

'If you attack a town you must be prepared to sacrifice a great many of us. That will leave the ships undermanned. The slaves, not exactly your happiest of crew members right now, will outnumber you, gods forbid! If we return from battle spent and short-handed, you may find a rebellion waiting for you. Gods know that is what I would be planning if I were them.'

Troan paced the castle, obviously unhappy with the Gal Meshedi's dour prophesies. He had taken to carrying a whip of late and often used it on the slaves. He thrashed it angrily through the air as he paced about.

Ani knew that Troan often took Purdu's council shortly after these sessions, perhaps seeking to cheer himself up. She was becoming restless and he could tell she was not looking forward to it.

'What does he talk to you about?' Ani asked her once more, trying to get to the bottom of things. 'Is he kind, or is he, well, you know, strange? Does he hurt you?'

'It doesn't matter, Ani. It keeps us safe. What choice do we have? Where can we go?'

'It matters to me!' he said angrily, 'and it should to you too!' He gripped the rail so tightly his fingers hurt. He had noticed she had strange welts on her arms and face of late and he could only guess how she had received them. 'If he hurts you...,' he stifled a strike against the rail.

Purdu walked over and put her arms around Ani. 'Don't worry about me, Ani. Remember, I still have my knife,' she whispered. 'If he hurts me badly, I will use it. Maybe we can escape when we land this time.'

He searched her face and saw the deep unhappiness there. He nodded. 'Yes.' He wanted that more than anything now.

He looked over at where Mezarus was deep in conversation with one of the Meshedi. They seemed to have taken a special liking to Mezarus and often invited him into their inner circle, playing dice with him and keeping him full of food and wine. Ani was suspicious about this and noticed the sly looks the Meshedi gave him. Mezarus was a kind man and too trusting, and Ani knew he was often blind to the darker side of people. Ani also had not forgotten that the Gal Meshedi had promised to one day punish them.

*

One evening, Ani asked Mezarus what the Meshedi wanted.

'They know about our plan to make iron swords and to fight back against the demons. The Gal Meshedi thinks it is a good plan, and he has promised to help us achieve it. They say they know where we can find the tools and materials we need. That we must go to Canaan to find them. I think we should work together with them Ani. They want to help us.'

Ani sighed. It was Lelwan's plan! It was the very reason they had fetched Mezarus from the rock temple to begin with. Ani could not help but be cynical. He knew the Meshedi had no intention of helping them, only of using Mezarus to further their own aims, and now they knew about Mezarus' skills, he was sure they would work on separating Mezarus from them. What fate the Gal Meshedi had in store for them, Ani dreaded to think.

*

There was a growing tension on board that Ani could sense in the air around him. He noticed the slaves cast knowing glances at one another while bent at their work, and once or twice he thought he saw signals exchanged between ships by slaves in the rigging or atop the mast. He sensed that Troan's men were also aware of it and a dangerous mood was growing, especially now they had sighted land again. But before anyone could give vent to such feelings, a thick pall of smoke was noticed rising from the south.

Like everyone, Ani and Purdu climbed into the rigging to get a better look. Speculation and conjecture spread through the ship like wildfire, wondering at what the smoke could mean.

'Cut sail!' Troan cried from the castle, and the slaves immediately jumped to work with renewed vigor. Signals were waved off the side of the castle as the order was relayed to the rest of the fleet.

'Uncle, come here!' Troan bellowed impetuously.

The Gal Meshedi left his little congregation and paced reluctantly down the deck to the rear castle.

Ani slipped out of the ropes and made his way slowly and inconspicuously to his usual position beneath the castle.

'But if it is a battle,' he heard Troan saying, 'we may be able to swoop in and defeat the already weakened parties. Just think what booty we might take! Full bellies and decent weapons for all,' Troan was effusing in his usual over-inflated way.

'Alternatively, we turn out to be the most foolish and ill-fated fleet ever to have picked an unprovoked sea battle in the history of the world,' the Gal Meshedi replied coldly.

'I have told you before that a sea battle is what we need, to test our metal, boost our confidence and strengthen our morale. We need a battle we know we can win, and this is it!'

'We have no idea if this even is a battle, but for once you may be right.'

'I'm glad to hear you finally admit it, uncle.'

'Admit what?'

'That I am always right.'

Ani could hear a now-familiar strangled choking noise coming from the castle.

'Do not dare to speak in such an impetuous tone to me ever again or I will have one of your slaves cut your tongue from your mouth! Do you understand?'

There was a sniveling wailing sound from the castle followed by some heavy gasping.

'As I was saying,' the Meshedi continued, 'there may be some sense in preparing an attack should we stray upon a recent battle with one man left standing, albeit beaten and bloodied. Order it!'

Troan gave a hoarse order to one of his men waiting on deck beside Ani. The order was relayed across the ship and then across the fleet, and the crew got to work hauling up the weapons and armor from the hold.

The ships made sail again and readied themselves for battle. A sense of excitement replaced the mutinous mood of only hours before.

Ani and Purdu tightened the straps on each other's armor and found their favorite lighter than normal swords and shields. Arrows and boarding spears were stacked against the mast and braziers for fire arrows were lit.

Ani had butterflies in his stomach, just as he had had on each previous raid. This time he knew he was much better prepared, but he was also keenly aware that life or death may not be his to choose.

As they sailed closer it became clear that a sea battle of some kind had recently been fought. Burning ships sat low in the water, their masts and rigging already consumed by the flames. Surrounding them was a group of ten or more sleek warships with striped red and white sails, fighting castles fore and aft, rows of ten oars to a side, and a huge steering oar at the stern. The prow of each ship curled back elegantly like a swan preening itself. Gleaming helmets of soldiers could be seen in the fighting castles and the sound of drums timing the oar strokes could be heard over the singing rigging.

An apprehensiveness immediately seized the crew, and many shook their heads worriedly or murmured anxiously about the size and hardiness of the fleet.

As their ships approached within a few leagues, their presence seemed suddenly to become noticed. Horns blew and the drums beat a new rhythm, and the ships began to turn. Initially, they turned towards the oncoming fleet, but a few moments later, they turned again and began rowing hard away from them.

Unfortunately for Troan, the wind was light, and their fleet could barely gain on the retreating enemy. One ship, however, had messed up its turning maneuver and had fallen significantly behind the others.

'That one!' Troan cried gleefully. 'It is ours!' He gave a long string of excited and impatient orders to the crew, each of which amounted to much the same thing – 'hurry up and catch the stragglers before they get away!'

For all its finesse and power, the last ship could not gain speed quickly enough, and Ani watched with growing excitement and trepidation as the two ships slowly drew alongside one another.

24.

The gunfire stopped as quickly as it had begun, and all was now quiet. Michael's ears were still ringing as he lay still beneath the solid stainless-steel bench, his body draped over Nathan's.

A moment later he felt himself tugged to his feet. A soldier in a heavy helmet was shining a torch into his face. A medic was already checking him over quickly. Next, he realized a woman had her arms around him in a hurried embrace. 'It's me, Arla!' she whispered hoarsely, her lungs full of the same dust as Michael's. 'I'm so glad to see you!'

He did not recognize her in battledress but smiled all the same. 'More than words can say,' he rasped back. 'Nathan,' he added hurriedly, 'he's hurt!'

'I know, we saw him. We're getting him out.'

'And the drug?' he croaked.

'Yes, we know about that too. Where is it?'

'In the freezer.' He realized he was still clutching the primed syringe in his dusty hand. He slipped it into his pocket.

The soldier quickly strapped a bulletproof vest onto Michael and pushed on a helmet, then left him with Arla while he turned his attention to Nathan.

Michael spun around and looked for Nathan. The soldier and medic were lifting Nathan's limp body from the floor and back into his wheelchair.

Gunfire recommenced further inside the building. 'Come on!' Arla urged, turning him back towards the opening and pushing him forward. 'We can't stay here. Bad people. Can you walk?'

'Yes, I'm fine. Nathan was only just recovering from the last one,' he said worriedly, looking back at the medic hastily bandaging Nathan's bleeding face.

'I can't believe he's even alive. We were sure he was dead.'

'So was I. I guess they make them tough Down Under, or else he's just too darn stubborn to die.'

'Either way, it's a good thing. I'm sure he'll be fine once we get him out of here.'

They reached the entrance and Michael was very relieved to see the sun and breathe fresh air again. Suddenly everything seemed like it was going to be alright. He had been rescued, he was in safe hands, and he was back among friends. How good it felt! But as soon as that thought crossed his mind, he realized it was not to be, for at that instant there was another explosion that knocked him off his feet.

*

As his mind cleared, he found himself on top of Arla. Blood was streaming down his face. His helmet was gone, and Arla was unconscious.

'Arla!' he cried, trying to bring her around. There was blood oozing from her nose. 'Oh Jesus, why does this keep happening?!' He rolled off her and took his bearings. There was heated gunfire all around and bullets were whizzing through the air and punching holes in the concrete walls around him, sending stinging dust into his face. He could not make out who was firing at whom. There was gunfire overhead on the overpass and coming from the park opposite. Instinctively he grabbed Arla and dragged her back through the opening and behind a pile of rubble. The soldier and medic suddenly appeared at his side, the soldier clutching a Styrofoam box to his chest. The medic immediately set to work on Arla.

'What's happening?' the soldier yelled in mixed confusion and concern.

'I have no idea. There was an explosion and then gunfire.'

The soldier unslung his rifle and crawled carefully to the shattered opening and peered outside, hailing his team on his radio as he did so. A puff of concrete near his head made it clear the entranceway was being closely guarded by someone outside.

He yelled into his radio in rapid Hebrew. An answer came that only made him look more worried. He replied and withdrew back from the entrance to Michael and Arla. 'We're not getting out that way.'

'Who is it? What's going on?' Michael asked, trying to think through the jackhammer headache that had started up in his head.

'Unfriendlies,' he replied flatly.

'Who?' Arla asked, conscious now and struggling to sit up.

'Maybe your old friends from the compound,' the soldier replied.

'Shit!' she cursed under her breath. 'Of course! They've been waiting for us. It's an ambush and they've planned it all along. Bloody Demir! Where are Ariel and

Yosef?' she asked worriedly.

He fired a question into the radio. 'They're pinned down in the park. Heavy encircling fire.'

'Goddammit!' she swore again and rubbed her face anxiously.

'Don't worry,' he added, 'the gunships will flush them out.'

Michael's brain now felt like it was being repeatedly prodded with a fork. The medic noticed him clutching his head and scurried over from where he was bandaging the wound on Nathan's face. He dug into his bag and produced some pills.

'Thanks,' Michael said after taking a quick look at the pills. 'I reckon I'm going to need my wits about me for the next while,' he said and swallowed them.

The medic nodded and offered a canteen to wash them down with.

A thundering noise filled the entrance and leaves and rubbish blew inside as an attack helicopter hovered low in front of their position, the guns spewing a confetti of brass casings over the road outside. A moment later it was gone.

'Change of plan,' the soldier relayed after another short radio conversation. 'New pickup point.'

Michael shot a worried glance towards Nathan, still unconscious in his wheelchair.

Arla nodded grimly. 'We will get him there, don't worry. We're going to make it!' she said resolutely and began to stand on shaky legs.

Gunfire was intensifying inside the building and growing louder. A moment later two soldiers dived back into the lab out of the darkness, panting and beating a hasty retreat. 'Go, go!' they shouted in Michael and Arla's direction and made a beeline for the exit themselves. Tracers flashed around the room as the Meshedi began firing into the lab.

Michael and Arla were on their feet and carrying Nathan through the gash in the wall in seconds, the wheelchair abandoned in the panic. A spray of bullets hit the walls around them and showered them in concrete fragments. Obviously, the attack helicopter had failed to dislodge Demir's men. The soldier beside them opened fire towards the park, then scurried out through the hole after them with the medic in tow. The remaining two soldiers dived through the exit after them, firing as they ran.

Michael was barely able to stay upright after the concussion he had received from the blast, and Arla looked no better off, but he knew they had little time to get away before the Meshedi reappeared behind them. The soldiers kept up a constant hail of fire towards the park as they backed into the dark tunnel beneath the overpass and headed towards the distant light at the other end. Before long Michael realized the shooting had stopped and they were out of sight of Demir's men.

Michael staggered on under Nathan's dead weight, the soldiers taking the lead towards their new pickup point. The tunnel entrance drew closer, but as they approached, Michael became aware of a sound that sent a chill down his spine. There in the entrance was a virtual sea of INS victims, all staggering into the entrance of the tunnel, drawn by the noise of explosions and gunfire. The conflict with Demir in the park had left their flanks unguarded and now his worst nightmare was coming true. They were trapped between the Meshedi, Demir's men and an impenetrable wall of gurgling, staggering figures intent on tearing them to pieces.

'Oh, lord!' Michael breathed as he came to a shaky halt, almost dropping Nathan as a wave of fear washed over him.

The soldiers raised their guns, about to fire.

'No!' Arla cried and pushed their barrels down. 'That will only bring more!'

'Then what?' the medic asked in terror.

'We have to run.'

'Where to? Demir will blow us to bits if we go back.'

'Radio the chopper,' she said. 'Maybe they can wipe them out before they get into the tunnel.'

Michael's body was shaking, he felt limp, and his throat seemed to tighten so much he could barely breathe. He lowered Nathan gently to the ground, then knelt beside him, preparing himself mentally for what was to come. His last reserves of strength deserted him.

Arla was animated. She wrenched the radio from the soldier and barked into it in Hebrew.

'What's happening? Are the choppers coming?' Michael asked quietly, his voice strangled and thin.

'I don't know,' she replied. 'They're low on fuel and the men are pinned down. We're going to have to fight our way through.'

'Arla,' Michael said slowly and with forced calm. 'I honestly don't think I can. My legs just won't allow it and Nathan is as heavy as a log.'

Arla heaved a sigh, then seized the radio again as the soldiers raised their guns again. The hoard was entering the tunnel. Their wailing, rasping, and barking echoed off the dark interior, multiplying Michael's fear tenfold.

'We have the cure but it's of no use to anyone if we're all torn to pieces. Get here now!' she screamed into the radio in English, her face bright red and her hands trembling.

Michael found himself on his knees, unable to stand or even move in the face of the horror advancing on him. How had it all come to this? Everything he had done to survive, to find a cure and to save his friends and loved ones had come to naught. It was all a huge tragic waste. He felt the vial in his wet pocket, cold and covered in condensation. The silver bullet, the cure humanity needed so badly, was potentially right there in his palm, yet he now saw no hope of delivering it. It would be lost in a pile of litter, leaves, and chewed bones in a dark and disused tunnel, a tragic end to a tragic tale.

Arla knelt beside him and he felt her hand on his shoulder. He looked up and saw sadness in her eyes. The hoards were close. Their horrifying noise was deafening. The soldiers opened fire, and a few dropped, but behind there came many, many more. Suddenly there came a crackle over the soldier's radio.

'They said to lie down!' Arla suddenly cried, translating the command.

Still paralyzed, Michael felt Arla push him forcefully to the ground. He sprawled, face down, in the musty leaves and litter, his cheek pressed hard against the cool tarmac. With one eye and one ear, he observed the dark machine descend over the mouth of the tunnel as if in slow motion, blocking out the light. It swiveled slowly, turning its fearsome guns directly towards them. Then, in a deafening, blinding halo of light, the sea of staggering figures fell to pieces before his eyes. The mass of bodies thinned and seemed sure to be entirely eradicated, but suddenly the helicopter was gone, and many open-mouthed grimacing figures remained.

Arla was on her feet at once. She pulled a pistol from a holster and began to fire into the oncoming crowd. The soldiers jumped up and did the same, changing magazines and continuing to fire.

'There are still too many!' Arla said as she expended the last of her ammunition.

A moment later the soldier's guns clicked and were empty also. A fast-approaching group of gurgling men and women continued towards them, running with talon-like hands outstretched and hideous guttural sounds issuing from the gaping mouths.

'Run!' Arla yelled. 'We can't fight them!'

'What about Nathan!' Michael cried. He stood, adrenaline now suddenly charging through his body. He reached down and took hold of Nathan's arm. He was not leaving him to that fate!

He soon found Arla had Nathan's other arm and a soldier his legs, and they ran as fast as they could back the way they had come. It soon became obvious they could not run fast enough while carrying Nathan, and the soldier dropped him and charged on ahead.

Michael looked imploringly at Arla. 'Please!' he pleaded.

She stopped and looked back at him. She let go of Nathan's arm, but to Michael's surprise, she did not run. Instead, she took his hand. 'We did our best, didn't we?' she said quietly, squeezing his hand.

'Yes, we did,' he replied and closed his eyes. He could smell the musty odor and the foul breath of the approaching creatures. He braced himself for the moment he had long feared.

But instead of pain, there was a sudden eruption of gunfire only meters from him. He fell back in shock and disbelief as the head of the INS victim only several feet from his face, vanished, showering him in gore. Then the next and the next in the huddle of figures descending on them fell as they were gunned down from behind. The last two figures turned and fell upon their savior.

Michael could not make out who it was, but the poor soul was overwhelmed almost at once. He went down screaming as the last two dropped and writhed on top of him, their teeth quickly going to work.

'No!' Arla screamed. She managed to heave one of them off and kicked it savagely in the head. For a moment the creature seemed stunned, and Arla wasted no time in yanking a knife from her boot and plunging into its blood-drenched face. It sagged with a weary groan and lay still.

Michael was having less success. The creature writhed feverishly and tore flesh away from its victim in ghastly strips. Then Arla was there, and the knife sunk deep into its skull. It stooped with a groan and lay still.

At once Michael yanked the lifeless body from the whimpering victim beneath.

Arla gasped in recognition. 'Yosef!'

25.

'Loose!' Troan shouted, and a smoky cloud of fire arrows sailed across the narrow gap and embedded themselves in the timbers of the opposing ship or cut ragged holes in its sails. Almost at once, a fire began to spread through the rigging as crew members rushed about trying to douse the spreading blaze.

The rest of the foreign fleet was now little more than a white foamy mark on the horizon, leaving their stricken comrade at the mercy of Troan's encircling ships. But mercy was clearly not what Troan had in mind. He appeared openly gleeful at what must now be a certain victory over the hapless crew.

As they closed the remaining distance and prepared to board, Ani saw those on board the stricken ship toss down their weapons and hold their hands in the air in surrender. Troan, however, seemed unmoved by the gesture and ordered his men to board and spare no one.

'You can't!' Purdu yelled in horror, running to the castle and scaling the short ladder. 'They are survivors like us! They will be useful to us. Spare their lives, please!'

Ani began to move after her.

'Foolish girl!' Troan shouted and flung Purdu to the ground. 'How dare you tell me what to do! I am your king! You swore an oath to me, now kneel and beg forgiveness!'

Ani threw himself up the ladder behind her. He saw Purdu reluctantly begin to kneel before Troan as he stood threateningly over her. Ani scowled, feeling hot anger surging up in him. He advanced on Troan, sword in hand. 'Stand up, Purdu!' he said when he got beside her. 'I won't let you kneel before this monster.'

'What did you say?' Troan said, straightening up in outraged disbelief.

'I said she is not to kneel before you. I know what you've been doing to her.

You're are a sick man, and I won't have you touch her ever again. Stand up Purdu!'

Troan took a threatening step towards Ani, lifting his whip as his face twisted horribly. 'You'll be flogged for that insolence, boy! It's all the harder to take from you since I've saved your life numerous times,' he spat. He flicked his whip and was about to strike when their ship suddenly collided with their opponent. They all lost their footing and staggered and fell. A cry went up from the boarding party as they jumped from ship to ship and instantly set to work on their unarmed foe. Those who had thrown down their arms now hastened to retrieve them, but it was too late. The screams of those cut down without mercy filled the air.

Ani helped Purdu to her feet and forced her behind him protectively as Troan also regained his footing. At once Ani felt the blinding pain of Troan's whip as it lashed his face. He staggered and fell, blood running into his eyes. Again, and again, the whip fell across his neck and back, driving him down with each blow like a nail being hammered into the deck. Purdu screamed as Ani struggled to get up, but again the whip forced him to his knees.

'Don't you dare hurt my brother!' Purdu cried as she leaped over him, her small dagger in her hand.

'Hah, haven't you had enough of a whipping girl?' Troan cried in sadistic delight. Ani heard the whip buzz through the air again, and this time Purdu cried out in pain.

Ani wiped the blood from his eyes and stood up. Purdu had fallen and Troan was whipping her savagely, a brutal expression on his face. Boiling with rage, Ani was determined to put an end to Troan right there and then. He found his sword on the deck and made a lunge for Troan. But Troan was ready for him, and another mean flick of his whip and Ani's sword arm was tangled and smarting with pain. He dropped his blade and jerked his throbbing arm away.

'You don't give up, boy, I'll give you that!' Troan snarled. 'Well you've grown too big for your boots and it's time to teach you both a lesson you won't forget.' He raised his whip again, this time directing it at Purdu. It was about to fall when Troan suddenly staggered strangely to one side and blood began to drip from his mouth. Troan stood still for a second, then groaned and began to stagger, blood now erupting from his mouth in huge torrents. As he dropped to his knees, Ani saw the perpetrator standing behind him - a dark-skinned muscular man holding a bloody sword. It was Jeemah, the slave who Ani had befriended, and who he had suspected of planning mutiny for some time. Now that had come to pass amid the sea battle. Although Ani was not surprised, he regretted that he had missed his chance to deal Troan what was coming to him for his mistreatment of Purdu. Purdu, on the other hand, did not miss her chance, and even as Troan drew his last breath, she sunk her knife deep into his chest and twisted it for good measure, then kicked his lifeless body to the ground.

Ani realized he was trembling. He looked around, frightened at what recrimination might come from the crew. But he realized now that they were all aboard the other ship. Instead, a group of slaves surrounded the castle, swords and shields in hand, guarding it against any who might challenge them. Only the Gal

Meshedi remained aboard, standing at the far end of the ship with arms folded and a look of quiet satisfaction on his face. Ani caught his eye as he watched them cautiously. He nodded and turned and joined the others aboard the other ship.

'Thank you Jeemah,' Ani said even as Purdu was throwing her arms around him.

'That is quite alright, Ani,' he replied, smiling grimly. 'We had had enough of him.'

'So had we. But what now? Is there going to be more fighting?'

'Not it if I can help it,' Jeemah replied. 'The other slaves will join us. They knew this was coming. We plan to take ships and go our own way. Will you come with us?' Jeemah asked kindly, obviously not intending to force a choice upon them.

'Yes of course,' Purdu answered at once.

'Good! We will be needing a new leader. One who is kind and clever, opposed to tyranny and slavery. I think you would make a very good leader, Purdu,' Jeemah said, looking down at her as she clasped him around the waist.

Ani could not tell if he was joking, but something made him tingle with glee.

Inevitably, the crew soon noticed the throng of slaves guarding the castle and raised the alarm. 'A slave rebellion!' someone called. 'Kill the slaves!' another yelled. All those who were not still engaged in combat turned and made to rejoin the ship. But it was too late. A group of slaves had wasted no time in using long poles to push the two ships apart so that the crew could no longer leap back aboard.

Ani spied Mezarus standing on the rail of the other ship, a look of alarm on his face. He made to dive into the water when several Meshedi leaped forward and held him back. 'Ani, Purdu!' he yelled in desperation, trying to free himself of their grip, but still they held him fast.

'Our friend, Mezarus!' Ani cried to Jeemah, pointing to their struggling friend.

'I'm sorry unless he can break free, we cannot help him.'

Mezarus made another attempt to throw off his captors, but the Meshedi held him fast. He called their names again in grief as the two ships drifted further apart.

Ani waved to Mezarus. Sadness filled his heart, but he could see that Mezarus was never going to be allowed to leave. There was nothing he could do to change that now. 'Goodbye Mezarus!' he called with tears in his eyes.

Purdu began to sob as the ships drifted further apart. She could not make words come and only waved goodbye until they could no longer see Mezarus in the smoky twilight.

Many slaves began arriving aboard on small boats from the other ships as the sails were hoisted. It was not long before they had made sail on the rising breeze, headed for the distant coastline.

26.

'Arla! Thank god you're alive!' Ariel cried as he ran into the underpass, a team of soldiers jogging alongside. 'Who's hurt?' he asked as he ran up and kneeled beside her. 'Oh god, it's Yosef! And who's this?'

'Nathan. They need a doctor right now!' Arla cried in desperation as she tried to stop Yosef's bleeding. 'Where are the choppers! Get us out of here now!'

Ariel barked an order into his radio. 'They're coming, they're coming. We'll be out of here in a second.'

'What about Demir?' she said bitterly.

'He won't be a problem.'

'Did you kill him?'

'No, but they've gone. They set a very good ambush. We've lost a lot of men.'

'The Meshedi?'

'Gone too. I told Yosef he was a bloody fool to come down here. He's no soldier.'

'Don't you dare start on him. He's a hero! He saved our lives!'

Ariel nodded and helped her with the bandages.

Michael could see that beneath his bluster, Ariel was very upset.

The thunder of helicopters soon shook the tunnel as the Blackhawks set down in front of the underpass. A team of medics rushed over. Nathan was stretchered away immediately, while the medics got straight to work on Yosef, staunching the bleeding and inserting a drip.

Michael sat on his haunches, still in shock and feeling helpless. 'His wounds,' he said at last, suddenly realizing Yosef's plight was far greater than mere loss of blood.

'I know,' Arla said looking up, ashen faced, from where she sat holding Yosef's hand.

'What about them?' Ariel asked.

'We're about to find out if my drug really works.'

Ariel frowned. 'Of course it does, right?'

'I don't know, we've never tested it.'

'Well it's been paid for with a lot of good lives today, so it damn well better work,' Ariel replied hotly.

Michael turned away from Ariel's glare. That a man's life now depended on his crude attempts to replicate a ludicrously complex drug under duress from scribbled notes and protocols downloaded from a defunct internet was beyond rhyme or reason. And if it failed, what then? His rescue would have been in vain and their last chance at a cure may have faded forever. 'The notes!' he suddenly gasped. 'If it doesn't work, we'll need them.'

'It had better bloody work fella or you're in very deep shit.'

'Ariel, shut up and leave him alone!' Arla snapped. 'None of this is his fault. You're as much to blame for all this as anyone. You came back here without telling anyone where you were going, then we had to come and bail you out. Besides, you may yet thank him.'

Ariel nodded to the group of soldiers awaiting orders and a group of them took off back into the labs to search for the notes.

With Yosef's condition stabilized for the time being, the medics carefully lifted the stretcher and hurried off back to the helicopter.

Michael pulled the syringe from his pocket and examined it again as he limped out of the tunnel and back into the afternoon sunlight. The rays passing through the pinkish liquid inside the syringe made the ferrous particles inside sparkle like the finest glitter. He would soon know how this was all going to end…

*

Nathan had become conscious again almost as soon as they were aboard the chopper. At first, he was in great pain from his concussion, but he was soon rendered speechless by a huge dose of morphine. His only comment to Michael before slipping into a morphine-induced stupor had been, 'Have I told you before this is all your fault?'

Yosef stirred and Michael feared what they must now tell him –that he most certainly had INS, that he must be given an experimental drug that had never before been tested, and should it not work, that his hours were numbered. It was not a conversation he looked forward to having with a man who had just saved his life and nearly lost his own in the process.

The helicopters had headed straight for the Israeli border, as fuel was low, and they feared another attack. Now, as they approached the border, Yosef awoke and took in his surroundings. His face was heavily bandaged so that only one eye was visible.

'Yosef,' Arla breathed in relief and smiled down at him. 'Thank you. You saved us! You're a hero!'

Yosef nodded slightly and moaned a response.

Arla shot an anxious look at Michael before turning back to Yosef. It was clear she did not want to say what she was about to say, but also that she did not want to waste any precious time. 'Yosef, I hate to tell you this, but you've been bitten. I'm so sorry, and it was all because of us,' she said, anguish carving deep lines of sorrow in her face. 'Do you know what this means?' she asked softly, involuntarily look away.

Yosef nodded slowly, resignation and sadness filling his eyes.

'There is still hope. We rescued Michael and he has the drug,' she continued. 'We can give it to you right now. We need to give it to you now.'

Michael nodded, leaning in so Yosef could see him. 'We've never met. I'm Michael. You have no idea how grateful I am to you. You saved our lives!'

Yosef nodded.

'I have tried to make this drug exactly as it was designed by the man who invented it. Are you happy for me to give it to you now? I have to inform you there is some risk it will not work.'

Yosef gave a heavily bandaged thumbs up.

'You're sure?' Arla croaked, tears filling her eyes.

Yosef nodded but looked worried.

Arla nodded at Michael.

He unscrewed the cap on the line into Yosef's arm and with one last look at the assembled group, and after a final nod from Yosef, injected the drug into the tube.

No one spoke for some time as Yosef lay back and closed his one unbandaged eye.

A blaring alarm suddenly sounded in the cabin of the helicopter.

'What the hell is that?' Arla cried.

Ariel jumped up and peered into the cockpit. 'Missile lock!' he yelled. 'We're under attack!'

Michael jerked his head to the window. He could see a smoky trail zigzagging up from the ground below and tearing across the sky towards them. The attack helicopters on either side broke formation and dived away to right and left. Flares suddenly erupted from the sides of the helicopter and streaked away below. To Michael's horror, a missile seemed to pass almost within arm's reach of his window as the chopper suddenly jerked to the left, throwing him off balance and straight on top of Arla. The alarm ceased momentarily, then began again.

'Oh no, another one!' she cried, as they strapped themselves back into their seats in anticipation of further acrobatics.

The helicopter swerved erratically and dived this way and that as Michael saw another rocket narrowly miss the side of the helicopter and sail off to the right, chasing more flares before finally exploding far below. A series of booms followed, and looking out the window once more, he saw huge clouds of fire, smoke, and dirt rising where the attack helicopters had turned and were unleashing hell on the missile batteries below. As he watched, more rockets zigzagged up towards them.

'We're out of flares!' Ariel bellowed, peering into the cockpit. 'It's going to get hectic, so hold on!'

The helicopter suddenly dived, then turned rapidly to the left and right, shuddering under the huge gravitational forces it was being subjected to. Michael gripped the edge of Nathan's stretcher so tightly his knuckles turned white. He saw another missile roar past, its fiery tail glowing brightly. It suddenly swerved to the right and a second later it struck one of the nearby attack helicopters side-on. The helicopter exploded in a gigantic fireball, and smoldering wreckage spun away from the blast in every direction. Large fragments crashed into their chopper with terrifying force and noise. Michael realized a fragment must have hit the rotors, for a loud alarm suddenly sounded in the cockpit and the chopper began to shudder and spin round and round with growing speed. He could see out the window that they were dropping rapidly and that the ground was fast approaching.

'We're going down!' Ariel cried.

Arla gripped his hand and Nathan looked up at him in wide-eyed terror. In what seemed like dreadful slow motion, the chopper spun round and round as the ground came rapidly up to meet them…

27.

'That sounds like a solid bottom,' Jeemah remarked cheerfully as the keel of the small boat grated against the sandy bottom. The ocean had turned steadily more turquoise as they approached the beach, which appeared oddly dark compared to the golden dunes behind. Sea birds lined the shore and hovered in swarms above the beach. A foul reek was also carried in on the breeze from the shore. 'And none too soon,' Jeemah croaked hoarsely, licking his dry lips.

Provisions had run short in the last week aboard the breakaway ships, and all had been forced to suffer nagging thirst as they eeked out the remaining water from skins stored below the baking hot deck.

Ani scanned the shoreline and ran his gaze over the tops of the dunes and ridgeline that stood back from the beach. Houses and walls caught the sun faintly in the distance but not a living soul could he see in any direction. A small stone platform stood atop a cliff further down the beach, a beacon perhaps, but this too was deserted. But his gaze was quickly drawn to the dark swathe that marked the meeting of water and sand.

'No welcoming party is a good thing in my view,' Jeemah stated as he picked up his oar and paddled hard over the crest of a wave to send them gliding swiftly in towards the beach.

Ani prepared to jump out into the shallows as they plowed into the foamy swell, eager to get ashore after months at sea. He put a hand and foot up on the side, then suddenly pulled himself back from the edge in shock. The shore was thick with dark tangled shapes that defied logic.

Jeemah was about to jump in too when he also fell back into the boat with a gasp.

'What is it?' someone said as the rest of the boat's occupants leaned over Ani to get a view of the tangled mass of dark shapes liming the shore.

'Bodies!' someone cried in horror. 'Thousands of bodies!'

Everyone retracted back from the edge of the boat, but it was too late, the waves sent the boat crunching onto the sand amid the rolling and tumbling mass of bodies.

Out of the foam appeared leathery limbs, black with decomposition, tossing this way and that like driftwood as the waves sucked them in and spat them back onto the dark-stained sand. The lips of the horrid faces staring up at them were thin and drawn back, revealing large and jagged teeth in lifeless grinning mouths, the withered hands and fingers curled and talon-like. The eyes in those tightly drawn faces remained open, and though glassy and dead, a feverish hunger still lingered in them. The beach was piled with bodies as far as Ani could see in either direction, all infested with swarms of tiny crabs feasting upon the decomposing filth. Beyond the churning surf, higher up on the beach, sea birds picked at the shreds of dried, salt-encrusted flesh.

The boat was taking on water as it rocked and swirled in the shallows, all aboard too fearful to jump into the putrid water that seethed and boiled around them.

'Let's go Ani!' Purdu cried as a wave spilled over the edge, washing foul-smelling body parts into the bottom of the boat, its occupants wailing in horror.

Sickened but desperate to escape, Ani flopped over the edge into the noisome sea of gore, then helped Purdu over the edge after him. They waded forcefully to the shore, then picked their way through the thick carpet of bodies to the dunes behind. The others were running up the beach behind them, some retching as they came. Their injured lungs gasping for fresh air as they flopped down among the shady shrubs and trees behind the dunes.

'I thought this was supposed to be a land of milk and honey,' Ani said, still gagging from the stench of death clinging to their legs and clothing.

Jeemah did not reply but nodded despondently.

'What happened here?' Purdu asked, her voice thick with revulsion.

'A massacre?' someone suggested.

'No, didn't you see them? They were not like us. They were demons,' Ani replied quietly, trying to force out words despite his churning stomach.

'Yes, you're right lad,' Jeemah agreed. 'It's like that time we raided the coast and the demons chased us to the sea but wouldn't come in after us. It's like they had no place else to go. They just stopped there and stared at us.'

'So, do you think they just died there? Why would they do that?' Ani asked, confused.

'I don't know lad, I don't know.'

Slowly they recovered their spirits and crept out from the trees toward the small hamlet they had seen from further out to sea, higher up on the ridge behind the dunes. They followed a deep gully as they climbed the slope, fearful that other demons might be nearby. Reaching the edge of the settlement, Ani and the rest of the group remained hidden while Jeemah climbed out of the gully and crawled away to investigate the nearby houses. Looking back down from where they had climbed, Ani could see their tiny fleet of ships stretched out across the blue, rippled expanse of ocean below. If anyone were here, they would have had no difficulty spotting their arrival on such a clear morning.

Before long, Jeemah reappeared at the edge of the gully. 'All clear. No one here.'

They climbed out of the gully and made their way to the closest house. Beyond that lay several other houses built close together, all facing the sea. They were all small thatched cottages with whitewashed walls and tiny square windows tightly shuttered against the sea air.

Ani and Purdu waited outside as the others entered to check it was safe. Seconds later Jeemah strode cheerfully out through the door, his chin dripping wet, and handed Ani and Purdu a jug of water, much to their relief.

Ani entered the vacant house once the others had left. It had a single room, with several beds set into alcoves in the far wall, but all the bedding was gone. The house was bare of common effects and it was clear its former occupants had fled, taking all they had with them.

As Ani stepped back out onto the threshold and gazed out over the broad expanse of water, he immediately drew in a sharp breath.

'What is it?' Purdu asked from within.

'The ships, they're leaving!'

'What?' Purdu cried, immediately reappearing beside him. 'Oh gods, you're right!'

Their fleet of six ships had hauled anchor and was sailing away back the way they had come.

'Why are they abandoning us?' Purdu wailed.

Ani scanned the horizon and soon found what he thought must be the case. A large fleet of ships was beating up out of the south, their large, brightly striped sails billowing before the mast.

'Who are they? Is it the Gal Meshedi returned?' Purdu said, concerned.

'No, it's not them. They are the same sails we saw when we parted from the others. Those ships fled south remember, but now it looks like they're back, and in greater numbers. Oh, I hope they hurry up. They'll be caught before long at this rate.'

Ani called to Jeemah who soon reappeared with a sack over his shoulder. He followed their gaze out to sea and dropped his sack in disbelief. 'Traitors!'

'No, look!' Ani said and pointed to the fleet fast approaching from the south, already close enough to make out the scores of soldiers aboard.

'They are doomed, poor buggers,' Jeemah lamented.

'They still have a chance,' Purdu replied hopefully. 'May the gods give them speed.'

Before long the ships grew distant and vanished over the horizon, the outcome not yet determined.

'Well that leaves us in a pretty spot,' Jeemah said, throwing himself on the ground and placing his head in his hands.

'Is there food here?' Ani asked, eyeing the sack.

'Help yourself, though I have to say the rumors are much exaggerated.'

Ani reached into the sack and produced an onion and some very moldy bread. He didn't care. He was famished. He took a huge bite out of the onion then handed it to Purdu who quickly did the same. The flavor was overpowering, and his eyes began watering at once, but the juiciness of the onion was like a dream come true.

Morning turned to afternoon and then evening as they made their way from house to house, hamlet to hamlet, along that line of hills and cliffs overlooking the beach. The situation was the same at each one they came to – a hasty abandonment leaving little behind.

'Where to now?' some asked over a dinner of hearty soup made from the scanty grains, lentils and stale bread scavenged from the houses along with herbs growing wild on the hillsides. 'Do we wait for them to return or move on?' asked another.

Jeemah shrugged, unable to decide.

'I think there is little point in staying,' Purdu ventured, her forthrightness provoking surprised looks from around the table.

'Why is that miss?' the same man asked.

'Because I don't think they'll return here any time soon. That is the second time we have seen the ships with the striped sails in only a week, and I think they must be patrolling this coastline. And that's assuming they got away at all.'

'What if they do come back though?' Jeemah cut in. 'And how will we survive ashore for long? Demons will soon find us, and we can't hold them off here.'

'I know. I think we should leave.'

'How will leaving help that? It seems safe enough here. If we go somewhere else, it might be much worse.'

'Yes, but do you not see what those ships are telling us?'

There was a confused murmur around the table.

'It means there is a large kingdom in the south, big enough to have a fleet, and unharmed enough not to have suffered the fate of our own lands.'

As soon as this fact dawned on those around the table a rowdy discussion ensued until Jeemah banged the table and demanded silence. 'What the girl says is true.' He turned to Purdu. 'Are you saying Purdu that we should head south, to find safety and protection in this great kingdom, whatever it may be?'

'Precisely. I am not learned like our father Amuurana was, but I think I know what land it must be.'

'Yes?' they cried impatiently.

'It must be the land of a great army and of a great king. That land must be Egypt!'

28.

'This is crap!' Michael heard Nathan mutter in the darkness and choking smoke of the shattered cabin. Nathan's words somehow pierced the thick wall of agony that cloaked his throbbing head. 'When is this going to get any better, Michael?' Nathan continued. 'This is all your bloody fault, you know.'

'What, you mean that Gökmen betrayed us, that Corinne died, that you got shot, that the Meshedi captured us, that we ran out of flares and were shot down, and that we are now trapped in a smoldering wreck with an INS victim trapped between my legs? How is that all my fault? How is any of this my goddamn fault? Is that really the most useful thing you could think of to say right now! To blame me for EVERYTHING!' His frustration, pain, and fear boiled over into a sudden uncontrollable rage, then quickly broke into a fit of coughing as the noxious smoke filled his lungs. 'Every time something goes wrong you say it's my fault. How is that fair exactly?' he continued, coughing between each word.

'OK, calm down for Christ's sake, and stop being such a sissy. It's too cramped in here to be yelling like that. It's giving me a bloody headache. OK, so maybe it's not all your fault, just the bits after you came to my house and my life turned to crap.'

'Well, I'm so sorry, Nathan. Would you rather be a zombie pacing the streets of DC and eating your own leg off? Is that what you'd rather be doing? Because if it hadn't been for me, the total prick that I apparently was in coming to your house and dragging you away, that's probably what you'd be doing right now, OK, stuffing your mouth with butt cheeks and human entrails.' Michael stopped yelling. He realized he was raving. He was incredibly hot and thirsty and was struggling to breathe. No one else seemed to be moving or making any noise.

'Arla? Ariel?' he wheezed into the darkness, wondering where they were. There was no response. 'Can you see anyone, Nathan?'

'Yep, Ariel. He's bleeding on me, but he's still breathing. Smells like he ate a turd for breakfast though.'

'Well he was locked in a cell for a week without his toothbrush. Where's Arla?' he said, trying to free his right leg from the mangled steel frame that was once the folding bench seat. He wriggled himself upright and wiped what he thought was sweat from his face, but soon realized it was blood.

'Arla?' he repeated. He now realized that not only was he trapped in the mangled seating, but a huge amount of earth had entered the cabin, blocking out the light and burying Arla beneath it. 'Nathan, she's buried!' he said quickly. 'We need to dig her out. Can you move?'

Michael could hear Nathan groaning and swearing for a few moments as he struggled to free himself. 'Nope! Um, you said we're trapped in here with an infected patient. Did you mean Yosef? Didn't you give him the new batch already?'

'Yes, I did, thank God, but we don't know if it works, remember.'

'Well, we soon will.'

Michael clawed at the earth heaped against his side. His knuckles banged against Arla's helmet, protruding from the dry earth. 'I've found her!' he cried and dug feverishly with his left hand, the exertion making him gag on the foul charring plastic smoke smell in the cabin. He cleared away the dirt from around her face, feeling for her mouth and nose to make sure they were clear. A second later she gasped like one risen from the dead, then began coughing violently.

'Arla, can you hear me?' Michael said as he continued to excavate the dirt carefully from around her.

'Yes,' she rasped, coughing hard. 'I think I'm OK,' she added between coughing fits. 'I've just got a lung full of dirt. How is everyone else?' she spluttered.

'I'm fine,' Nathan answered.

'Yes, he's fine again, unfortunately. Ariel is breathing but unconscious and we don't know about Yosef, the medics and the pilots.'

'We hit the ground nose first,' Nathan said soberly. 'I doubt the pilots are…,' his words trailed off.

Michael hadn't been sure what had happened exactly, only that plummeting to earth in a spinning, flaming, alarm screaming helicopter had been the most terrifying thing he had ever experienced. It felt to him like he had passed out before they even hit the ground. 'Yosef is under my right leg, I don't know where the medics are, but I can't help anyone while I'm trapped. I think Yosef's unconscious. Can you get to him, Arla?'

With much writhing, coughing, and spluttering, Arla pushed off the remaining earth covering her legs and crawled over the top of Michael. She switched on the torch attached to her combat vest and light flooded the cabin, blinding all within. She crawled into the wreckage between Michael's legs. Eventually, she found Yosef trapped beneath his own sickeningly bent and distorted stretcher. She began work trying to free him from the twisted metal and eventually managed to get close enough to try and check his breathing. 'Yosef,' she called quietly. 'Yosef, it's me, Arla.'

Yosef did not respond.

'I can't hear any breathing!' she said worriedly. She passed her hands through the bars of the stretcher and managed to clasp onto one of Yosef's hands. 'I'm not feeling a pulse either,' she said, sounding panicked now. 'How long have we been down?'

'I don't know. Believe it or not, I forgot to check the time as we plummeted to our deaths,' Michael snapped, his discomfort and distress getting the better of him again.

'Don't be a sod, Michael,' Nathan chimed in. 'Probably only ten minutes or so. I wasn't knocked out like you pussies.'

'Well, he's not good. I need to see if he's breathing. Ariel!' she shouted almost reproachfully at her unconscious brother. 'Ariel, wake up!'

Ariel stirred and lifted his head and groaned.

'Ariel, Yosef's hurt. We're all OK, but Yosef is under us all and he's been crushed. I'm not getting a pulse.'

Ariel looked around blankly, his face a study in confusion. 'What happened?'

'We were shot down, remember? Now can you move? I need help freeing Yosef so we can see how bad he is.'

Ariel struggled to make his body move, then slowly sat up and began to crawl over to Arla. 'Yosef, can you hear me?'

Ariel had just reached Yosef when loud explosions rocked the cabin once more.

'What the hell was that?' Nathan cried. 'Can't they leave us to die in peace?'

No one replied and Ariel continued to maneuver himself down beside Yosef, then began disentangling and removing the bent chairs and stretcher bed.

'Is he breathing?' Arla asked worriedly.

'I… don't… know,' Ariel grunted as he pried an oxygen tank out from beneath Michael's left leg.

Soon Ariel had removed enough of the wreckage that he could get down low enough to check Yosef's breathing. 'There's nothing,' he said a moment later. 'Yosef!' he shouted and shook Yosef's still body.

There came a loud banging on the outside of the fuselage and muffled voices calling out. Everyone froze. Ariel plucked a pistol from his holster and pointed it warily at the fuselage sliding door, now directly above them. Footsteps thundered across the roof above, then suddenly the door flung open and light and fresh air poured in. An Israeli soldier stood straddling the opening above them, staring down at their alarmed faces. 'Come, we go!' he said with some urgency. 'Enemy close.'

Behind the soldier, Michael could see another Blackhawk hovering not far away, and the attack helicopters racing about higher up.

Ariel burst into Hebrew and issued some hurried commands. The solider quickly grunted into his radio then dropped down into the pile of earth and tangled wires beside Ariel. Together they quickly freed Michael's legs, then helped him and Arla out through the opening and into the fierce heat and sunlight. Next Nathan was lifted out, then Ariel and the soldier got to work feverishly trying to rescue Yosef.

Michael looked on helplessly, his fears for Yosef deepening with each passing minute.

Arla could not restrain herself and jumped back into the wreck. 'Come on,' she cried, as she stooped over Yosef. 'Don't you do this to me!'

Michael had plucked his batch of vials from the wreckage, dirt-stained but still safe in their foam container under his arm. He hoped desperately that Yosef would pull through, not only because he was a good man and had saved his life, but also because he had to know if the drug might actually work at last. If Yosef died now he would have lost a vital chance to test the drug.

Another Blackhawk landed in the dusty wheat field in which their smoking chopper lay. A woman jumped out and came running over with a large medical bag. She stepped over Michael and lowered herself nimbly down into the ruined shell and got straight to work on Yosef.

A few minutes later Ariel stood up and climbed out, his face ashen. He heaved a sigh as he flopped onto the ground beside the fuselage.

'You better not leave us!' Arla was still shouting angrily at Yosef inside, her voice stricken.

Michael caught Ariel's eye briefly and he gave a small shake of his head. Michael hung his head, forlorn that yet another good man had met a brutal and untimely death, and that yet again he had no proof whether his serum worked.

Arla crawled slowly up out of the fuselage, her eyes red and her dusty, blood-stained face streaked with tears. She fell to the ground and hung her head. 'When will this end?' she said quietly.

Ariel only shook his head.

*

'Poor chap. No result then?' Nathan commented quietly to Michael as he was stretchered over to the waiting Blackhawk.

'Hmm?' Michael replied, deep in reverie. 'No, quite right. No result.' He pulled himself into the chopper and stowed the vials under his seat and strapped in. 'Let's hope we actually make it out of here this time,' he mumbled as the rotors began to spin up.

Ariel was leaning into the cockpit talking rapidly to the pilots. He scratched his head and looked around at them in the back, his face puzzled.

'There's someone waiting for you in Jerusalem, Arla. Someone I was not expecting to ever hear from again.'

29.

Ani lay awake, listening, his ears working like an athlete in the darkness until they roared with the silence. There was a claustrophobia to sleeping in a house again, and a sense of dread; the fear of being trapped inside with nowhere to run to. That fear had vanished while sleeping on deck beneath the stars, far out to sea and far from the horrors of the land. Memories of the last time he had slept indoors oozed into his mind like a thin mist under a locked door. Amuurana, Sidani, and Lelwan had been with him then, the demons scratching and banging on the walls and door, but he had felt safe with them. He felt no harm could really befall them. But it had, and his heart ached for them.

A cool hand touched his. 'Are you awake?' Purdu's voice came whispering out of the void.

'Yes.'

She did not speak for a long while, but he could sense her fear. He squeezed her hand. 'Don't worry, we're safe here. Go back to sleep. I'll keep watch.'

Before too long her soft slow breathing resumed, like a faint summer breeze, and he knew she was asleep. But he could not sleep. It was stifling in the sealed-up room full of sleeping bodies and he needed to relieve himself. He rose, feeling for the cool stone wall, and made his way slowly and carefully through the bodies and outstretched limbs, occasionally kicking an arm here or treading on a finger there, to be greeted by off-tempo snores, sudden rustlings or an indignant grunt.

He lifted the latch and yanked the door open a crack. The cool night air descended on his face and ruffled his shoulder-length hair. There was no moon and it was almost as dark without as within. He stepped out into the night air, the door squeaking a little as he shut it behind him, the sound masked only by the rhythmic sighing of the dark and distant waves on the shore. He searched the faintest of lines that he knew must be the horizon far out to sea for any sign of a ship. Nothing.

Finding his way through the dark a few paces from the house he found a place to relieve himself. He had turned to go back inside when a faint noise caught his attention, carried on the gentle breeze. It was the sound of footsteps. Footsteps on rocky ground. Instinctively he crouched low on the ground, listening with all his might. Then he heard it again, far off, and to his astonishment, it was accompanied by a faint glow atop the cliffs above. Then a voice came carried on the breeze, clear and young. A youth's voice, but he could not understand the words.

Keeping low, he made his way further from the house until he came again to the deep gully. He slipped over the edge and found his way to the rocky bottom. There he clambered up the other side, just far enough to be able to peek over the top without being seen.

'Where are you going? Don't leave me!' came a quiet whimper from behind him.

He spun around. The silhouette of a small body was perched on the other side of the gully. It was Purdu.

'Shhh!' he hissed and beckoned her down. 'There are voices.'

She slithered into the gully after him and clambered over to his side.

'Listen!'

They both clung to the lip of the gully, straining their ears for the faintest sound. The glow on the clifftop grew and receded as someone made their way along the edge, talking as they came.

'Who are they?' Purdu asked in concern.

'Listen, they do not use our tongue.'

Now they could both clearly hear a youth and an older man talking as the torches bobbed along the cliff edge, their speech audible but unintelligible. Soon their silhouettes emerged at the edge, and then remarkably, they appeared to begin a descent vertically down the cliff face.

'How are they doing that? Are they some kind of spirits?' Purdu whispered in fear.

'I don't think so. Maybe they have ropes? Come on.' Ani took Purdu's hand and they crept quietly up the gully, closer to the cliffs where the glowing figures now seemed to be nearing the bottom. Sure enough, in the torchlight carried by each person, Ani made out two figures sliding down thin ropes to the base of the cliff. One light remained at the top.

The two figures let go of their ropes and drew short gleaming blades from under their cloaks and made their way toward the houses. Soon they must cross the gully in which Ani and Purdu lay without cover or hiding place.

'They're going to see us!' Purdu hissed in alarm, looking around in desperation.

Ani did not care. His joy and curiosity at the thought of another living being still inhabiting this land was more than he could contain.

'Hello!' he said at once loudly, standing so as to be seen before they were stumbled upon.

The stranger's shock and surprise at having been suddenly ambushed by someone appearing out of the gully were both audible and significant. One of the torches was dropped into the gully and immediately extinguished. The other torch was waved furiously about with shouts of alarm and the thrusting of swords.

'Do not fear us!' Ani cried, showing his empty hands and standing still. 'Stand up, show yourself,' he hissed down at Purdu.

'What on earth are you doing Ani?' she hissed back in horror. 'You're going to get us killed!'

A long string of unintelligible expletives erupted from the man who was now sheltering the boy behind him. He waved the torch at them to keep back. Ani knew he must fear they were demons.

'Ani,' he said slapping his chest. 'Purdu,' he added as he banged her on the shoulder.

'Ow!' she winced and glared reproachfully at him in the torchlight.

'Help us, we are lost,' Ani said quietly.

The man slowly lowered his blade as it dawned on him these were no demons, but two children, seemingly alone. His look of alarm changed suddenly to one of bewilderment and even concern. 'You speak the north tongue,' he said slowly in accented Neshili. 'Where are you from? How did you get here?' he asked suspiciously.

The boy, a lad of around ten, now emerged from behind the man and stared in open amazement.

'By boat. We're stranded. We are from…' Ani paused.

'We're Hatti,' Purdu finished for him. 'We are friends.'

The man looked them up and down and circled them warily, shining the torch over them as if searching for something. 'And where are you going to little Hatti?' he said at last, saying the final word with obvious distaste.

'We are friends,' Ani repeated Purdu's words, sensing his displeasure. 'We're lost.'

At that moment a third torch approached and a middle-aged woman, wiry and gaunt, suddenly appeared beside the boy. Like the man had done, she forced the boy behind her. Then she broke into a rapid diatribe directed at the man. She reached for his blade, but he held it high, away from her. Finally, unable to take the short sword, she turned and stormed off a few paces.

'Does she wish to kill us?' Ani asked, shaken by her obvious hatred of them.

'These are hard times and there is little to eat and more hungry mouths mean less for her son. Don't worry.'

'Thank you,' Ani said nervously, eyeing the woman warily lest she return and try again. 'Where are you from and where do you go?'

'Here. This land by the sea was once our home,' he said waving a hand toward the moonlit coast. 'We came back for food, tools and to see if it is safe to return, but there is little left to be found here.'

'Where is everyone?'

'Dead,' he replied as if it were obvious, 'or gone. We do not stay long. The withered ones are coming.' He made a move towards the house. Ani feared what might happen if they discovered a room full of sleeping bodies. He threw his hand out in panic and grabbed the man by the arm. The man jerked away from him, spun around and raised his sword to strike, when Ani suddenly blurted out, 'Don't go in there. Demons!'

The man stopped, lowered his sword and eyed Ani warily. 'What did you say?'

'The house, the houses, they're full of demons – withered ones. That's why we were running away.' He put on his most earnest and terrified face.

'Let's see,' the man said, shook off Ani's hand and paced off towards the house. Ani and Purdu ran quickly along behind, their fears mounting that all would soon be lost, and their companions discovered.

The man stopped in front of the house. He felt the latch. He listened at the door. At that moment a sudden, explosive guttural snoring erupted from the house.

'See!' Ani cried. 'Demons! Let us get away from here.'

The man hesitated, looking suspicious. He put his ear to the door again.

A choking, rasping snore erupted once more from within, even louder this time. The man needed no further evidence. He turned and was running as fast as he could back the way he had come, with Ani and Purdu hot on his heels. He stopped only once they had reached the woman and the boy and rapidly explained the situation in their guttural tongue. The three of them beat a hasty retreat back to the ropes.

'Please,' Ani gasped, catching them as they prepared to climb. 'Where are you going? How did you survive? We have no one and don't know where to go.'

The man stopped, silencing the woman with a stern look as she began another tirade. 'We are nomads now. We go back to our new home. There are many there from all lands. We are under the protection of god.'

'Where is it? What's there? Is it safe?' Ani cared little for any mention of gods.

'Come. You will see.'

30.

Arla drummed on her leg impatiently as the armored truck tore by the stark white stone buildings of Jerusalem's inner suburbs. She was torn between grief and mounting excitement. She had tried to find out who was waiting for her, but Ariel had clammed up and was now riding in one of the other armored cars in the convoy. Her brother did that when he was upset, and Yosef's death was clearly weighing heavily on him.

The streets were strangely empty and there were no people and no traffic on the roads that evening as they sped through the city. Army helicopters hovered over the city, circling slowly, while a little swarm had gathered over the Old City.

'It's not the Shabbat is it?' Arla said vaguely, suddenly aware she had no idea what day of the week it was.

'No miss,' one of Ariel's colleagues said gravely. 'The sickness has spread.'

'Wait, it's here too now?' Nathan burst out in poorly concealed panic.

'It is everywhere. Soon it may be like Turkey.'

Arla now noticed a line of tanks parked along the entrance to the Old City as they passed. A group of young male and female soldiers stood nervously in a huddle beside the tanks. A waste disposal truck stood oddly to one side; its putrid mouth open at the back. She gasped as she noticed a bloody arm hanging out of the back.

'What's happening there?' she asked.

'There's been a big outbreak in the Old City. It is closed off now. Any sick that wander out must be taken away.'

'Jesus!' Nathan exclaimed under his breath.

Arla raised an eyebrow.

'Sorry, but he lived here too didn't he?'

She nodded effusively and resumed her weary gaze out the window as another line of armored cars screamed past in the opposite direction and rumbled off down the hill toward the Islamic half of the city.

'The Palestinians probably brought it here,' the spook grumbled.

'Don't be ridiculous,' Arla snapped.

'What, you think they wouldn't do that? They would.'

'It's spreading everywhere. Any person could have brought it. They'll be blaming us for it too. I don't see how a comment like that is in any way helpful. They'll be suffering just as much as us, maybe more.'

The spook snorted and fell silent.

At that moment the armored car swerved crazily then leaped into the air a few inches, sending everyone hurtling. Arla saw bodies, gaunt, unkempt and red-eyed hit the side of the vehicle and disappear. The heavy machine gun above their heads swung around and barked momentarily then fell silent.

'Man! What was that?' Arla shrieked.

'A pack of frigging zombies,' a soldier in the front seat called back. 'They're everywhere now.'

'And there I was thinking we'd finally come to a safe place,' Michael murmured despairingly.

The vehicle made a sharp right turn through a heavy steel gate and into a walled compound full of soldiers and military vehicles.

'What is this place?' Arla said, looking around at the unfamiliar compound. She knew they were in the hills just outside the city, but she had never been inside this compound with Ariel before.

'Our headquarters are no longer safe,' the spook said. 'All essential personnel are being brought here now.'

'Quarantine, more likely,' Nathan said as they all climbed out into the cool evening air.

'Did you see that?' Ariel said gravely as he fell in beside her as they made for a low concrete building that made no pretense at being anything other than a bunker.

Arla nodded and put her arm around her brother. 'Let's hope Michael's drug works a whole lot better than it did for poor Yosef.'

Ariel looked away at the mention of him. 'I'm going to have to tell his parents.'

'My poor brother. At least it will be no lie to tell them he died a hero.'

'He did it for you, not for Israel.'

She stared at her brother.

'You knew right?'

She nodded sadly. 'I don't know why. I'd never met him before.'

'Well, he noticed you a long time ago.'

They filed past a sandbagged entryway into a dour and noisy concrete corridor busy with military personnel and others coming and going. The noise increased as they turned a corner into a hectic operations room full of screens, desks, and people on phones or in rapid conversation over maps and documents.

'Arla?' a voice came from behind.

She stopped in her tracks. The sound of that voice made her legs wobbly and her pulse quicken. 'James?'

Her body found his amid the chaos and she slid into his arms, not daring to open her eyes as her head pressed tightly into his shoulder. 'But…,'

'I know,' he replied. 'I should be dead, or worse.'

'But how?'

'They came for me. Actually, they came for Michael, but they found me instead.'

'Who?'

'The CIA.'

'I heard they evacuated people, and I hoped…'

She opened her eyes and found him staring down at her, his eyes filled with joyful tears. A dark void suddenly fled her broken and empty heart. 'But how?' she mumbled through tears as the guilt of having left him so close to death got the better of her. She shot a dark look at Ariel. She would never forgive him for forcing her to leave when they did.

'We have Michael to thank for that.'

She looked around. Michael stood open-mouthed a few feet away, still clutching his foam box of vials.

'It actually works?' Michael croaked in disbelief.

'Living proof of it,' James smiled.

Arla tightened her hug. 'I can't believe it. I looked so hard for you.'

'I know,' James said tenderly as he ran his hand through her hair. 'You never cease to amaze me, Arla,' and with that, he kissed her.

'Wait, are you saying the drug is here? That there is a cure?' Michael pushed on eagerly.

'Just give us a few more minutes hey mate?' James said distractedly, taking Arla's hand and leading her out of the room.

31.

'Where are you taking us?' Purdu rasped, her lips cracked with thirst and her nose reddened by the fierce sun after a long day traipsing over dry hills.

Ani and Purdu had tagged along behind the family as they walked on without rest through the night and into the following day, stumbling over rocks and through prickly shrubs.

'We should never have left Jeemah,' Ani murmured sadly as he stubbed his aching toes on yet another sharp rock. They had no shoes after so long at sea, and their feet were ablaze with cuts, bruises, and burns from the searing hot ground.

The man, known to them now as Achan, did not answer this or any other question they had asked of late, only gesticulating for them to remain completely silent. Once he had clouted Ani severely over the head with his heavy coil of rope for talking loudly. Ani knew it was dangerous to make any noise that might attract the demons, but he was so tired and feeling so sorry for himself by that point that he had ceased to care. The blows had brought him quickly to his senses and now he only ever whispered to Purdu as they marched on.

After a long climb, they reached the top of a high hill, white like bones where the ridges of limestone poked through the shallow soil. The family stopped and squatted on the ground; their gaze turned to the north. Ani and Purdu threw themselves to the ground, brushing the ever-present flies from their eyes and mouth. At last, Ani lifted his weary gaze from the ground and fixed on what the family seemed to be staring at. A few leagues away nestled within wooded hills stood a city with huge walls, white and glimmering in the sun. Ani sucked in his breath, completely taken aback by the dazzling sight. A curious stillness hung over the city. 'What is that place?' he whispered.

'Uru-shalim.'

'It looks like an important city.'

'Yes, it was. It holds the Great Temple of Shalim.'

'Who is that? A mighty god I suppose. I have not heard of him,' Ani said puzzled.

'He is god of the setting sun, though I now know him to be a false god.'

'I think our gods abandoned us, too,' Purdu muttered despondently.

Achan gave her a tender look and put his hand gently on her shoulder. 'There is only one god, child, and he has chosen us above all others. He has not abandoned us. You will see. But we must hurry away from this place now. It is no place for us,' Achan answered, scratching in the dust with the tip of his finger as if remembering its layout.

'Why? It has walls. Is it not safe?' Ani asked, wishing it to be true.

Achan pointed to an area beyond the farthest edge of the wall where a thick knot of green trees stood out amid the dry countryside. Beside it, Ani made out a gateway with a low tower on either side, but his blood chilled as he beheld the distant shapes of hundreds of bent and shuffling figures, wandering aimlessly to and fro in front of the gates. Though far away, their posture and motion were unmistakable.

'When did this happen?' Ani asked, saddened at the sight before him.

'Some time ago. They came from the east. They headed west toward the setting sun. One might have thought Shalim himself had summoned them.'

'Demons?'

'Yes, the withered ones. The dead.' He turned to Ani for a moment, his dark eyes red-rimmed and filled with sadness. 'Now all of Canaan is in ruin. Only the possessed go to the temple and market. The rest of us wander the desert and await our Lord's bidding.'

'The desert? Is that where you're taking us?' Purdu asked in shock.

He nodded.

Ani felt his heart sink. To think they had abandoned Jeemah and the others without even so much as a goodbye only to find themselves on a journey into what must be a hellishly dry and dismal place. He stood up and gazed around the surrounding landscape, searching desperately for some alternative to the hot and desolate existence that otherwise awaited him.

'Here they come!' the man suddenly announced, standing and grabbing the boy by the shoulder and leading him quickly down the slope away from their vantage point.

Ani searched the vista for what Achan had seen, and there below, a long trail of dark shapes was hurrying over the dusty ground towards them in an off-balance and lurching run. 'But how did they see us?' Ani gasped.

'They didn't. They can smell us!' Archan held out his hand to the breeze as if reprimanding Ani for not noticing that the wind was blowing stiffly from behind them towards the city. 'We have to hurry now!'

The five of them scrambled down the rocky slope to escape the swarm clambering up the steep hills towards them, snarling and barking as they came.

'I won't live in a desert!' Purdu huffed as they scrambled down the slope, voicing Ani's feelings as well.

The man stopped and turned to face her. 'Do not worry, Rephidim is a safe place. The dead do not walk there. We are protected.'

'By what, a wall or an army? We have seen the demons tear down walls and destroy armies. You saw that city just now. Nowhere is safe!' Purdu cried accusingly.

'By *He* who is greatest.'

'No man can do that,' she replied cynically.

Achan chuckled quietly for the first time since they had met him. '*He* is no man. You will see him, perhaps, in time.'

Achan would answer no further questions on the subject as they scrambled through the rough country surrounding Uru-Shalim, over hills and through valleys, through abandoned farmlands, the sounds of barking and snarling echoing constantly through the hills behind them as they hurried on. Late in the afternoon as they crested another scrubby hill, a heavily wooded valley, shady and cooler looking, opened out beneath them. A large river flowed lazily between wide banks and beds of reeds. Beyond they could see bone dry hills rising above the banks and disappearing into a thick light brown haze that erased the horizon.

'Once we cross this river we will soon be safe, but we must hurry on,' Achan called over the rushing water as they waded across the river at a wide and shallow point. 'The evil ones will not follow us there, and to the north, there is a Great Lake that stops them crossing.'

Looking back, Ani saw a swarm of disheveled creatures, with their hideous wounds and claw-like hands, descending the wooded slopes towards the river.

'But we have seen them cross rivers. It will not stop them,' Ani replied in terror, his legs beginning to tremble as he beheld the ravening pack approaching the water's edge.

'It is the desert they will not enter. *He* will protect us there.'

32.

'Even though I knew you had to go, all I longed for was for you to come back,' James said as he held Arla tightly against him. 'I gave up caring about anything else - the Meshedi, INS, everything. I just wanted my last time to be with you; to lie with you as we did in the storm at Keskin Dağ and die in your arms if that was to be my fate.'

'I went back for you James, I really did. It's all I could think about too. As much as my brother can be a jerk, he went back to look for you too, almost immediately after we returned. You know how things had become. He couldn't get to you, and then he fell in with the wrong people. I would have given anything to have stayed with you and lie with you too. I'm so sorry!'

Arla buried her head on his shoulder, and he felt her hot tears on his neck.

'It's a miracle, James,' she said, looking up, her eyes wet and red-rimmed. 'I thought I'd never see you again. Are you really better?'

He nodded.

'But how?' she asked, shaking her head disbelievingly.

'I will tell you all about it soon. But first, you have to know something.'

'What?' she said, steeling herself for the blow.

'I was talking to Mossad agents and ministers before you arrived. I was pretty popular when I brought them the thing they wanted most of all and that the Americans were failing to deliver.'

'You mean the drug? You have it?' Arla gasped.

'Yes, but I'll explain all that soon. The thing is, they told me things about what's happening, not just outside, but in here as well.'

'It's bad isn't it?' she said gravely. 'We saw it on the way here.'

'Yes, and worse than you might think. This place is not going to last, Arla. Jerusalem, Israel, everywhere – it's all gone or on the edge of collapse. They told me America has fallen to pieces, China is a wasteland, and so is most of Europe. They're desperate. They have no idea what to do next. They can't stop it. No one can.'

'I'd feared as much. But how long do we have?'

'Days at the most.'

'Shit! But the drug, can't we use it? Can't we still turn the tide?'

'They say they don't know how to make it.'

'But Michael does!'

'Yes, so I hear, and that's why they put everything behind getting him out. I hope to god he knows what he's doing. I'm not sure what he's told you, but they're pretty sure that even if he could make it, he's not going to be able to make enough to save everyone, or should I say, to save anyone besides a few important people. The Americans told them before communications more or less ceased that they just couldn't make it anything like fast enough. They'd only made a few hundred doses before things basically shut down.'

'Are you saying they've stopped making it? Has it really gone that far already?'

James nodded gravely. 'We need a plan Arla, and we need one fast.'

'I don't think I… no one does.'

'I do, but you may think I'm mad when you hear it.'

*

Arla sat close to James on the narrow bench seat, her hand grasped tightly in his lap. The concrete room, deep underground, was small and stuffy, the air conditioning having been long since switched off to save what little backup power remained. Michael, Nathan, Ariel, and two senior Mossad agents sat crammed together around the small wooden table, a jug of warm water and a stack of glasses lying untouched in the middle. A tall thin agent named Taavi, and a short dark-skinned agent called Addi, watched silently in front of a digital sound recorder.

Ariel sat slouched back in his chair, his eyes burning into James. 'How the fuck are you still alive?' he asked, his tone more than a little hostile. 'Do you know what I, we, went through to try and find you? And how the fuck did you get here before us? Did the CIA deliver you?' he asked, his fingers drumming on the table irritably.

'Good questions,' James replied calmly, trying to ignore Ariel's gruff manner. 'I'll try to answer them all.' He looked around the group pensively before continuing. 'I was barely conscious by the end; my fever was that bad. I'd been taken to a military hospital and I could hear the chaos in the place. It's hard to believe, but it was spreading so quickly that the staff just fled in terror. Soon after that, but I don't know how long exactly, the place became silent, which was far more terrifying in a way. Occasionally I could hear something like growling or gurgling in the hall outside my room. It reminded me of Katrina,' he said quietly to Arla. 'Strangely I wasn't that worried. I'd already resigned myself to a fate worse than death. I guess I was ready for my own end, but the thought of becoming one of those things was more than I could stomach. That's when the incredible thing happened. I must have passed out for some time because when I woke up I was in the back of an armored car of some kind. I guessed we were escaping the city. There were screams and people kept hitting the sides making a terrible noise - they were just running people down - and guns were firing continuously. It was absolute hell. There was a man in the back of the truck, he was terrified too, but he seemed to know who I was and what was wrong with me. He said I was very lucky - that I was one of only a handful they had saved. I asked what he meant by 'saved', but I already knew what he meant. My fever had gone, and my mind was clear again for the first time, but I was still very weak. We were heading somewhere safe apparently, to sit out the end. It was pretty damn grim stuff I can tell you, but as you know, it came to pass very quickly. Ankara became a ghost town, the victims walking the streets picking off anyone who had been unfortunate enough to stay behind.'

'I was taken to a place where senior officials, soldiers, scientists, and doctors were being accommodated in extremely cramped and filthy camps. They called it Orion's Belt. It was a group of fortified compounds around the city that would allow important people to survive the outbreak and keep strategic command going. But it failed. The aim was to try and fight back and to come up with a cure for the disease or destroy the sick before they could devour or further infect the healthy. But it was doomed from the start. My helper, a man called Jack, knew better. He'd already seen it take hold in the US, and he knew it couldn't be stopped. He told me my recovery was a huge secret; that the Turks knew nothing of it, and that I must not breathe a word of it. I wanted to know why I'd been saved, and why it was so secret, but he wouldn't say any more. It was pretty surreal.'

'Within a few days of being there, the compound became a waking nightmare. Outbreaks were out of control within the compound and there were constant brutal executions of anyone suspected of being infected. Before long the place was overrun with those things, and I was rushed out of what had become a scene from a horror movie. We moved to a remote place far from the capital where two other American agents were also hiding. I'm not sure what the long-term plan was, but they seemed to be waiting for further instructions.'

'Were they CIA or CBT?' Michael interrupted. 'Did they mention a Martin Kruzinger? He's the one who sent us to find you and Akbulut in the first place.'

'No, they didn't. But I know who you mean, and I'll get to that in a second. So, I tried to find out more about who they were and who else they were trying to rescue, but they didn't trust me enough to tell me anything. We were there three days, and in that time, I busied myself again with transcribing the tablets, which I still had, since there was little else to do. Then, one night, I overheard two of the agents arguing. At first, I thought they were drunk. Jack wasn't there. One of them was accusing the other of sabotaging their mission. They didn't say what the mission was, but it seems they were freaked out after losing one of their team to INS before I got there, and now one of the agents was feeling ill himself. They still had some of the drug they'd used on me leftover, but they were supposed to keep it for someone else – and there wasn't enough for themselves. But this guy was freaking out because he was sure he had caught it. He started getting very agitated. He was insisting they use what was left on themselves and get out of Turkey and go somewhere safer. The other guy was torn up about it, accusing him of being a traitor. The discussion got heated and soon there was a fight. They were shouting and swearing, and then finally, there was a gunshot.'

'I rushed out of the room only to find one of the guys' head blown off. The other guy was sweating profusely, swearing to himself and muttering, and he was crouched down unlocking a big box that was connected to the generator power. It was obvious what he was after. He soon noticed me, and I could see at once he was out of his mind. I asked him what was in the box. He started swearing at me and telling me it was all my fault, and accusing me of being a pointless waste of the drug - that I'd cost them their only chance of survival, and for what? He got so enraged that he picked up his gun and fired at me but missed owing to how shaky he was. I noticed then that his nose was running like mad. Luckily Jack, the guy who had rescued me from the hospital, rushed in and pulled me out of there. He wanted to go back in and calm the crazy guy down. I warned him not to. I told him he was sick and out of his mind, but he wouldn't listen and went back in. I was right, the guy was crazy, and he just spun around and shot him down. The bastard went straight back to unlocking the box as though nothing had happened.'

Arla grabbed his hand tightly as he began to tremble, remembering the ordeal.

'He got it open after a lot of fumbling around. I kept watching him all the while, hoping he would soon pass out, as he was looking very sick by this time. There was a syringe in the box, and it looked like it was being kept at low temperature because a lot of cold vapor escaped from the box as he opened it. He took out the syringe and began rolling up his sleeve. He was about to inject himself, but then… I don't know why, but I just couldn't let him save himself after he had killed two people. I was so bloody angry. I took Jack's gun and, well, I shot him.' James stopped talking and hung his head in silence.

'It's OK,' Arla said after a long pause, putting her arm around him. 'He tried to kill you, right? And he would have again.'

'Yes, but I still shouldn't have done it,' he cried, angry and ashamed of himself. 'He had the disease for Christ's sakes. He didn't know what he was doing. If I'd just let him take it, he would have been fine soon enough, and then he would have realized what he'd done. But I was too damn angry.'

'You didn't have a choice, mate,' Nathan offered. 'I'd have shot him too, the greedy bastard. Don't worry, if it helps, Michael's done much worse.'

Michael gave Nathan a horrified and injured look.

'So how did you get back here then?' Nathan continued. 'And what did you do with the drug?'

'Well, that's when things got weirder still. Mobile phones had stopped working by this time, but a little later a satphone in the house started ringing. It was that guy you mentioned, Martin Kruzinger.'

Michael and Nathan nodded knowingly. 'So, he was behind the rescue?' Michael said.

'Yes, he said he knew about me and had ordered my rescue because of what I knew about the last outbreak and how it ended. He was looking for answers for how to stop it, how to survive. He was sounding seriously worried. I think the place was in total shut down. He obviously hadn't heard anything from anyone in ages. He wanted to know what had become of the drug and of you both. I told him there was a single syringe left, still frozen, and that I had saved it from misuse. As for you two, of course I had no idea. He told me to stay put and he would send someone for me, and that under no circumstances was I to talk to or give the drug to anyone until they arrived and identified themselves as his agents.'

'So it was CBT that brought you back,' Michael stated, sounding pleased.

James shook his head, then nodded toward the two intelligence officers opposite him. 'Nope, they did.'

'OK, so everyone is working together now?' Michael asked, looking confused. 'That's good.'

'Erm, not exactly,' James said awkwardly. 'I think Martin meant to send his own people to collect me, but these two can probably explain better what actually happened.'

Ariel beamed and threw his hands behind his head and kicked his feet up on the table, clearly enjoying the story more and more. 'Tell us,' he encouraged them. 'What did actually happen?'

'You'd left your post to find James,' Taavi, the tall thin agent with spectacles began in a reprimanding tone directed at Ariel. 'We overheard the conversation between James and Kruzinger. There's a lot less chatter on the airwaves these days and this conversation definitely caught our interest.'

'You mean you seized the drug before the Americans could get it back?' Michael said in disbelief.

The man looked blankly past Michael, avoiding eye contact and the question.

'For fuck's sake, Michael, don't such a baby,' Ariel burst out. 'The stakes are pretty high right now, you know. Perhaps you failed to notice on the way in here that we're teetering on the edge of the abyss too? No goddamn American was planning on giving us anything to help our plight. I'm fucking glad we took it!'

'From your conversation with Kruzinger,' the other agent continued, a squat man with dark skin who ignored Ariel's outburst, 'we knew this drug worked, whereas our own attempts were failing. The Americans could make their own, this much we knew, but they were not sharing, so we saw no harm in taking it. We cannot let millions of our own people die.'

'And what about the agents? You killed them I suppose?' Michael asked in outrage.

'Oh, grow up, Michael,' Ariel interjected again peevishly. 'This was a piece of clever espionage for our survival, not a cheap back street mugging. Anyway, you can't honestly be complaining about our actions after we just saved your neck. Your own people did nothing for you.'

'OK, that's enough,' Arla cut in angrily as Michael began to bristle and his face grew flushed. 'Let's not forget Michael is the only one here who actually knows how to make the drug,' she said caustically to her brother. 'I think you should treat him and James with a lot more respect, don't you?'

'Hey, don't cast me as the villain,' Ariel said, throwing his arms up in mock chagrin. 'If not for me you'd still have been in Turkey with a boyfriend who was about to eat you.'

'You're such an arsehole,' she spat.

'And proud of it! But of course you're right my sister, as usual. My apologies, Michael and James, that was rude of me,' he said with a slight nod of his head in apology. 'Now, if we could continue. I'd like to know, James, and I hope this is not too disrespectful, why you were rescued at all. What information do you have that was worth the last few drops of this precious drug and the lives of three agents?'

James brushed off the dig again. 'Like I said, I don't really know.'

'But James,' Arla said reassuringly, 'you said you knew something, that you had a plan, however crazy it might sound. What is it?'

'I did find something out,' James continued, his expression distant. 'Something I've thought about a lot since. I've lacked the materials to do the research, but I've worked a lot out in my head. I think I know why some groups survived and how they survived. It is obvious really, once you think about it. We need to do it too.'

'Who? Who survived? What do you mean? Explain,' Ariel asked, suddenly sitting to attention.

'You should know,' James replied a little smugly. 'It's in the Torah after all.'

33.

The hills became dry and dusty as they hurried ever on, the shrubs becoming small and withered, the creek beds dry and sandy. The horizon became an indistinct blur of haze where the blue sky above merged imperceptibly into the brown earth below. The barks and howls of the pursuing demons grew fainter as time drew on, and as the ruggedness of the landscape made their pursuit more difficult. Once or twice Ani noticed a withered body lying in the sand, desiccated like the dried fish he had seen sold in the markets in Arzihapas long ago. They reminded him too of the bodies he had seen on the beach - the same haunted staring eyes and drawn back lips surrounding savage-looking teeth.

'Are these demon bodies, like those on the beach?' Ani asked as he gave one a wide berth.

'You saw those? Yes, they are.'

Ani and Purdu exchanged glances.

'Soon these demons, as you call them, will no longer follow us. After several days in the desert, they drop like flies.'

'Why? What kills them? The heat?'

'No, the dryness I think.'

'I have never seen them drink,' Ani thought out loud.

'Indeed, they do not, and that is their doom, for they soon dry out. Their skin becomes like tanned leather and their bodies shrivel with such thirst, as might any man's body that ventures far into the Negev without enough water.'

Ani licked his parched lips at the mention of it. 'Is that the name of the place we are going to?'

'What, Negev? Yes, that is what we call this place, for it simply means southern land in the Canaanite tongue. But Rephidim is where we are headed.'

'And what lies beyond that?' Purdu asked, wondering at these lands she had never seen or heard of before.

'Egypt.'

Purdu looked up at her brother. 'See, I was right!' she said, and punched him hard in the arm.

Ani winced, but nodded and smiled at his clever sister.

'We saw ships,' Purdu explained to Achan. 'They came the night we came ashore. They were great warships we think. Are they from Egypt?'

'Very likely I'd say. They remain strong, and some say an army will soon come north to try and destroy us.'

'Why?'

'Because those who we shall join are from there. The Pharaoh is not pleased with them and wishes to destroy them all.'

'Was it the demons that made them flee?'

'No, they were led here. They escaped great torment in Egypt, so they say, but now they have joined with survivors from many lands.'

Ani was baffled by this talk of a mysterious leader.

'Is he a great warrior, the man who led them here?'

'No. You will see. *He* has chosen us to survive the horrors that have taken all others.'

*

For another day and night, they marched without rest, walking faster by night than by day, eating only dried mutton that Achan carried in his sack and drinking from his near-empty water skin. Ani was so tired that he walked even as he slept, becoming alert again only when he stumbled and fell or walked into a spiky shrub. As the hills became drier still, so that little at all grew on them, Ani began to see dry corpses everywhere. They were naked for the most part, but some still wore armor or clothing. There were men and women, adults and children, dark and withered, their corpses drier than Amuurana's clay tablets. The numbers grew throughout the following day from dozens to hundreds, even thousands, scattered randomly about, all facing west, and seemingly having dropped as they walked, never to rise again.

'There was a great sea of them when they first came from the east,' Achan explained as they picked their way through the musty smelling corpses. 'In the north, they devoured all in their path until they reached the western sea, and there they simply perished with nothing left to eat and nowhere left to go. I saw that with my own eyes. Here they met the fate of all unlucky creatures that venture into and became lost in the desert.'

'But how do you survive out here when not even the demons can?'

'We are nomads, as I told you before, and we keep flocks that can survive on meager forage. If you know how to live, there is milk and there is honey. There are wells too, and springs, in the desert that have been revealed to us. We cannot return to our homeland until this scourge has passed, as I know it one day shall. Then we will return to the land that is promised to us by god.'

'How do you know this?' Ani asked, long since disavowed of any trust in gods or talk of good fortune.

'*He* will tell us. *He* will lead us when we are ready.'

'But who is he? Who is your leader?' Ani asked again.

Achan avoided the question again. 'Twelve of us return to the north as often as we dare to find food and to watch for the appointed hour when we shall take back our land from the withered ones. We have taken in many strangers, both from the sea and from surrounding lands, and our numbers grow stronger day by day. We have even found some who claim to know how to defeat these creatures with new weapons of their making.'

'Who? Tell us!' they both cried in unison.

'Hatti folk like yourselves, from the north. Soon we will be ready to take back what is ours.'

Ani and Purdu exchanged puzzled looks.

*

For several days more they walked into the heart of the desert. The sounds of the pursuing demons had long since departed, and now a new sound greeted them. It was that of bleating animals and the calls of shepherds to their flocks. Below them lay a wide sandy valley filled with faded tents and many people. Flocks of animals were dispersed along the length of the valley floor and shining here and there amid the parched landscape were pools of clear and life-giving water.

The woman and boy threw their hands into the air and wailed, apparently offering a prayer of thanks for their safe return. The woman and the boy had ignored Ani and Purdu for days and looked on bitterly at every meager morsel or sip of water they took from Achan's supplies. Now, for some reason, the woman turned and smiled at them. She said something in a foreign language then turned and began her descent into the valley, the boy running eagerly along behind.

Ani stood dumbfounded for several moments, staring after her.

'She has decided,' Achan said smiling, obviously relieved by her change of heart. 'She said welcome to our home.'

34.

'Is this some kind of academic joke? What's any of this got to do with the Torah?' Ariel asked combatively, tapping a cigarette irritably on the table before stuffing it between to his lips.

'You can't smoke in here!' Taavi said sternly.

'I know, I wasn't going to,' Ariel fired back, then reluctantly yanked the cigarette from his mouth and shoved it into his top pocket.

'Look, if this is of no relevance to you then fine, I'll shut up and you can figure it all out without me. I've put a lot of thought into this, and I don't hear any of you coming up with solutions.'

'Solutions?' Ariel retorted. 'I don't see how a lot of old biblical guff is going to offer a solution. This is the twenty-first century, James, as if any of that old religious nonsense is going to have any relevance today.'

'Shut up Ariel and let him speak,' Arla snapped angrily. 'James is an expert, now listen for all our sakes.' She nodded to James to keep going.

James waited until he had Ariel's reluctant attention. 'The Merneptah Stele, found by our old friend Flinders Petrie in the late 19th Century in the forecourt of the temple of the same name in Thebes, is an ancient Egyptian text that gives us a faint clue as to what happened to Canaan, that is, Israel and Palestine, at the end of the Bronze Age and the beginning of the Dark Age, or Iron Age 1A as it is also called. The stele refers to the destruction of Canaan but also makes the oldest known reference to the people of Israel. The two most pertinent lines in the engraving tell us that Canaan has become an evil place, essentially a wasteland. It says Israel, and this refers to its people and not just the place, is fallow and has no seed. It names other societies too, including the Hittites, that have also met a nasty end. Most scholars think it refers to an Egyptian conquest and destruction of troublesome neighbors, and while that is one possible interpretation, I think it is wrong, like pretty much everything we thought we knew about the collapse. I think it is the only real mention we have from antiquity of the fate of those lands bordering Egypt. The other mention we have, as I was saying, is from the Old Testament and Torah. Scholars have always said those texts, though written down long after the actual events, record a distant memory of the collapse and the travails of the wandering Hebrews before they came into the land of Israel as we know it today, that is, the land of Canaan. The Bible says,' he flicked open his notebook and found a page, then read, 'and I quote:

Sorrow shall take hold on the inhabitants of Palestina... All the inhabitants of Canaan shall melt away. Fear and dread shall fall upon them; by the greatness of thine arm, they shall be as still as a stone.

'I think these early texts speak of the horrible end, but they might also hold a vital clue to their survival, a lesson we should heed if we want to survive the thing that's beating in our doors this very minute. Jerusalem, like every other city on earth, will soon suffer the same fate as elsewhere. It is being eaten out from the inside like a corpse-filled with maggots and we may only have days left - if that - before it is doomed along with all those left inside it.'

The tall thin agent looked uncomfortable at what James was saying, either because he did not believe it, or he was concerned by James talking about it.

'Are you saying the Bible actually tells us how to survive this?' Michael asked, incredulous.

'Maybe. It may be the very reason it was originally written - as a warning and a memory of how to survive, though it had been diluted and altered with the passing of many generations before it was finally written down.'

Now Ariel sat still and focused on what James was saying.

James flicked through some more pages in his notebook for a second before continuing. 'I think the early people of Israel survived in the desert for a long time while INS ran its course and petered out, then gradually they returned and settled the highlands of Samara, Galilee and Judea and founded the three provinces of Israel. Archaeologists consider a lot of the early scriptures apocryphal, but I think they are wrong, in part at least. The Old Testament records that the Israelites wandered the desert for forty years, knowing that the inhabitants of Canaan – the land they believed promised to them by God – could not be ousted. The twelve spies they sent north to investigate the promised land returned telling tales of an unbeatable foe, and they themselves all apparently later died of 'plague'. I think the Bible gives us at least this one solid germ of truth, a germ that is vitally important for understanding how to survive this. I contend that these early texts are of course muddied by various influences and retellings over the centuries, but they record a fundamentally important way in which this small population survived the INS onslaught and later recolonized Canaan and renamed it Israel. It's also thought that the early Israelites took in many refugees from surrounding lands, including some of the Sea Peoples, who were probably just refugees from INS, coming from stricken lands like Turkey, Greece, Macedonia, Cyprus, Sardinia, Corsica and Crete, and other eastern Mediterranean regions. The Sea Peoples raided and battled the Egyptians for three decades before Ramesses III finally dealt with them once and for all in a great sea battle in a bay in Libya. He resettled many of the captives in southern Canaan, and they probably became the Philistines, a collective group of survivors who would later become Israel's greatest enemy for hundreds of years afterward.'

'But why only the eastern Mediterranean?' Nathan suddenly interjected. 'Why not everywhere? Why didn't we all go extinct? Why are humans still here at all?'

'I don't have good answers for that, only a gut feeling. Places like Egypt did survive, though much diminished and heavily harried by the Sea Peoples. Their survival may have been due to their geography.

'How so?' Michael asked.

'Egypt is bordered by oceans and deserts.'

'What's that got to do with it?' Ariel challenged.

'Well, they lived in an oasis protected by a girdle of natural barriers through which INS could not easily spread. Amuurana's text tells us that the INS victims wandered ever westward. He opened his notes again. His second tablet says:

The demons walk tirelessly toward the setting sun, as though Arinna calls them to her chamber.

'Arinna was the god of the sun, as you've no doubt worked out. If this account is true, then no INS victims heading west could have reached Egypt without crossing huge deserts.'

'So where did it start then?' Michael asked, looking puzzled.

'No idea, I'm just guessing here, but maybe in India or Mesopotamia, but it spread quickly westward. Amuurana writes that by the time he brought word of the catastrophe to the king, emissaries had already arrived from other lands in the east telling of their demise, so it is likely the disease spread from somewhere east of the fertile crescent, maybe even Asia. As for why humanity wasn't entirely snuffed out, I don't know, but maybe INS reached a point where it couldn't spread any further.

'Well, if they were moving westward, they would eventually have reached the edge of the deserts and then the ocean,' Arla stated, looking at a huge map of the Middle East hanging on the opposite wall.

'Yes, I think you're right. Amuurana mentions several times that as victims became scarce, the 'demons' just dried up and died. Maybe when they reached the ocean they also had nowhere else to go and just died.'

'I find this all very hard to believe,' Ariel cut in. 'If a fifty-caliber bullet won't take them out then why would a bit of sunburn? These fucking creatures are like super-humans. You can't kill them.'

'You can, but you have to sever the spinal column at the base of the skull. That's what Akbulut's notes said. But even so, they're still animals. Like us, they have to stay hydrated or they eventually die.'

'That makes sense,' Michael offered, nodding.

James continued, spurred on by Michael's support. 'I think they probably hit their physiological limits in deserts and at the edge of the oceans and just expired. The Israelites remained in the desert a long time until INS just faded away with no new victims to feed on. I'm not saying they were the only survivors, there were probably lots in other refuges, but I think the secret to our own survival lies in those texts.'

'Are you saying we should all just pack up and head for the desert?' Ariel said doubtfully, fishing his cigarette out of his pocket again and tapping it on the table nervously. 'How the fuck would we all survive out there in the middle of nowhere for forty years?'

James shrugged. 'True, but forty years may just be poetic license.'

'It's worth a go,' Nathan said seriously. 'I'd prefer that to waking up with my leg gnawed off.'

'Is this even possible?' Ariel asked, directing the question at the two other agents at the table.

They looked at each other doubtfully. 'There are military bases in the Negev, depots and bunkers, missile silos and other installations. Some people might survive there for a while. Essential personnel for instance.'

'Essential. Oh well, that counts us out, mate,' Nathan said jokingly and whacked Michael on the shoulder.

'On the contrary, my friend,' Taavi, replied. 'I don't think you are going anywhere. We have a job for you. Quite an urgent job.'

35.

The old man had clearly once been tall and powerful but was now frail and stiff. His long grey beard hung down over his white tunic, and huge bushy eyebrows thrust outwards from his face. He sat regally on a carved wooden chair in the center of the tent, a line of servants standing behind him awaiting his bidding. He gestured for Achan, Ani, and Purdu to enter the tent and take a seat on the striped rugs that lay before his chair. A ram's horn trumpet lent against his chair and behind him a wooden box wrapped in gold bands. He spoke to Achan a long time in a foreign tongue while the children sat and waited, wilting in the heat and dying of thirst. Ani could see Purdu swaying slightly like she might be about to faint.

'He welcomes you and asks you to tell him your tale,' Achan said at last, turning to them, and giving them a reassuring smile. 'I will translate for you.'

Ani opened his mouth, but his dry lips stuck together and only a strange croak emanated from his parched throat.

The old man smiled and beckoned a servant to bring forth water and some strong-smelling white cheese.

'He asks you to eat and drink, then he will hear your tale,' Achan said and sat down next to them while they filled their grumbling bellies.

At last, Ani licked his fingers, a burp slipping between his lips by accident. 'Sorry,' he said, a little embarrassed, and slapped his hand over his mouth.

'I'm glad you liked it,' Achan said.

The old man smiled, his bright eyes piercing Ani and holding his attention, then nodded for Ani to begin.

Ani recounted the tale of their journey with Amuurana, the fall of Hattusha, the last battle in the fort, and their escape to the sea. This was hard for him to talk about, and he often fell silent for long stretches while he held back tears and gathered the strength to go on. He continued with the ill-fated voyage with the Sea

Peoples and Troan's usurpation of the fleet. He omitted to mention the Gal Meshedi or the slave revolt led by Jeemah. He wondered as he spoke what had become of the Gal Meshedi, and most of all, Mezarus. Achan had mentioned something that had made them hope he might even be here, however unlikely that seemed, but did that mean the Gal Meshedi was here too? When he had finished his tale he fell silent for a long time while Achan translated. Purdu stared at him consolingly, knowing how hard it must have been for him to tell their story.

At last, the old man nodded and sat back thinking for some time. Then he stood up a little shakily and approached them. He spoke for a minute then looked expectantly at Achan.

'He thanks you for your fascinating tale. He has learned much that he did not know. He also says he is sorry for your suffering. He feels sorrow for all you have been through. He says his people have also suffered much and he knows how hard it is to be an orphan. He asks, if you are willing, will you abide with us here?'

Ani and Purdu looked at each other, unsure whether to agree or not. Ani was unsure what agreeing would mean, how long they must stay or how safe it would really be. But he already trusted Achan, and if Achan followed this man, then perhaps he could too.

'But the old man also says that if you stay, you must renounce your old gods - those that led your people to ruin and must place your heart before the one true god.'

Ani was shocked. He had never really felt the presence of any god, and he truly believed if any gods had watched over the Hatti, they had forsaken them to their doom at the last. 'Who is the one true god?' Ani said, unsure who this could be.

'The Lord, Yaweh. We are his chosen people,' Achan replied.

Ani looked around the tent at the meager furnishings, the worn rugs, the tattered clothing, and thin-looking servants, he sucked in the dusty hot, dry air like the fumes from a forge, and he wondered how these people could possibly think themselves the chosen people. And then another thought crossed his mind. They lived! They had survived when no others had. Indeed, he agreed, in this sense at least, they were chosen. He looked at Purdu, trying to read her thoughts. She nodded slowly but meaningfully and that told him all he needed to know.

He turned back to the old man. 'Yes, we wish to stay with you, and we will abandon our gods and follow the one true god as you ask. But can I also ask you something?'

Once Achan had translated this request, the old man smiled and nodded and opened his hands for Ani to ask his question.

'What is your name? And what are your people called?' Ani asked.

'His name is Aaron,' Achan replied, 'and we are the people of Israel.'

'Can I ask another question?' Purdu asked, speaking for the first time.

'Yes child,' Achan answered, 'ask what you like.' 'Is Mezarus here?'

36.

Talk of leaving had made the Mossad agents come to life. The shorter, darker one, Addi, had left the room shortly after they began to discuss it, while Taavi had watched and listened attentively as Ariel mused over the existence of desert installations and survival systems that should exist in secret bunkers in the Negev.

Soon Addi returned with two more officials, one in senior military uniform and another - a woman - wearing a tight suit. The suit looked highly incongruous with the bare bunker and military uniforms. To James, it signaled a last ditched effort to cling to the last shreds of normality in a rapidly crumbling world.

'This is Brigadier-General Menuen, in charge of the defense of the Negev sector,' Addi introduced the high-ranking military officer, 'and this is former Minister of Tourism, Dr Hillel, now in charge of the evacuation of Jerusalem. They wish to speak to you about your ideas, James.'

'Oh,' James replied, taken aback. 'I didn't think you would be that interested.'

'Addi has mentioned to us that you think there might be some hope of some refuge in the desert, that the disease would be unable to spread there,' The Brigadier-General asked in good English.

'I didn't say it wouldn't be able to spread. It probably would I suppose. What I said was, that is, what I think is, that INS victims will be unable to survive in the desert and that so long as no one goes there that is already infected, it may be possible to set up a safe haven, the desert acting as a kind of quarantine – a shield if you like. I gather that the INS victims do not drink. As living beings like us, though unrecognizable in many hideous ways, they will soon expire in the extreme dryness and heat, prohibiting them from reaching a refuge deep in the desert.'

'So, you are saying we should evacuate the population of Jerusalem to the Negev? You really think this is our best chance of survival?' Dr Hillel asked, sounding extremely skeptical.

'No, I'm not saying that at all. If you simply transplanted everyone here into the desert, you would just be taking the problem with you. The situation would be exactly the same as here. I doubt the desert would kill the sick faster than it kills the healthy, and if so, then we would likely all be dead before INS could run its course. I have no idea how long it will take for INS to die out.'

'A pandemic will usually run for weeks to months,' Michael chipped in. 'The only way we can survive that is if our immune system bounces back at some point, or we have a cure.'

'Well I'm not subjecting my men and women to a dangerous and risky mission when they are perfectly safe inside this compound,' the Brigadier-General stated firmly. 'I don't place any faith in ancient texts, and we're certainly not going anywhere without a cure!'

'But we do have a cure!' Dr Hillel said forcefully to the Brigadier, then turned her gaze imploringly towards Michael.

Michael nodded but said nothing.

'It won't help us!' James insisted.

'Where is it now?' Nathan whispered to Michael as Dr Hillel and James began to argue about the virtues of the cure.

Michael shrugged. 'You really think they were going to let me keep it?' he answered quietly. 'They took it off me as soon as we got here of course.'

'But aren't you going to make some more? Do they have the gear?'

'I sure as hell hope so, but I haven't seen any yet. I've told them what they need. They seemed worried about it.'

'The truth is,' Michael said angrily, forcing his way back into the conversation. 'We have very few doses of the drug, as you well know, we have a whole country on the verge of collapse, most people around us probably have the disease or soon will have, including people inside this bunker. The desert could well offer a last chance of survival as James says, and if some of us don't make a break for it soon there's not going to be anyone left to find out if he's right or not. I want out of here, I want my drug back, and I want the machines to make more of it. If you make this happen, I can offer you the only thing that's going to save your lives. You get us out of here, out into the desert with the right equipment, and I'll save your lives. Can you do that for me Dr Hillel? Because if you can't, we might as well kiss our own sorry asses goodbye.'

A sudden silence fell on the room.

'Erm… well,' Dr Hillel stammered and frowned. She looked at Menuen who was staring down at the table, then she fell silent again.

'What about you Brigadier-General?' Michael said, following her gaze. 'Can you get me and my friends somewhere safe while we do what's needed to stop this thing?'

'Like I said, I'm not risking the safety of my people and equipment for a fanciful story based on some over-literal reading of the Tora,' Brigadier-General Menuen replied angrily.

Michael looked at Ariel who was shaking his head disappointedly, then back at the Brigadier. 'We don't have long, sir. That is a very short-sighted response.'

'How long do we have?' Arla asked quietly.

'I don't know,' he replied. 'How quickly has it taken hold everywhere else?' he asked Taavi.

He shook his head. 'Most places are pretty silent now. There are a few outposts, but it's probably only a matter of time. There has been no response from any government agency in America for a week,' he answered gravely.

'And elsewhere?'

Taavi shook his head. 'There are isolated, desperate pleas, but that is all. Phone lines, radio, the internet, satellites, … most are dead or silent.'

Michael shook his head. 'So, as you can see, we move fast, or we go down too. Do you really want to die in this bunker? Because that's what's going to happen sooner or later! You're going to catch the disease or you're going to get your throats torn out!'

James sighed noisily, furious that no one seemed prepared to support his plan.

Then Taavi spoke up. 'I think your plan has some merit, James. You could be onto something, if what you're saying is true,' he continued, 'then you may be right that a refuge in the desert is worth a try. How soon could we do that?' he asked the Brigadier-General.

'I already told you, there'll be no convoy into the desert on my watch. No one can survive there for long, there is no water, no food, and the bunkers are for very short-term use only and rely on frequent resupply. We are safest here. I suggest you abandon this foolish plan and we get to work on the thing we lost good men and women to bring Michael here to do. Make the drug and do it now or we'll rethink your situation! Now good day,' he said and stood up and left. Hillel left quietly as well, but she shot James a perplexed look as she left.

'Fuck him,' Ariel said angrily. 'We can do it ourselves!'

'You don't have permission for that,' Taavi stated flatly, but he smiled slightly as if somewhat approving of the idea.

'I don't give a fuck!' Ariel cried and jumped to his feet. 'We could organize a convoy pretty quickly if we have the resources and the right connections,' he added walking to the door.

Taavi sat for a moment and thought. 'While they will never officially ratify this mission, bear in mind the bunkers won't hold many people or for very long, assuming we can find out where they are. Your escape must remain secret or it will not work. You would also have to get your hands on some vehicles and getting them out of the compound will not be easy now that the Brigadier-General knows your intentions.'

'And don't forget the drug,' Michael piped up. 'We have to get the drug back if we're going to test it and make more. I need the serum, the notes, the machines and a source of prions. How are we going to get all of that?'

'Leave that to me,' Ariel said. Prepare your things, and keep this meeting secret,' Ariel said sternly, looking at James and the others in turn. 'There will be many here that will not be happy to hear of it. Are you in or out?' he said turning to Taavi and Addi.

They looked at each other for a second, then Taavi nodded. 'In!'

37.

Ani sat on the hot stony ground beside their little tent on the valley slope, watching the dust devils swirl through the dry riverbed below as the warm wind shook the shrubs around him. The stars grew began to appear in the darkening sky and Purdu lay on the ground beside him, silently staring up at the brightening firmament.

Footsteps soon became audible on the stony path leading to their new dwelling. Ani looked over and saw Achan trudging up the path towards them, looking thoughtful.

'I thought you'd already be asleep,' he said when he reached them. 'Are you comfortable here?'

'Yes, very,' Purdu replied. Their tent was indeed comfortable, with woolen rugs and cushions to lie on, but it was too hot to stay inside for long.

'I'm glad.' He paused pensively for a moment. 'You asked today whether Mezarus was here. How do you know that name?'

Ani looked guiltily at the ground. He had omitted all mention of Mezarus and the Gal Meshedi from his recollection of recent events. 'He is a friend. He came with us from Hattusha. We hoped, maybe, he might be here.'

'And what gave you that impression?'

'You said foreigners had brought knowledge of new weapons. Mezarus was the High Smith's apprentice in Hattusha. Our friend, Lelwan who I told you about, brought him with us because he thought he could make the great iron swords that can easily kill the demons. We hoped he had come here somehow after he was separated from us at sea.'

'Interesting,' Achan said, smirking deviously to himself. 'Well it is getting late, children, and you have walked many, many miles. Why don't you sleep now and tomorrow you will learn more of our customs and our Lord?'

'Thank you,' Purdu said, though there was sadness in her voice. 'Thank you for bringing us here. Our parents, our old parents and Amuurana too, would be very happy that you have brought us somewhere safe at last to be among your people. I hope we will be welcome as foreigners.'

'Do not forget, I am a foreigner too, but I am sure you shall be as welcome as I have found myself. Now sleep.'

Ani and Purdu did as they bid. They crawled in through the tent flap into the stuffy interior, collapsed onto the hot cushions and were soon deep in their usual dark and troubled slumbers.

*

Ani woke to the sound of a distant horn, muffled and two-toned, like the ones he had sometimes heard priests use in Arzhiapas during festivals. The long deep hooting was soon taken up by another and another horn, all of different pitch, and seemingly coming closer over the hills surrounding the valley and into the camp itself.

Ani sat up, looked around, and realized he had overslept. The morning was already well upon them, and his rumbling stomach told him that it was well past time for breakfast. Purdu stirred too and rubbed the dust from her eyes. She looked around as if she had no recollection of where she was or how she got here.

The horns died away as quickly as they had begun, leaving a heavy silence in the valley. This was soon broken by the sound of someone approaching the tent. The tent flap was thrown open and Achan peered in. 'Good morning!' he said cheerily. 'There is an important meeting to take place today. You must come!'

Ani's heart sank at the thought of leaving. All he longed for was to lie on a bed for a full two days without moving so that his feet may heal, and his legs lose their stiffness. 'No more walking,' he blurted out, still half asleep. 'I can't walk anymore.'

'But you will want to come and see this. It will be worth the sore feet. I am four times your age. Believe me, I feel it too!'

'What is it then? What are to we to go and see?' Purdu asked sleepily, a tiny hint of excitement in her voice as she brushed back her thick shock of black hair from her face.

'Something marvelous, miraculous you might say!'

Ani forced himself up off the bed and pulled on his shirt. 'Is there any food?' he found himself asking rather rudely while searching around for water.

'There will be food on the way if we leave soon.'

Ani was confused by this nonsensical statement. His stomach growled loudly again, and he overturned a pile of cushions, desperate for water.

'You are looking for this I think,' Achan said and held out a water skin.

Ani seized it and began chugging down the sweet cold water inside, then passed it to Purdu. She sat up and drained the last of it. 'Sorry,' she said unapologetically and handed it back to Achan, who had taken a seat on a small wooden chair inside the tent and smiled while he watched them.

'Here!' Achan said and took from behind his back two pairs of rawhide sandals. 'Put these on. You'll need them.'

*

A small party of men and women wound their way along twisting stony paths through the hot and barren hillside as they climbed their way up out of the shady valley and into the surrounding hills, exposed to the searing sun that rose rapidly in the cloudless blue sky. Four of the largest men carried the old man, Aaron, on a shaded sedan chair on long poles. This meant the pace was slow and Ani and Purdu could easily keep up.

They trudged along near the back of the line, their heads bent away from the sun, their sore and swollen feet picking their way among the jagged rocks and thorn bushes. Achan came last in the line, ensuring they did not fall behind the rest of the group. The new sandals Achan had given them kept their feet from being pin cushioned by the nasty thorns that grew along the edge of the path, but unfortunately also presented a new problem – blisters.

As they came up out of the valley. Ani could see sunshades of stripy cloth erected atop the highest hilltops, with a person sheltering beneath each one.

'You heard the horns this morning?' Achan asked as Ani stopped and stared at the closest of these shelters.

Ani nodded.

'Well, they were the horns of our sentries up here on the hilltops. They send word between the valleys and alert us of any demons that wander this far into the desert. They were inviting us to a council today. It is not too far away now. We will be there by noon.'

They descended into a shady gully filled with scrubby shrubs where the dew still lay thick on the ground. Suddenly there was excitement in the group. 'Look!' Achan cried, pointing up ahead. Ani noticed the rest of the party were bent double, picking up small flakes and little round yellow balls from around the scrubby trees and shrubs that grew in deep shade, and eating them. 'You may fill your bellies, for it will be soon gone until tomorrow.'

Ani hurried forward, his belly screaming for some nourishment. Little white flakes lay around the base of the trees, and rings of small yellow mushrooms the size of coriander seeds grew in the still damp soil between the rocks. 'Eat them! For soon it will be gone.'

'But what is it?' Purdu asked in wonder as she put a little white flake to her tongue and smiled at the pleasantly sweet taste.

'It is manna. The Lord has given sustenance to his chosen people so that we may survive here in the desert. Now that you have joined us and learn our ways and beliefs, he has revealed it to you too!'

Ani frowned at this strange talk. He quickly gathered a handful of the little crunchy flakes from around the base of a tree no one else had yet visited and popped them into his mouth one by one. The taste was pleasant, like honey cakes, and the little flakes dissolved quickly on his tongue. Next, he tried the little mushrooms the size of coriander seeds. They were like cheese to taste, pleasant and strangely satisfying. After several handfuls of these, his hunger subsided, and he began to feel pleasantly euphoric.

'Behold the holy gift of the Lord,' Aaron was announcing from his sedan chair, feasting on the handfuls of mushrooms and honeydew brought to him by his followers. 'Tomorrow is the Sabbath, so eat doubly now my good people so that we may rest contented tomorrow.'

Ani felt a strange feeling creeping over him as he digested the unusual meal. He found himself reflecting on what a wondrous gift from nature, or from God, this food truly was. Soon he felt deliriously happy, filled with jubilation that he now realized must come from this god of which they spoke with such love and devotion.

'You see now, don't you?' Achan was saying as he sat smiling on a rock watching them gather and scoff the bounty from the glade. 'You see the power of the Lord. You see that he has chosen us!'

'Yes, I see it,' Ani said, sitting down on the ground to keep from swaying. 'I believe you!'

*

Having eaten their fill and enjoying the euphoric sensation, the party left the shady glade and climbed high into the hills again, the temperatures soaring high enough that the soles of Ani's feet felt like they had cooked and separated from the bone like a well-cooked joint of lamb. Mercifully, the sandals had kept this from actually happening, and meant his feet had fared much better than on the journey into the desert.

Before them lay another deeply dissected and twisting valley with lines of rock that jutted out along the edges like vertebrae on a skinny dog. Clusters of tents were visible in the valley bottom beside a small swathe of green that sat deeply shaded beneath a huge rock outcrop at a sharp bend in the valley.

They waded through flocks of goats browsing on the tough shrubs, and down the steep valley sides to the soft silty bottom, then trudged on up the dry riverbed towards the tents.

Ani could hear a rhythmic metallic pounding that had grown louder and louder as they approached the little tent city. He could also see groups of men lined up in front of the tents, practicing some kind of drill.

'You will soon meet our great leader, the instrument of god, who has delivered these people from untold suffering,' Achan said as they made their way between the tents. Their companions on the march had already begun to break off and enter some of the tents to a chorus of excited greetings.

At last, they came to the center of the camp, and there the rhythmic pounding was loudest. A tall tent, high peaked, stood open before a central area where men with tall spears dressed in long shirts were drawn up in ranks, their backs to Ani. Someone was instructing them, but Ani could not see them over the lines of tall men and spears.

'This way,' Achan said, leading them directly toward an area where cloth shades were hung around a mud-brick chimney belching fire and smoke. 'Go on in. I will see you soon,' he said and left them.

They rounded the tall stack and the source of the noise came into full view. A group of young men were pumping a large leather bellows and heaping charcoal onto a red-hot fire that sizzled and belched sparks as the charcoal dust hit the white-hot coals. Before it stood a large stone, squared off, flat-topped and blackened by the smoke. On it lay a red-hot rod of metal, held by bronze tongs in the hands of an apprentice in deep concentration. A huge man stood over the glowing bar, belting it again and again with a massive hammer while the apprentice moved it backward and forward, then whipped it off the stone and plunged it back into the glowing coals.

The huge man looked up and wiped his sweaty brow with a blackened cloth hanging around his neck. At once his knitted and weary brow relaxed and his face lightened and broke into a huge smile. 'A miracle!' he cried in his deep and familiar voice.

'Mezarus!' Ani and Purdu cried together and ran and threw their arms around the filthy, bear-sized man.

38.

A series of loud muffled bangs woke James. He rolled over and checked the clock – it was nearly midnight. Arla moaned and rolled over beside him. He delicately brushed her long hair away from his face and sat up. He slipped on his shirt and pants and tiptoed quietly over the concrete floor to the door, just as another series of loud bangs reverberated through the solid concrete bunker and along the metal air duct.

'That's gunfire!' Arla said, suddenly out of bed and pulling on clothes.

'Jesus!' James muttered under his breath and opened the door a little. He looked out into the brightly lit hallway onto which dozens and dozens of bedrooms joined, housing the senior ranking politicians, military and their families that now resided in the compound.

Soldiers in battledress were running fast down the hallway, jostling concerned people unceremoniously out of the way as they emerged from their bedrooms to enquire as to the source of the commotion.

Arla shot a question in Hebrew at a passing soldier. He replied fleetingly between heaving breaths as he ran past.

'What is it?' James asked.

'He said 'critical mass',' she replied, looking confused.

'What do you think he meant?'

'I don't know, but it sounds bad.'

Arla switched on the lights, pulled on her boots and began throwing the last few personal effects lying around the room into her already bulging backpack. James did the same, a mood of urgency suddenly overwhelming them both as more muffled automatic gunfire reverberated down the hallway.

'Come with me, quickly!' a familiar voice shouted in through the doorway.

James spun around and saw Ariel panting at the door. He had a large backpack over his shoulder and a large folded sheet of paper under his arm.

'What is it? What is critical mass?'

'I'll explain later.' He waved them out of the room. The hallway was now filled with people pushing past in both directions and more soldiers trying to force their way through the congestion.

'Where are Nathan and Michael?' James asked.

'Gone with Addi,' Ariel said, taking Arla by the hand, and fighting his way through the panicked crowd towards the end of the hall. 'They've gone to get more machines and stuff they need to make the drug.'

'That sounds dangerous. Who's with them?'

'They'll be alright, don't worry about them. Hillel's sent an elite Sayeret unit with them,' Ariel said as he pushed past some soldiers talking on radios. 'It's us I'm worried about right now.'

After much struggling, swearing and trodden on toes, they reached the end of the long hall.

'Wait, what about the drug? Do we have it?' asked Arla.

'I'm fine, you're fine, we're all fine. Let's keep it that way and we won't need it.'

'We have to get it!' Arla said, stopping and grabbing Ariel by the arm. 'What future is there for any of us if we can't save ourselves or if there's an outbreak? What is the point of leaving at all?'

'You needn't worry on that score,' a woman's voice said from behind them.

James spun around to find Dr Hillel forcing her way through the crowd behind them, several soldiers clearing a path for her. She was holding the precious cold box gingerly in her hands like a ticking time bomb. 'But,' James stammered, 'how did you get it, and what are you doing with it?'

'I thought about your plan, Dr Bindley. I think it will work. In fact, I think it is our only hope, but I won't let you leave alone. I am coming too, and I want to evacuate many of our people - important people.'

Ariel stepped forward and whispered a word in her ear, something that sounded to James like a name: 'Miriam'.

Dr Hillel smiled faintly and nodded.

'Miriam, is that your name? Your first name I mean?' James asked out of curiosity.

'No,' she said, 'why do you ask?'

James frowned and looked to Arla.

'Come on,' she said and pushed James onwards toward the exit.

They hurried along behind Ariel, heading for a large transport bay at the rear of the compound which James had seen when he had first come to the bunker. Many people were pushing their way towards it. The sounds of gunfire and revving vehicles grew louder as they climbed a metal staircase to the depot.

'What is critical mass?' James asked again as they reached the top of the stairs and saw the long lines of vehicles parked behind heavy metal roller doors.

'It means the sick now outnumber the healthy. It means Jerusalem is overrun. It's the code word for evacuation. It's the end, my friend.'

'Oh shit! So what now?'

'What we're doing, but we'd better hurry or we may get left behind.'

To James' relief, Taavi was waiting anxiously by the roller door at the end of the large room which appeared to be an assembly area. He waved to them over the bustling crowd. Lines of soldiers were guarding the large doorway through to the vehicles, letting only a few people though with appropriate security badges. Automatic fire was erupting in heavy bursts outside.

'Good, you're here!' Taavi said, pulling them out of the crowd and leading them out of the assembly area through a side door.

'What's happening? What are all these people doing?' James said, looking back at the anxious, jostling crowd being held back by soldiers.

'It's total chaos,' Taavi answered, the sweat pouring off his forehead.

'But isn't there an evacuation plan?'

'There was. The President is sick and so are most of his cabinet. I think this is the only evacuation plan that is going to work now.'

'What plan is that?'

'Your plan. Hillel has organized vehicles and most of the VIPs are already loaded,' he said, turning to her.

'Good' she said, sounding relieved. She handed the cold box to Taavi meaningfully. 'Keep it safe and pray god we don't need it.'

He nodded and kissed her on the cheek. 'Good luck!' he said and turned and led them out into the high walled rear transport yard.

'What's all the shooting?' James asked as he hurried alongside Taavi, the noise deafening now.

'The compound is surrounded, and the walls have been breached in places. We're going to have to dash for it.'

A line of revving armored personnel carriers was parked in front of the huge steel roller gate, their taillights glowing faintly in the shroud of exhaust fumes. All had their gun turrets pointed squarely at the huge steel gate that stood shut in front of them. Between gunshots, James could hear a blood-curdling roar of gurgling, barking, hissing and moaning from just beyond the gate.

'In!' Taavi instructed as he brought them to a large armored truck whose back doors hung open.

James climbed into the dark and cramped interior beside Arla. Ariel and Taavi jumped in after them. They took their seats along the sides and the doors slammed closed behind them.

'What about Dr Hillel?' James asked, noticing she was absent.

'She is up the front of the convoy,' Taavi replied.

'Why did you call her Miriam if that was not her real name?' he asked as the engines began to rev in anticipation of departure.

Ariel smiled. 'It's not *her* name, it's our name for what we are doing now. The plan we hatched last night.'

'Huh?' James replied, confused.

'I thought you said you'd been studying the Tora. Catch up!'

James nodded sagely, but he was stumped. Then he remembered where he had read that name. 'Miriam was the sister of Aaron and Moses. But what's that got to do with anything?'

'And in what book is she named?'

James thought again for a moment, trying to overcome the fog of fear and anxiety shrouding his normally sharp mind. 'Oh, of course, how stupid of me! Exodus! Their escape to the desert. This is our exodus!'

39.

'But how are you even here?' Purdu asked, clasping tightly onto Mezarus' waist and shedding tears of joy.

'I could ask you the same question,' he laughed in his deep, bear-like laugh.

'Well, I asked first!' Purdu retorted merrily.

'Well, we didn't last long on our own. Our ships were attacked only a day or so after we separated.' His face grew long for a moment as he remembered their sad parting. 'The ships were huge and fast with striped sails. They were absolutely piled full of black soldiers. We were lucky to escape.'

'Who escaped?' Ani asked, suspiciously.

Mezarus looked down for a second. 'You won't like what I have to say I'm afraid.'

'He's here isn't he!' Purdu cried in anguish. 'The man who had our father beaten and imprisoned, who tore him and Sidani apart for decades, who made his life a living hell! How could you stay with him after all he's done?' Purdu cried accusingly, separating herself from Mezarus and stepping back indignantly.

'It's not how it looks. They tore me from you. It was never my intention to leave you. I would have stayed and protected you. You know that don't you?' he said, sounding wounded.

'Well that may be so, but we won't hang around here only to taste more of his cruelty!'

'It may be too late to argue about that,' Mezarus said. 'He's here now, and so are his men. They pulled me from a burning ship and brought me ashore when all the others lay dead or dying. I owe them my life.'

'Well he owes us a good deal more than that,' Ani said, furious and desperately unhappy that their worst enemy should turn up in the very place that seemed to offer them refuge at last.

Mezarus remained silent for a minute, nodding slowly and thinking. 'I know you hate him, and with good reason, but he is behind all of this,' he waved his hands around the forge. Ani followed his gaze and saw four or five huge iron sickle swords, like those Lelwan and Mezarus had wielded, standing propped against a bench.

'That's not true, making those swords was Lelwan's idea!'

'Yes, I know that. I mean he is the one who persuaded them to fetch things from infested places so we may arm ourselves again and kill off the demons. Many died to bring us these things.'

'So he is stealing Lelwan's ideas now and claiming it as his own after he cruelly beat him and sentenced him to death?'

'I'm sorry children, I know you're angry…,'

'Angry! That doesn't do it justice. Send him away! Make him go!' Purdu cried angrily. 'I will tell the leader of these people to send him away - and he will once he knows what an evil man he is. What is his name, this leader? I want to speak to him!'

'Moses. His name is Moses.'

'Well tell this Moses the Gal Meshedi has to be kicked out. He'll ruin everything! Nothing ever goes right when he is around.'

'What is all the commotion in here?' a woman asked in concern as she entered the forge behind them.

Ani turned to see a middle-aged woman, tall and thin and clad in grey linen.

'Perhaps you can tell his sister, Miriam,' Mezarus whispered with a look of warning. 'Nothing, nothing,' he said cheerfully and greeted the woman warmly. 'It's just that these new strangers Aachan dragged in now turn out to be two of my dearest friends, Ani and Purdu,' he said, turning them to face the woman. 'We have been through a terrible journey together and were separated, but now we are reunited.'

'Oh,' she said and looked the children up and down. 'You look like fine young people,' she said cheerfully. 'Welcome to the Valley of the Springs. I am very happy you have found each other again. I was coming to fetch you and Arnuwanda to the great meeting,' she said, looking past the children to Mezarus. 'It is about to begin.'

Mezarus nodded and she was gone.

'Who is Arnuwanda?' Ani asked as Mezarus took off his apron and wiped his face with the dirty cloth tied around his neck.

'Come and you will meet him… again.'

'No, not him! I don't want to see the Gal Meshedi!' Purdu railed.

'But listen, Purdu and Ani,' he said dropping to one knee to speak with them face to face. 'He and his men are turning this group of famished nomads into a powerful force, or at least they soon will be. His men venture far into Canaan to gather materials and watch the movements of the demons. With my great swords and his training, we are nearly ready to conquer our foes. Now come!'

Ani and Purdu tagged reluctantly along behind Mezarus, with Purdu cursing the Gal Meshedi's name as they went.

*

A large throng had gathered in front of the tall A-frame tent that stood within an enclosure of woven thorn branches. In front of it was the flat open area where soldiers had been drilling earlier. Mezarus led them through the small crowd to large rugs laid out in front of two unoccupied wooden chairs. The crowd huddled close around the rugs and murmured in anticipation. Ani sensed there was a mood of dissatisfaction in the crowd, with angry looks and words exchanged between those assembled.

'We'll sit here,' Mezarus said, taking a seat on the rug. 'Aaron and Moses will soon come and then it will begin.'

Ani took in his surroundings. Armed men stood on either side of the wooden chairs wearing large shields on one arm and clutching iron-tipped spears. Large sickle swords hung at their sides in leather scabbards. They looked identical to the swords they had just seen in Mezarus' forge. Ani gasped as he suddenly became aware that he knew these men. He looked quickly around the rest of the assembly area and spied other soldiers among the crowd or guarding the high tent. He realized he knew them all. They were the Gal Meshedi's men!

Ani quickly counted twelve in number, and each had a great iron sword at his side and iron-tipped spear in his hands. They wore shirts of iron scales that shone brightly in the sun, and helmets of leather-bound with iron bands. The Gal Meshedi was nowhere to be seen.

Achan soon appeared from out of the noisy crowd and took his place beside the children. 'You will soon see our great leader, though you will not hear him speak. Few have that privilege.'

At last, the tent flap opened, and a young man stepped out holding Aaron's ram's horn trumpet. He sounded a long-muffled note, to which the crowd instantly hushed. Aaron then emerged and rather feebly took his seat in the smaller of the wooden chairs. Behind him came an even older man, though hale in comparison, with a handsome and intelligent face and a long grey beard. He took his seat in the larger chair and began speaking quietly but rapidly to Aaron.

'That is Moses,' Achan said quietly, tipping his head towards the older, bearded man.

Before long, Aaron stood and turned his hands skyward, as if in prayer. The crowd murmured with anticipation, then grew silent. Moses began to speak quietly to Aaron and then Aaron relayed his words in a loud voice that easily reached all those assembled. Achan translated quickly for the children as he spoke.

'Since leaving Egypt and coming to Rephidim and Masa we have faced many trials and have suffered, not least of which from thirst and hunger. But the Lord in his mercy has provided for us, revealing to us manna and leading us to springs of sweet water from the rocks. He has taken hunger from our bellies and nourished our children. He has given us victory over the accursed Amalekites time and time again, who attacked our sick, our elderly and our lame as we fled the horrors of Egypt. He has taken us to this place of refuge and has given us laws to abide by and an altar to worship at,' at this last he gestured to the large tent behind him. 'Has he not proven to you many times that we are his chosen people? Has he not led us here to spare us pestilence, cruelty and the horrors that now dwell in the land of Egypt? Yet still, you ask, why has he led us here? Why are we still impoverished, living as nomads eating only manna and mutton? Why are we being punished? Listen now, children of Israel, when I tell you that one day soon the Lord *will* lead us into the promised land of Canaan. But first, we must show him our obedience and devotion. Only then will he help us to overcome the fearsome creatures that dwell there. The Lord has brought to us many strangers to help us take what is promised to us. He has brought us sailors from the west who will one day build us a strong fleet. He has brought strangers from the north who bring us miracles and new weapons to overcome the foul and putrid beasts that surround us and to bring us victory over the murderous tribes that wish us gone. He shall one day lead us into the promised land. Arnuwanda, guardian of a northern kingdom, brother to a King, has brought us this gift.' At this Aaron turned and looked back into the tent.

To Ani and Purdu's horror, out strode the Gal Meshedi and took his place behind Aaron and Moses. He drew from its sheath his huge iron sword and handed it to Moses, who stood and held it high above his head for all to see. He then continued relating his speech to Aaron.

'His twelve men go forth into Canaan to flush out the beasts that dwell there and spy on their movements. Soon, that land shall again be ours, as it was once Abraham's and all our forefathers. And we shall call it Judah. And the people of Israel shall again be as numerous as the grains of sand in the desert and the drops of rain in a storm.'

To this, a great cheer went up and Ani sensed the mood had changed from dissatisfaction to jubilation. At this moment Moses stood up and raised his arms to his side and held them aloft as if feeling raindrops on his hand. The Gal Meshedi stepped forwards and signaled to his men, who at once hurried forward from the crowd and formed two tight lines in front of Moses and Aaron. Moses continued to hold his arms high at his sides. On another command, the iron-clad soldiers lowered the tips of their spears into a bristling wall of spikes protruding from behind their large shields and began advancing quickly toward the crowd as if intent on impaling those in the front row.

For a second the crowd panicked, a cry went up and they retreated quickly back away from the advancing line of spearmen. The Gal Meshedi barked another command and at once they dropped their spears and drew their great iron sickle swords, quickly reforming into a single long shield wall with swords held high. The crowd fell back still further, undecided if this was just a display of arms or an impending slaughter. Then Moses dropped his arms to his side and sat down. The Gal Meshedi issued another command and the soldiers instantly sheathed their swords and stood to silent attention.

Ani had to admit it, the demonstration was terrifying and awe-inspiring. If this was the kind of military force Mezarus mentioned, then it was indeed imposing and very likely to be entirely devastating to any enemies they faced. But he still wondered if it was enough to defeat the demons. They cared not if they were impaled or hacked with a sword. And worse, one bite from them would not only reduce any soldier to a sweating heap before long but actually turn them into the very foe they were fighting. Such things Ani had seen before, and he dreaded seeing them again. But he had also seen the great sword in Lelwan's hands and knew what a fearsome weapon it could be. With such a sword, victory was likely to be snatched from both man and beast.

Moses left his chair and walked forward to stand beside the two lines of soldiers. Aaron hobbled along beside him.

'You see the gifts the Lord has provided,' Aaron said, relating Moses' words again. 'Soon our armies, trained by these men of the north, will take what is ours and destroy the evil ones and the Amalekites and any who challenges us. Go now, my people, lower your tent poles and roll up your rugs, for the Lord beckons us once more. Follow me now, people of Israel, sons and daughters of Abraham, for I have seen signs that the Lord wishes to commune with me once again.'

*

Ani and Purdu followed Mezarus back to the forge. 'I can't believe he is here and in charge of an army!' he fumed.

'Well it doesn't end there my friend,' he said, directing him not to the forge but towards a tent further on.

'What do you mean?' Ani asked worriedly.

'He is also betrothed to Moses' sister. He will soon be royalty and at the heart of the household. It is not to your advantage to dislike him any longer, Ani, or you, Purdu. It is time to put aside your hatred. The Gal Meshedi is reborn now and he has taken a new name, though not many know it yet. He may be a future leader.'

'What is it then?' Ani scowled.

'Joshua.'

*

For weeks Ani and Purdu stayed with Mezarus, slowly learning the ways of the people of Israel, and in turn, telling them of their own lands and the terrifying journey they had been on. During this time the Meshedi's men ventured north on foot out of their valley, further and further, in search of better-watered valleys while also keeping a watchful eye on once-inhabited areas of Canaan.

After many weeks working in the forge with Mezarus, one hot dry afternoon a group of Meshedi came stumbling into camp. One was wounded with an arrow, the other three had taken bites. There was a huge commotion as the Meshedi were helped into Moses' tent. Mezarus took Ani and Purdu with him to see what was afoot.

The Gal Meshedi - Joshua, as he was now called - looked furious at his men. 'To think you three, the highest knights of Hattusha, should allow yourselves to be bitten like that! How careless and stupid,' he was yelling in Neshili.

The three bleeding Meshedi hung their heads in shame.

'And you, what do you have to say?' he turned to the fourth Meshedi with a broken arrow shaft protruding from his shoulder. 'Are you telling me demons fire arrows now?'

'No, of course not,' the Meshedi said between gasps of pain.

'Then speak! What happened?'

'I took some trainees to a far valley in the desert looking for water. There were amazing cliffs and gorges there, and pools of water seeping from the rocks. We found the perfect place for us all there. But then we were attacked. From between the rocks came dark men with bows and arrows and deadly aim. They shot at us and the two trainees were killed. I was wounded but got away.'

'Amelakites!' Aaron spat.

'There is more,' the Meshedi said forlornly. 'They followed me here. It is not long now until they will attack us!'

'We must prepare to fight!' the Gal Meshedi said, his translator relaying his words rapidly to Moses and Aaron. 'We have little time to prepare. How many swords and how much armor have you made Mezarus?'

Mezarus shook his head forlornly. 'Not enough!'

The Gal Meshedi stared at Mezarus with disappointment for a moment, then turned and whispered to the translator who spoke quietly to Moses. Moses nodded and spoke to Aaron.

'As I said at our last meeting,' Aaron spoke loudly so all the assembled menfolk could hear. 'God has beckoned us north to the mountain where we can defend ourselves. Lower your tent poles, roll your mats and fetch in your children. We march tonight!'

*

Ani trudged along behind the caravan through the gorge, his feet sore and his back hurting from the weight of Mezarus' tools wrapped in a bundle and handing over his shoulder. Before long he had fallen behind the others. Exhausted, he found a shady rock ledge and crawled beneath it.

'Come on Ani, you can't rest now,' Purdu said, coming back for him and hurrying him on.

'I'll catch up soon,' he said, and lay back against the wall and closed his eyes. 'Just a short rest. Mezarus won't notice, he's too busy with the stupid donkeys.'

Purdu sighed huffily and plonked down beside him.

After a while, Ani took a scrap of iron from his pocket that he had taken from Mezarus' forge and stared at it. He doodled in the dirt with it for a while, the stiff iron making white marks on the soft sandstone beneath the dust. Then something struck him. 'You know how Amuurana wanted to write it all down – all the terrible things that happened to us?'

Purdu nodded and wiped the sweat from her eyes.

'Well, I was thinking, we should do that too.'

'How? Neither of us can write!'

'True, but we can draw. I was thinking we could sketch it out. Sketch it on the rocks likes some of those drawings we saw back there.'

Purdu stared into the distance thoughtfully. 'But who will read it?'

'I don't know, but I want to do it for him. For Amuurana.'

Purdu nodded wearily.

'Besides, I do know how to write something.'

'You? What? How?'

'My lucky charm. It had words on it that I've memorized.'

'Saman,' she said, her voice suddenly sad at saying the name. 'He saved our lives.'

'Yes, he did. I want to do it for him too. I will do a drawing for each of the people we've loved and who have helped us.'

With that, the two children began furiously scratching symbols and drawings into the rock with the iron rod. At last, when they were done, they bundled their equipment back together, and ran on after the caravan, eventually finding Mezarus waiting for them and shouting for them to hurry up.

40.

Radios crackled and the vehicles revved forwards towards the gates. The glow of taillights in front and behind and a thick cloud of blinking lights circling overhead was all James could make out through the small plate glass windows beside his head. Then suddenly the guns started firing, rapidly and continuously. James could see the gates were now opening and the trucks accelerated hard towards the exit. To James' horror, ghastly, disfigured and blood-stained faces appeared at his window as they rushed in through the open gates, champing their fang-like teeth at him through the glass, dashing their heads against the fast-moving window, then disappearing as quickly as they had appeared. Arla and James clung to each other in horror as the vehicle smashed a path through the huge press of the infected surrounding the compound, jerking and bumping over the bodies that went beneath the wheels. The glass was soon smeared with blood and his view of the outside world gone. The guns kept firing deafeningly overhead, a rain of spent and smoking cases clattering into the cabin around them. Then, just as suddenly as it had begun, the firing stopped, and the truck's roaring engines eased back to a rhythmic hum.

James changed seats to take a look out of the rear window, which was still clear, though covered in thick dust. The whole city around them was blacked out, but frequent flashes accompanied by deep rumbles briefly silhouetted buildings and walls as they rushed through the outskirts of Jerusalem. Ariel and Taavi kept up a steady conversation with the drivers and the gunner as they sped out of town, pausing to listen the radio chatter or check in with the other vehicles.

'We are clear of the main danger now,' Taavi said at last. 'Everyone is out and unharmed. Hopefully, we'll have no further trouble now, but we still have a long journey ahead of us.'

James nodded but had no words to say. He was still shaking, and it took time to settle his racing pulse. Eventually, he resumed his seat next to Arla and tried to settle in for the long journey ahead. As he sat in a weary, half-doze, he noticed the box of vials beneath Taavi's seat.

Ariel and Taavi meanwhile extracted a large map from a tube and unfurled it across both of their laps. They were discussing some important landmarks by the light of a small torch clamped between Ariel's teeth.

'Where are we going exactly?' James asked after watching them for some time.

'Here!' Ariel said and flipped the map around for James and Arla to see. He was pointing to a valley in what was otherwise an uninhabited and desolate-looking spot deep in the Negev Desert. He could not read the writing on the map.

'It's near Timna Park!' Arla said, translating for James.

'There are bunkers there? With supplies?' James asked hopefully.

'Yes, thereabouts. Enough for some time, and we have more supplies in two of the trucks.'

'And we have the drug with us too?' Arla asked, sounding exhausted.

Taavi nodded but said nothing. James noticed him instinctively kick the cool box under his seat as if checking it was still there.

'So how many doses do we have?' she continued.

'Three.'

'Three!' she choked. 'What the fuck! Whose bright idea was this?'

Ariel and Taavi sighed but said nothing. It was clear this had not been their idea.

'Do you mean we went through hell to rescue Michael, Yosef and others lost their lives, and now we only have three doses? Tell me we can make more.'

'If Michael turns up with the right equipment,' Ariel replied.

'It is coming, believe me,' Taavi said quickly. 'Michael and Nathan and a team have gone to collect the last of it from Tel Aviv. They will meet us on the road to Be'er Sheva tomorrow.'

'Let's hope no one gets sick along the way then,' James mused gravely. 'But why do we have so little? I thought Michael made several batches. That's what he told us.'

Taavi looked uncomfortable for a moment. 'The truth is,' Taavi answered, 'that the deal we struck with the emergency council meant they got to keep most of the drug. In return, we were able to evacuate many people. It was the only way we were going to get vehicles. Otherwise, we would still be back there, and I didn't like the look of how that was turning out.'

'They let us leave in return for most of the drug,' James stated flatly. 'What's going to happen if people get sick? I mean a lot of people, which is, let's face it, very likely.'

'Did you screen everyone coming with us for any signs of infection?' Arla asked, sounding frightened.

'Yes, of course,' Taavi answered evasively. 'As much as time allowed.'

'As much as time allowed?' Arla repeated in disdain. 'So no in other words.' She shook her head in disbelief. 'We'd really better hope no one gets sick!'

*

James rocked sleepily from side to side with the motion of the truck as they drove south along Highway Sixty towards Be'er Sheva, through dark Bethlehem, Hebron and other Palestinian towns. The radio chatter was almost continuous as they drove, keeping James from falling deeply asleep, though Arla slept with her head on his shoulder most of the way. People roamed the streets and highways everywhere, arms limp by their sides, eyes staring. They emerged out of the darkness towards the vehicles as soon as they heard them, only to be gunned down or run over if they came too near. Each time Arla would jolt awake in a panic, but James would do his best to soothe her back to sleep.

James found himself waking with a start as the truck came to a sudden halt. He looked through the dusty blood-streaked window and saw the sun rising between high rise buildings in the distance. Their convoy had come to a halt on the highway some way out of the city. Ariel and Taavi had squeezed into the front and were talking hurriedly on the radio with Hillel.

'What is it?' James asked, rubbing his eyes and trying to wake up.

'We can't go this way,' Ariel said between bursts of conversation.

'Why, what's happening?' Arla said, climbing further forwards to listen in.

'Roadblock. There's some military action in the city. It's not safe to enter.'

As soon as he spoke the air-tearing shriek of fighter planes screamed overhead. Seconds later the truck was rocked by huge explosions up ahead. Out of the tiny window, James could see clouds of dust, smoke and concrete plume over the city.

'Christ!' he cried involuntarily as the second wave of jets brought another gut-wrenching set of explosions within the city, only to get a withering stare from Ariel.

The trucks immediately began to reverse and slowly turn around.

'Change of plan!' Ariel shouted back to them. 'We're going around.'

'What about Michael and Nathan? They're supposed to meet us here.'

Ariel conversed for a moment with Taavi. 'We can get a message through to them most likely. They'll have to make their own way there.'

'But how will they know where to go?'

'The commandos will figure something out.'

*

Ariel relayed reports of the worsening situation as radio traffic intensified during the morning. Jerusalem was in a state of chaos. Tel Aviv was faring better but was now surrounded by a huge mass of INS victims traveling westward towards the sea. There were also reports of terrible scenes of carnage as people were attacked on mass, and of INS victims entering homes and apartments and killing whole families. The situation was so ghastly that Ariel eventually stopped listening.

Their attempts to get around Be'er Sheeva were foiled on several counts by roadblocks, rough terrain and congested roads as people tried to flee the city, while continued airstrikes made heading further into the center too risky to try.

Around midday, Arla came up with a plan. She suggested they backtrack to Tsahal Boulevard and cut through the Tel Sheva archaeological site. By following the dirt tracks around the site, they could eventually reconnect with Highway Forty heading south. Ariel radioed the plan through to Hillel and the others, and within minutes they were tearing through the outer suburbs heading for the Tel.

Their truck now took the lead, with Arla squeezing into the front beneath the turret gunner's feet. They found the gates to the site locked, but a little nudge from the truck soon had them open and speeding across the dry ground, skirting the mound and excavations and heading across open terrain. They sped across dry gullies and beneath train lines, knocking down loan or small groups of shuffling INS victims heading west towards the city. At last, the highway appeared ahead to James' relief.

The plan seemed to be working like a charm with the highway stretching out into the desert haze beyond. As sped up to a cracking pace, James finally began to feel their troubles were behind them, but it was not long before they came to a stop once more. He could see out of his window that where there had once been an overpass there was now a pile of tumbled concrete and shattered pillars; the road ahead was nothing but a series of craters and upturned tarmac.

'Why on earth would they destroy the road?' James asked in disbelief, interrupting intense discussions in Hebrew up the front as the radio chattered madly.

'There was a big pack coming up the road from Nevatim and Segev Shalom, apparently,' Arla said, shaking her head worriedly as she listened to the radio.

'So what now?'

'Back! We're going to have to go around and cut through the southern suburbs,' Taavi said, pawing over a map with the driver.

The vehicles turned and left the highway again, this time heading west across fields towards the suburban sprawl. Soon they climbed the side of the highway again and drove into the city.

Jets came racing overhead again and James watched in horror as a tightly packed cluster of apartment blocks ringed by palm trees to their left suddenly erupted in a volcano of flame, shattered concrete, smoke, and dust. The rubble came raining down on their vehicle, clattering off its thick armor and causing the turret gunner to retreat back inside the vehicle, swearing loudly, as chunks of shrapnel hit his turret.

'Why are they bombing us?' Arla shrieked as more rockets showered rubble over the road ahead.

'We've got to get out of here!' James yelled as more planes rent the air as they passed low overhead.

They turned off the main road, away from the zone of huge destruction ahead, and found themselves in suburban streets between towering apartment blocks. The place was a chaotic ruin. Clothing, belongings and junk lay everywhere. And then there were the bodies: bloated, covered in flies and chewed to the bone.

'Get us out of here!' Arla cried as they found themselves in a dead-end street surrounded by shabby buildings. Doors and windows hung open or were smashed in, rubbish was everywhere, and the smell of death soon infiltrated the cabin.

The driver yelled into the radio and tried to turn the truck. The convoy was backed up behind them with no way to easily turn around. The radio was blaring with what sounded like a hundred people shouting at once. Huge explosions shook the truck and seemed to be getting closer each second. To add to the chaos the turret gun began firing again. James shot a glance out of the side window and saw through the murky glass a thick pack of infected appearing from between the apartment blocks.

Ariel was screaming into the radio now as the gunner fired incessantly, empty shells clattering noisily around them. The trucks slowly began to move backward, but within seconds they were gridlocked again. Their driver began to attempt a turn, moving in tiny arcs forward and backward in the crowded street. Soon the horrid faces were at the window, peering in with ghastly bloodshot eyes, and champing their teeth incessantly as they snarled and gurgled inches from James' head. He jerked back from the glass, trying to get as far from the creatures as possible, but as he did so, dozens began climbing onto the truck. A moment later there were savage snarls above him and the turret gun was silenced. Blood began to drip through into the cabin as the horrific sound of teeth ripping into skin and bone and the swallowing of huge mouthfuls of flesh turned James' stomach. The gunner was torn out of the turret, leaving nothing but a bloodstain.

'Take this!' Ariel said and slid a pistol across the floor to James. Ariel, Taavi and Arla were holding pistols now, staring grimly up at the turret, and expecting the inevitable. Through the back window, James could see the other vehicles still trying to reverse or turn, but INS victims were now swarming over them like ants. Their guns kept firing, knocking down swathes of bodies as more and more surged in through the lanes between buildings, pouring in out of nowhere, but one by one, the guns began to fall silent.

'Oh god,' James muttered involuntarily as he saw the gunner in the truck behind them pulled from the turret and devoured on the bonnet.

James was stunned by the sudden percussive burst of gunshots inside the cabin as Arla, Ariel and Taavi began firing. He turned to see an unkempt, blood-soaked body slide through the turret and onto the floor, shattered and bleeding. Another followed, gurgling and slathering as it crawled like a reptilian predator finding a burrow full of eggs. It slid through the tight gap in the floor of the turret, snarling at James and struggling to gets its legs clear. Another was close behind it. James flung himself back against the back door as more and more squeezed in through the turret. Others were beating on the back doors behind his head. The snarling, gurgling and gunshots in the cabin were unbearable, with the driver screaming in panic as he tried to force an exit past the nearest truck, wedging the vehicle hard between steel and concrete.

James picked up the pistol still lying at his feet and aimed at the first of the creatures that finally squeezed through the gap and dropped on all fours in front of him and prepared to jump on him. It crumpled in a second as Arla shot it point-blank in the back of the head. Another dropped through after it, turning this time toward Ariel and Taavi. They fired the last of their rounds into it, but the beast was only thrown to one side and immediately came at them again.

'The head!' James screamed over the noise. 'In the head!'

Arla needed no reminding and destroyed the thing with her next shot.

More and more were struggling in through the turret with no way to hold them at bay. James still had to fight to pull the trigger, and in the end, his first shot was stray. It was only when a creature turned on Arla that he found the resolve he needed and took half its head from its shoulders. The cacophony built to a roar as dozens more grimacing, snarling heads forced their way in through the opening.

'We've got to get out of here!' James cried as the driver rammed the trucks on either side, again and again, sending them flying from their seats, as he tried in vain to squeeze between. The two trucks had ceased to move some time ago. James needed no explanation as to why. He could see the swarms of INS victims funneling down inside through the turrets. It was clear there was no hope for their occupants now, nor indeed for any of them unless they could get clear of the swarm. The radio too was eerily silent.

'Obviously!' Ariel replied tersely, fear etched on his face as he frantically reloaded his weapon. 'Got any ideas? Something from the ancient texts maybe?' he added sarcastically, then blew away a young man and an old woman who dropped through the roof in front of him.

James was trying to think, but all he could do was keep firing. Soon the turret was entirely blocked with lifeless bodies – a river of blood pouring into the cabin. James had to perch on the bench seats to keep his feet out of the deepening pool, his stomach churning at the mutilated corpses and body parts that now filled the truck. The smell was detestable. Then James had a terrifying thought. Wouldn't this swarm bring the bombers? 'I don't care what we have to do, we're getting out of here, now!'

The driver shook his head. 'We can't. We're completely stuck,' he sat back in his seat and threw his arms in the air as if surrendering to his fate.

'Then we'll go on foot!' James replied.

'Are you mad? We won't last ten seconds out there,' Ariel shot back. 'They'll rip us to pieces.'

'We've only got to get to the trucks at the other end of the convoy. Surely we can do that!'

'Oh, what makes you so sure? You do a lot of this sort of thing on your excavations and trips to the library do you?'

'Ariel, shut up! James is right!' Arla bust in. 'We can't just sit here. They'll force their way in soon and we can't fight them off forever. We'll run out of ammo sooner or later.'

At that moment jets screamed low overhead, shaking the truck slightly with their wash. Taavi whitened and suddenly looked terrified. He nodded, 'OK. How much ammo do we have left?' he asked nervously and checked the metal box half-submerged in the pool of blood at his feet. 'Only three clips left. That won't get us far!'

'We have these too!' the driver said as if suddenly waking up and leaned over Arla and opened a hatch behind her. Five high explosive grenades were clamped to the wall right behind her head.

'That's reassuring,' she said. 'I'm glad we didn't hit anything,' she said sarcastically.

The driver unclamped each one and handed them out.

'We could make a path with these,' Taavi commented, feeling the weight of the thing in his hands like he was about to pitch it at a batter.

Ariel nodded. 'Yes! We open the back doors, we throw a grenade and then shut them again before it goes off. Then we lob another, and as soon as it goes off we run for it, lob another and so on until we get there.' Ariel was trembling as he spoke. 'Yosef would have done it. He was a brave man. That's good enough for me.'

They all nodded but no one spoke. James was trembling too as he looked towards the back doors, blood-streaked now as champing, gurgling faces pushed so hard against the glass they were oozing blood on its dusty surface.

They gathered their things and crawled through the gore to the back door. The press of bodies, outstretched claw-like hands, and gnashing teeth outside the window was vast and terrifying. As James stared for a moment, he saw the back doors of another truck open and several people jump out and make a panicked attempt to flee the crowd. They were chased, pulled down and devoured in seconds.

'I don't think I can do this!' James said as he backed away from the doors in horror.

'You have to!' Ariel said, taking James firmly by the arm. 'Do it! Do it or we die anyway!'

'OK,' James said at last, forcing himself to focus.

'We have a plan. It will work. When the first grenade goes off, we shoot anyone close. Then I'll lob another, and we'll work our way forward. Go it?'

'OK, you can do this,' James whispered to himself, trying not to hyperventilate. Jets shot overhead again, and nearby explosions rocked the truck.

'It's now or never!' Ariel cried, pulled the pin, pushed open the door with a mighty thrust of his legs, hurled the grenade into the crowd. They worked together to try and pull the doors closed again, but a sea of heads and arms immediately thrust their way through the gap, jamming the doors so they could not be shut.

Taavi and Arla began firing furiously at point-blank.

'No! Save your ammunition!' Ariel cried.

Suddenly a huge blast sent a wave of limbs, gore and body parts splashing against the window and into the cabin. The shock was enough to force the doors closed again, and it knocked James back against the window.

Stunned for a second, he forced himself to clear his mind and seize the moment. He grabbed Arla's hand and leaped on trembling legs out of the truck into the tangle of dismembered bodies and immediately slipped over. He was lifted to his feet by Taavi. 'Come on,' Taavi said quietly but firmly.

'Wait!' James cried and dived back into the truck. At once he found what he was looking for. The cold box full of FaveBest lying forgotten beneath the seat. He grabbed it, tucked it under his arm, and fled after Ariel.

The pack was surging in again around them from beyond the blast radius. Ariel took Arla's grenade and hurled it further into the crowd ahead, between two trucks, while the rest of them fired incessantly into the crowd. 'Get ready to duck!' he yelled. 'Now!'

James threw himself to the ground as another blast and shower of body parts rained over them. They rose and began firing again as they dashed through the horrifying streetscape to the next two motionless, but still idling, trucks. Here they could cover ground quickly as the vehicles gave them cover on two sides. They paused for a second as James handed Ariel the next grenade. He lobbed it again, aiming it to give them a path through to the next group of trucks. They quickly reloaded with their last clips as they waited for the blast.

'And duck!' Ariel said almost comically this time as though they were performing in a bizarre pantomime.

The blast sent a human head ricocheting off the side of the wheel next to James' face where he crouched low to the ground. He resisted the urge to be violently ill and instead focused on the task ahead.

'Last dash!' Ariel cried as he jumped up and led them once more into the fray, guns blazing.

They reached what they thought was the final group of trucks at awkward angles to each other just as their ammunition ran out. It was then that James realized there was another group of trucks further on. Some had clearly fled, but two more stood idling with rear doors open around fifty yards away.

Arla shot James a worried look. Ariel suddenly looked beaten as the crowd surged in from beyond the blast radius.

'Oh shit!' Arla cried as her gun clicked and a powerful looking man set upon her.

James shoved the man aside, but in seconds he had his teeth wrapped around James' wrist. James felt for the first time the true horror of having one's flesh torn by one of these creatures. He realized to die in this way would be a death more horrible than any he could have imagined. He screamed in pain as a woman also grabbed him and bit off two fingers from his left hand. Suddenly both man and woman disappeared in a puff of brains and skull fragments. James looked up, incredulous to see that Taavi had climbed into the turret of one of the trucks and was blazing down a path for them.

'Come on sis!' Ariel shouted and dragged Arla away from another slathering brute. But something went wrong. A bullet passed so close to Arla's head and hit an INS victim beside her that the spray of blood made her flinch and she fell. Before James could catch her or pull her up, they were on her, their teeth at work on her arms.

'No!' James cried and kicked them away as hard as he could. Like ravenous wolves on a fresh kill, they did not even look up but latched on again as others surged forward. Then Ariel was beside James, a submachine gun blaring in his hands. James realized he had pulled it from the half-devoured body of a soldier lying close by. James did not hesitate but lifted her over his shoulder. She was still. He hoped with all his might she had only fainted.

They ran now through the last of the crowd, Ariel cutting down any that remained in their path. The last of the vehicles were in a terrible state, with bodies hanging out of the rear doors and blood everywhere. The engine was still idling as they climbed in. James lay Arla down on the bench seats and pulled the doors too and locked them. Blood was seeping out of his severed fingers over everything. He tore off the sleeve of his shirt and wrapped it around the stumps, whimpering in agony as he did so.

'Taavi!' Ariel said as he heaved the mutilated driver's body out of his seat and jumped in. But he had missed something in his haste. Crouching behind the drivers' seat beneath the gun turret was an INS victim, content in its full and satiated state. But the noise of the revving engines brought it to life. It jumped up as Ariel began to reverse and bit him on the shoulder. Ariel screamed in shock and sent the vehicle smashing into one of the other trucks. The creature began tearing into Ariel's back and neck. Ariel looked as though he was about to pass out. In one motion, James flipped the submachine gun up from where it lay on the seat and dispatched the foul thing.

Ariel was hyperventilating by the time James got to him. He had a nasty gash on the face and his neck and back were bleeding badly, but mercifully his jugular was intact. He helped Ariel out of the driver's seat and into the back beside Arla. A trauma kit was strapped to the wall above their heads. He ripped it open and lashed some thick pads over both their wounds.

James could hear Taavi had stopped firing.

'Help him,' Ariel said, wincing in pain.

James nodded, cast one last glance at Arla, and jumped through into the driver's seat. He could see that Taavi was out of ammunition and was trying to keep the grabbing, clawing, biting, creatures at bay by bashing them with a helmet as they clambered up over the edges.

'Oh, god!' James said as he saw Taavi suddenly pulled rapidly to one side, a young man biting into his back. He floored the truck and it surged forward with surprising speed, crushing a large number of infected as it beat a path to the other vehicles. He collided with the truck with such force that he flung most of those on top of it off in an instant. Taavi was also thrown savagely around, but as soon as he regained his senses he was up and out of the turret. He leaped onto the bonnet of James' truck and held on tightly as James threw it into reverse and charged blindly backward through the crowd. Reversing further and further, he began to realize he had passed the worst of the crowd and was now approaching their original turn off. He could see bloody tire tracks from those trucks that had escaped. He slowed to let Taavi climb stiffly back inside, then floored it in the direction of the tracks.

As he reached the long sort-after Highway Forty, he looked back and saw jet bombers turning the tightly packed apartment blocks they had just left into pillars of dust.

Arla, Taavi and Ariel were all groaning in the back by the time he finally felt it was safe to stop and check on them. Arla was conscious but looked sweaty and flushed. Ariel had his eyes closed against the pain and sat clutching the crimson trauma pad to his shoulder and neck.

'You have to get through to the bunker,' Arla said in a whisper. 'Go there and stay safe. Michael and Nathan will come to you if they can. You know what this means, James, you have to leave us here. I want you to survive.'

'Arla don't think like that,' James said, wiping sweat from her brow. 'As if I'm leaving you here. I can do better than that.' He reached down and with his bloodied hand and opened the cold box containing the vials. An icy vapor leaked out of the sides as he unlatched the lid. Inside were three syringes, covered in condensation, their contents still liquid despite the sub-zero temperatures. He lifted out a syringe with his wounded, trembling hand, and pulled back Arla's sleeve.

'It mightn't work, James, you know that don't you?' she whispered, her expression resigned and fearless.

James stared at her for a moment, the realization suddenly hitting that this was Michael's batch, and not the one that had been given to him. 'But… I thought they tested it?'

Arla shook her head. 'I don't think so.'

'Well it's going to work,' he said determinedly, not wanting to give any thought to the alternative.

'How long did it take you to get better?' Arla asked weakly.

'I don't know. I think I was in a coma. When I awoke I was better.'

She nodded and relaxed back onto the bench seat, a look of grim determination on her face. 'I want to wake up better…,' she said, then passed out.

James moved the syringe to her bloodied and bandaged arm. He had never given an injection before and had no idea really how to do it. He felt for a vein but could find none under all the blood. In the end, he simply jabbed the needle into the skin and pushed its contents into her. 'You're going to be fine now,' he said tenderly and smiled, trying to sound sure of his own words.

'Now me and Taavi,' Ariel said gruffly. 'It's not all about her you know.'

James nodded and looked hesitantly into the cold box. Two doses left. After Ariel and Taavi, none left. He had been bitten too. He looked down at the throbbing, agonizing stumps where the pinkie and ring finger had been savagely bitten off at the lowest joint near his palm. It made his stomach turn to see it, and the pain was excruciating, but it was nothing against the wounds the others bore. Even if he could cure the INS, he wondered how he could keep them from bleeding to death.

A question was now running through his mind: 'Am I immune, or am I done for?' But his introspection was shattered by Ariel's cry of pain. He grabbed a dose from the cold box and turned to Ariel.

'I can feel it taking hold inside me already,' Ariel said hoarsely through gritted teeth. 'It's making my mind foggy. I can feel the fever coming on, like vines wrapping around my brain.'

James frowned but said nothing. He remembered that feeling from when he was lying on the trolley after the battle with the Meshedi in Ankara. He knew they still had time for the drug to work, for it was not given to him until days later. He just hoped to god Michael had known what he was doing.

'Ah, you're probably imagining it,' he said reassuringly. 'It takes days to affect you.'

Ariel smiled weakly and accepted the situation.

'So where exactly are we going?' James asked once he had given Ariel and Taavi the doses and rebandaged their very frightening wounds – bite marks the size of fists, red and swollen, with flesh torn away in places.

'You brought the map, right?' Ariel asked, suddenly panicked.

'No!' James said in horror, suddenly remembering seeing it lying on the seat before they left.

'Oh shit!' Ariel said slowly, 'Now we're not just dying, we're completely fucked!'

'No, we're not!' Taavi said. 'I have it. I shoved it in my pocket. Can you take it out, James?'

James moved over to where Taavi was leaning heavily against the wall in the front passenger's seat, breathing hard with the pain. James had had to tightly bandage both his arms, so he had little use of them. James could see one large bulging pocket on the right leg of Taavi's pants.

'Here!' Taavi said and pointed to a red circle marked on the map near a place called Timna Park.

'OK, I'll do my best. You lot don't bleed to death on me now, you hear?' He leaned down and kissed Arla's unconscious lips. 'Sleep for a while, but not too long,' he said quietly in her ear, her breath falling softly on his face. 'I need you.'

41.

'Just bloody floor it!' Nathan cried as bodies bounced off the windshield. 'You drive like a granny. Don't you know how to drive yet!'

'Just shut up and look at the map!' Michael replied, frantically trying to steer the lorry full of equipment through the piles of detritus, shattered concrete and dead bodies on the road. The commando unit had left them hours earlier to return to Jerusalem and help defend the bunker, with promises to re-join them later, south of the city. Now they were very alone and very lost in the dark neighborhoods around Be'er Sheva. The street lighting was out and the mass of snarling, gurgling, staggering figures coming into the headlights was truly horrifying.

'Where the fuck are they all coming from?' Nathan screamed, throwing the map in front of his face as another head smashed against the glass.

'Out of that Soroka Hospital, I think,' Michael said, swerving again as more crazed INS victims raced in front of the lorry from behind the Soroka Hospital Emergency sign. 'This place is torn up. What's been happening here? Tel Aviv was like a holiday resort compared to this place.'

'Look out!' Nathan cried again as another large group came staggering towards the truck. It was too late to swerve and a few large bumps later and they were through the crowd.

'Is there anyone even left here that's not fucked up?' Nathan said. 'You know we don't have any weapons or anything right?' he added, terrified.

'We don't need them, we'll get through!' Michael said, amazed at the phony confidence in his voice. 'There's nothing that's going to prevent this truck from…,' even as he was about to say the words, the night sky lit up in front of them as huge balls of fire burst across the road far ahead of them. Michael swerved off the road in shock and hit the curb, a tire bursting loudly as it did so.

'Oh fuck, oh fuck!' Michael began screaming as the truck was showered in fist-sized debris, cracking the windscreen. Seconds later his side window came under assault from a frenzy of banging, gnashing teeth and bloody drool on the glass as more infected crowded the truck.

'Calm down, you big wimp,' Nathan cried and flung the wheel out from the curb. 'Step on it!'

Michael did as he was told and revved back out onto the street. Nathan had the map back on his lap now under the reading light, studying it hard, and their surroundings. 'The hospital helped,' he said more confidently. 'I can get us out of here I think.'

'Yes, do that!'

'Take a left and a right and we should be heading east towards Highway Forty.'

At the next junction, gunfire could be heard some way away.

'At least there's someone still alive here,' Nathan said, trying to take confidence from the sound.

At that moment a tank came clattering around the corner. A line of cars was following behind, sheltering behind its blazing machine guns, clearing a path through the dense mass of INS victims drawn to it by the noise. A gunner on top saw them and waved to them to follow. The tank turned away down the road and a long convoy of ordinary terrified citizens came trailing behind it in their cars, some sitting on the roof. Michael fell into line behind the slow convoy, another tank bringing up the rear.

'This is nice!' Nathan said happily, throwing his legs up on the huge dashboard and his hands behind his head, as though he were lying on a deck chair beside the pool at an expensive resort. 'I haven't felt this relaxed in a while.'

Michael gazed down at the map the commandos had given him, open on the seat between him and Nathan. 'They're taking us right through the middle,' Michael said, puzzled. 'Is that wise?'

'Who gives a fuck! We've got two tanks flanking us, dude.'

As if to reinforce his words the tank guns suddenly opened fire again, as did those riding shotgun on the roofs of the cars in front. The huge gun of the tank behind them also boomed concussively and nearly made Michael wet himself.

'This looks bad,' Michael said, observing a huge crowd of INS victims wading between cars and around the tank. It was too much for the tanks to deal with and the cars too were being surrounded. 'You don't think being in a convoy might be a bad idea, do you?' Michael said as they ground to a halt as more and more INS victims surged in around them.

'Well, yes, actually,' Nathan said, sitting back upright and beginning to look panicked again. 'They're surrounding us. This is a bad idea.'

'OK, screw this,' Michael said, revved the truck and turned slowly out from the convoy. The huge tank gun fired behind them again, sending a wall of flame, tarmac and body parts into the air to their right. He had turned into a dark back street. 'You'd better direct me.'

Nathan already had the map on his lap and was feverishly trying to find street signs and landmarks in the dark. 'Looks like we're on Yitshak Rager Boulevard. Now we're approaching Shi'mon Street, and yes, there's the performing arts complex. Take a left here and that will put us on the main highway, then a right back onto Yitshak and then south onto Highway Twenty-Five.'

'Sounds easy enough,' Michael said, swerving and knocking over a small group of shambling figures.

They found their way back onto the main route south and were approaching Highway Twenty-Five just as the first rays of dawn lightened the horizon. They took the ramp onto the highway past a shopping complex, but as they turned onto the highway, they could see over a park to what appeared to be the ancient buildings of the Old City behind that. Thousands upon thousands of the infected were crowded into the park, and the highway ahead was choked with them. Abandoned cars, jettisoned belongings and corpses became visible on the highway ahead for as far as they could see as the sun cleared the tops of the buildings and illuminated the dreadful scene. In the background, they could still hear the tank guns firing, and gunfire could be heard elsewhere through the city too.

'This is very not good, Michael,' Nathan said, staring in horror at the choked road ahead. 'Why didn't they warn us about this?'

'I guess they didn't know how bad it was.'

'So, what do we do? Can we get through?'

The sound of their engine running was now bringing hundreds of INS victims in their direction, shuffling between the cars and walking up the on and off-ramps.

'Put your seat belt on Nathan. Here goes!' Michael cried and put his foot down.

The truck gathered speed quickly, then in a steady series of spine jarring bangs, began to collide with cars, pushing them aside, knocking them over the edge of the highway, and sending INS victims flying like matchsticks. Their run seemed to be going well until suddenly they reached an intersection and beheld a solid wall of shuffling, staring figures.

'Shit! I don't' think we can get through this!' Michael cried, gripping the steering wheel with white knuckles.

'Relax, I have every confidence in your driving Michael. You've come a long way in four weeks. I think you'll probably be ready to sit a driving test when this is all over. I really mean that, buddy.'

Michael shot Nathan a bewildered look, then floored it. He gained as much speed as possible before the truck ripped into the pack, sending Michael and Nathan lurching painfully against their seat belt straps. Within seconds the windshield was a shattered mess, entirely covered in blood and caving in at a dangerous angle.

Michael wound down his side window to better see where he was going, only to pull his head back in immediately as limbs, heads and other things whipped past the window and nearly took his own head off. He kept his foot down, the roaring of the engines deafening and the wheels beginning to slip and slide as they lost traction due to the sheer quantity of gore beneath the wheels.

Then suddenly they were free. Michael instinctively turned on the windscreen wipers, only to send a jet of blood through his side window all over him. A lengthy dousing with the wipers on high and he was soon able to make out the beautiful sight of a clear highway ahead.

Shooting a glance at Nathan, Michael noticed he was still gripping the handle on the dashboard like a man in the ocean clinging to a life raft. Finally, he let go and let out one of his characteristic howls of excitement and punched the air. 'Don't you feel a bit like Santa Claus now?'

Michael gave another bewildered look.

'You know, delivering a sleigh full of toys to the needy kids and getting back home to the north pole in time for supper?'

Michael shook his head wearily and drove on towards the brightening desert skyline.

Postscript

A deep shadow cast by the cliff cut a swathe through the brilliance of the desert sunshine, a contrast so sharp it seemed the earth had been rent asunder and cast away. The sun was rising fast and soon the intense heat of the noonday sun would spill over into the valley.

James and Arla stood in the deep shade looking out over the hot desert expanse beyond the gorge into the hazy distance. Behind them stood jagged boulders at the foot of the cliff, carved with the images of sheep, hunters with bows, snakes and other symbols.

At last, Arla broke the silence. 'Do you think this is how it was at the end for them?'

'For whom?' James asked, turning to her and smiling a little at her thoughtful expression.

'Those that survived it last time. So quiet. So empty.'

'Well, we are in the middle of the desert.'

'Yes, I know that you dork. What I mean is, what comes next? We could be the last people left on earth for all we know. They must have wondered that back then too, after the last big collapse. How did they even cope, knowing it was all gone?'

James turned her gently to face him and touched her cheek. 'At least we still have each other,' he said and pulled her against him and kissed her. 'Truly I desire nothing more than that. But anyway, it's not all gone. Not yet. I guess they must have had love and hope, like us. Otherwise, they wouldn't have made it. They rose again, here in this place, and took the land of Canaan for themselves under Joshua, and so your people and the land of Israel were born.'

They sat down next to the engravings for a time, happy in each other's arms and snacking on survival rations.

'James,' Arla said at last, 'why do you keep coming back here to this gorge these last days? I never knew you liked rock art. What is it about this place?'

'I don't know. I haven't coped well with everything that's happened.' He pulled her tighter against him, knowing that she had been suffering from the same trauma and sense of loss. 'I find it reassuring somehow to see these engravings that are thousands and thousands of years old. It reminds me that although everything changes, civilizations rise and fall and disasters happen, we have carried on - as a species I mean. I guess it helps me believe we're not done yet.'

Arla nodded. 'We're definitely not done yet, James Bindley, I can assure you of that,' she said, smiling and rubbing her slightly swelling belly.

He leaned down, lifted her shirt a little and kissed the tightening skin beneath which his child was growing. 'Actually, there's another reason I came today too. Something a little strange and incredible. Something I saw yesterday when I came on my own but was unsure about it. Now I am sure.'

'What? What is it?' Arla said, sitting up, intrigued.

'I'll show you,' he said, standing and helping her up, then taking her by the hand and leading her up the dry riverbed deeper into the gorge. They stopped at an overhang under which faint engravings in the soft red stone could just be seen. They had to duck a little to fit beneath the ledge and get a closer look.

Arla leaned in under the rock ledge and peered closely at the small carvings. 'I didn't know there were carvings here.'

'Yes,' he said, pointing to faint lines and symbols. 'What do you make of that?' James pointed to a group of symbols, crudely executed for the most part and only barely discernible. The first was of a sword, hooked and sickle-like. The second looked a little like a hammer and anvil. There was a chariot, with crude horses drawn on either side of the draft pole, a dog, a square with lines on it, and a ship with a square sail. Next was a group of horrid, deformed-looking figures with their arms in the air, or outstretched. Arla shot James a baffled look. 'What does it mean? They're not like any of the other engravings around here.'

'Now this one,' he said, pointing to a very fine spidery engraving of two short sets of characters.

'Isn't that cuneiform?' she said in amazement.

'Yes, it is. I know you can't read it, but I've figured it out. It's very poorly executed, much like the writing of a child, but I know what it says and where I've seen it before.'

'You've seen it before? What does it say?'

'It says *Annitas* and *Saman*.'

Arla shook her head, unsure at first what it meant, but then understanding slowly dawned on her face. 'No way! They were here?' she gasped, incredulous.

'Yes, they were here,' he nodded slowly. 'Ani and Purdu.' Tears began to pool on his eyelids. 'I don't know why it moves me so much, but it does.'

'Because they have guided us on this journey together, James. They are what brought us together in the first place at Keskin Dağ. It is because of them that we are here. They somehow warned us – them and Amuurana. I can't believe my eyes to see that they actually did this. But I thought they died with the others at the tower?'

'Apparently not. They came here and their story must somehow be entwined with Exodus and beginnings of the great events that were to come.'

Their wonder was interrupted by the sound of footsteps crunching up the sandy creek bed.

'What are you two love birds up to?' Michael shouted from a distance. 'Canoodling like teenagers again I see.'

'How did it go?' Arla called back, smirking a little.

'Good. That's the last batch done. Nathan is waiting in the truck.'

With one last gentle touch of the rock face, James and Arla turned and crawled out from under the ledge and began scrambling back down the slope to where Michael was waiting. They embraced him and began the short walk back to the road. The truck was purring by the roadside as they marched out of the gorge into the bright sunlight.

'I hope you're right about this. It's going to get crazy!' Nathan called from the drivers' seat as they approached.

'At least I don't have to drive this time,' Michael added with relief as the back doors opened and Ariel climbed out.

'All set?' Arla asked as she hugged him.

'Yes, we'll start somewhere small. I was thinking Be'er Ora. Taavi is there now rounding up a few of the infected. It's not far. We can work our way north if all goes to plan and they make a full recovery.'

James and Arla jumped into the back of the truck, loaded with batches of frozen FaveBest. 'There's enough here to bring half of Be'er Sheva back!' James said as he admired the crate of neatly stacked foam cooler boxes in the back.

'Yes, and you're both going to need these,' Ariel said and handed them each riot gear. 'Nathan's right. It's going to get hectic.'

With a shriek of excitement, Nathan flung the truck into a tight U-turn and headed north, beginning the short journey back to Be'er Ora, and a much longer one to put humanity back on its feet.

Printed in Great Britain
by Amazon

74997888R00125